A LETTY D[

MW01258313

UNNATURAL INTENT

BROOKE L. FRENCH

Black Rose Writing | Texas

The author grants the final approval for this literary material.

First printing

ISBN: 978-1-68513-497-6
PUBLISHED BY BLACK ROSE WRITING
www.blackrosewriting.com

Printed in the United States of America
Suggested Retail Price (SRP) $22.95

Unnatural Intent is printed in Baskerville

*As a planet-friendly publisher, Black Rose Writing does its best to eliminate unnecessary waste to reduce paper usage and energy costs, while never compromising the reading experience. As a result, the final word count vs. page count may not meet common expectations.

PRAISE FOR
UNNATURAL INTENT

"Field research has never been so riveting–and potentially deadly. *Unnatural Intent* is a tense combination of scientific detective work and corporate intrigue, set within the brutal but starkly beautiful landscape of the Arctic, where man is no longer an apex predator."
–Regina Buttner, author of *The Revenge Paradox*

"*Unnatural Intent* is like Michael Crichton's *State of Fear* meets Michael Connelly's *The Rapture of the Deep,* except this author's first name isn't "Michael"…and her book's better!"
–Cam Torrens, award-winning author of *Stable* and *False Summit*

"French weaves a complex tale of corporate greed, ecological disaster, and survival in this thriller, inserting you deep into the minds of her characters. The science is as accurate as it is terrifying, and the plot twists will keep you engaged until the final chapters."
–Gary Gerlacher, author of the *AJ Docker thriller* series

For Alec.
You are pure joy.

UNNATURAL INTENT

PROLOGUE

Katmai National Park, Alaska
October 12, 2018

The river swirled around Scottie's legs, bracing and fresh, the midday sun glittering along its surface. He wagged a fly rod above his head and cast, the line flying free and landing a hundred feet downstream. He loved it here. Sunk hip deep in the water as he caught and released one giant rainbow trout after another from the Brooks River. Nothing made him feel closer to nature, like he was a living, breathing part of something greater than himself.

A gust carried Craig's voice from beyond the river's bend. "You know the deal. Loser buys." He laughed. "I can't help that it's always you."

Scottie waited for Paul's answer, but another swirl of wind swallowed it. Knowing Paul, it had probably been an impressive display of cursing virtuosity. Scottie grinned. Some things never changed, and thank God for that. The three of them had been joined at the hip since they'd met in second grade. And they had been making this same trip, standing in these same waters together, since Scottie's father first got it in his head to teach the three of them how to fly fish. No small feat. Fly fishing wasn't like other fishing. Not everyone could do it. It took skill, perseverance, patience. Things that did not come naturally to eight-year-olds. But his dad had made sure they all figured it out, even if it had taken Paul three summers to actually catch a fish.

Scottie's grin faded. How many summers would it be before they could come again? He pulled in his line. Every year, it got harder for him and his friends to find a time they could all get away from work and family.

And now Scottie had a baby due Christmas Day.

Michelle had said it would be the best gift ever. He grimaced. He didn't disagree, not really. He just wasn't sure he was ready. To be a dad. To share Michelle with a child.

To stop doing all the things he loved.

They'd only been married a year. And everything was already changing. Instead of lazy Saturdays in bed together, they spent their weekends at the baby superstore or in a never-ending cleaning spree her mama called "nesting." He couldn't imagine she'd want him to head off for any more week-long fishing trips. Not once they had a baby at home. She'd been sighing over the still un-grouted tile in the baby's bathroom the whole time he'd been packing for this one.

Scottie cast again. The line plopped down into water now darker than it had been moments before. He glanced up at the clouds, where they had shifted to cover the sun. Wisps of gray wreathed the tops of the snow-covered mountains in the distance, the sky above already cold as winter slate. The bit of sun they'd had earlier had been a gift, nature's send-off before the fishing season ended. This weather — windy, frigid, and wet — was more normal for mid-October.

He pulled out the hat Michelle had tucked in his coat pocket and tugged it on. She'd laughed when she gave it to him. It was light purple and fuzzy, made from the yarn she'd had left over after she'd knit booties for the baby. He might look like a fool, but it was warm and fit him perfectly. He reeled in his line. As much as he loved being here, he loved Michelle more. And the longer he thought about it, the more ready he was to get home and wrap his arms around her. Around the baby growing in her belly. Their baby.

A child he could teach to fish one day, just like his father had done.

A mini version of him, or of Michelle. In mini-waders.

The grin came back to his face.

Wind whipped around him, finding its way under the collar of his shirt to leave a misty chill on the back of his neck. Scottie wiped at it and shivered.

Yeah, time to go.

He waded back toward his friends, who, for once, weren't bickering like an old married couple. Scottie veered around a spindly spruce reclining out over the river, the water resisting his progress as he rounded the bend.

Paul and Craig both stood on the shoreline, faces creased in concentration, neither moving. Paul, as tall as he was thin. Craig, his exact opposite, barely five foot eight, with the build of a wrestler who'd given up on weigh-ins. Craig held his head cocked, like he was listening for something.

"What's going on?" Scottie called up to them.

Craig jerked a finger to his lips. Quiet.

What the hell? Scottie scanned the woods, listening for whatever it was that seemed to have his friends so spooked. He picked up the soft lap of the river against its banks. The growing rustle of wind through the leaves. A magpie's raspy chatter.

A shuffling in the forest.

Scottie stopped moving through the water, listening harder. A heavy, muffled shifting of brush. Branches cracking, then the thud of a log turned over. Something big coming through the woods to the right of his friends. Moving toward them from the area where Scottie had been fishing, as if it were following his progress from the shoreline.

"Hey, bear!" he called out as they always did when a bear was nearby, and he closed the distance to his friends, water running off his waders in rivulets as he stepped onto shore. This was brown bear country. This late in the season, there were fewer of them, but, still… More than two thousand lived in Katmai National Park. And Scottie had been knee-deep in their primary food source. It made sense to announce you were there. To make enough noise, maybe the bear would just go away.

Paul fumbled with his gear bag, his hands shaking as he pulled out a can of bear spray. Scottie gave him a quick nod.

Good call.

He kicked himself for not having thought to bring some of his own. It was a stupid, rookie mistake. Craig echoed Scottie's "hey, bear," caught his friends' gazes, and tilted his head to the trail, indicating they should go. Head back to where the sea plane was meant to pick them up. Paul raised his bag onto one shoulder, the bear spray still gripped in his other hand.

A rustling came from the bushes to their left. Something else moved through the woods. Of considerable size, by the sound of it. Too far from the previous noise to have been made by the same creature. And not the receding steps of an animal as it retreated through the woods. Whatever it was, it was coming closer.

Scottie froze.

"Hey, bear!" he called out again, this time louder. Black bears didn't want anything to do with people. If you made noise, made yourself look big, they'd wander off, more interested in catching fish or collecting berries than bothering with people. Brown bears, like those living here in Katmai, were a different story.

Craig stayed silent, his Adam's apple bobbing.

Another crash in the woods to their right.

A mother and cubs?

A chill ran down Scottie's spine, his stomach tightening. If a mother bear felt threatened by them… if they'd somehow cut her off from her babies… He looked back out into the woods on the far side of the river. She would do whatever it took to make sure they weren't a threat.

He jerked his thumb toward the trail. They needed to go. Now.

His friends nodded and, as Scottie led the way back, they followed in a tense silence. He made his way down the trail, which was really nothing more than an overgrown dirt path winding through the trees. Even this time of year, when the brush had thinned, he only had ten or fifteen yards of visibility. The forest, a dense mass of spruce trees and willow thickets. He listened hard, trying to detect the bear through the squelch of their footsteps in the mud, the shifting of their gear against the still-wet rubber waders, past Craig's heavy breath as he struggled to keep up. The thirty pounds he'd added in the decade since high school wasn't doing him any favors.

Scottie stepped into the clearing surrounding a usually crystal-blue lake, that was now only a choppy gray reflection of the clouds above. Any time now, their sea plane would land and take them back to their cabin. They'd pour a couple stiff drinks and laugh about how they'd been chased out of the forest by what had probably been a bunch of deer.

Except it didn't feel funny. Not yet, anyway.

Craig and Paul followed him into the clearing, none of them speaking.

Another rustling in the trees, this time behind them.

Scottie whipped around.

An enormous, scruffy white bear loomed in the center of the trail. Its eyes were red-rimmed, its massive jaws hinged open.

A polar bear?

What the fuck?

His heart clattered against his rib cage, beating so hard it felt like it might burst free. Why would a polar bear be here? They were a thousand miles from where a polar bear should be, far enough that Scottie had never thought to find out what he should do if he encountered one. Did you hold your ground? Or run?

The bear ambled forward, panting hard. Now only a few yards away. If it were to charge—

Scottie took a step back. He glanced at Paul, who still held the bear spray gripped tight in his hand. But his friend seemed frozen in place, his eyes wide, the can still pointing down toward the ground.

The animal snorted, scenting the air with a hard huff as it raised up onto its hind legs, towering ten feet above them. Each of its paws was the size of a dinner plate.

"Run!" Paul yelled as he finally loosed the spray, aiming for the space between them and the bear. A smell like hot peppers and engine oil filled the air, burning Scottie's eyes. He didn't wait to see if the spray hit its mark.

He made a run for the lake. If they could put some distance between them and the bear... Maybe swim to the other side. He listened for the sound of his friends behind him but couldn't tell their footfalls from the pounding of blood in his ears. He threw down his gear and splashed into the water, too afraid to look back.

A scream erupted from behind him. Craig.

Scottie turned. The bear loomed over where Craig lay sprawled in the dirt — his head a red mass where his hair should've been. The bear had peeled his scalp like an orange.

Holy God.

Scottie froze, knee deep in the water. Nausea swirled in his gut.

The bear pawed at Craig, a heavy swipe against his torso.

But Craig didn't move, didn't call out.

No.

Please God don't let him be dead. He couldn't be dead.

Scottie's throat squeezed tight. How could he not be?

Paul stood a few dozen yards down the shoreline, his gaze flicking from Craig's body out to Scottie, horror etched into his face.

"Go," Scottie mouthed the word. For the moment, the bear seemed distracted, sniffing at their friend. Scottie tried to make himself run while he could. But he couldn't just leave his friends like that. Paul still frozen in place, Craig lying helpless in the mud.

The bear opened its mouth wide, cocking its head to one side as if it were trying to figure out how to fit Craig's skull into its jaws.

"Hey, bear!" Scottie yelled without thinking.

The bear looked up to meet his gaze, the white fur of its muzzle smeared red with blood.

A sheen of sweat broke out on Scottie's forehead, his stomach clenching as he forced himself to hold his ground. He needed to keep the bear's attention. Give Paul time to snap out of it and get moving, it was the only way Paul would have any chance to get away. There was nothing more he could do for Craig; he wouldn't leave his other friend there, too.

Scottie waited until Paul's frantic gaze met his and jerked his head up the shoreline.

Go.

Paul seemed to hesitate but then, finally started to move.

Scottie let out a tight breath as he watched his friend stumble down the shoreline from his peripheral vision. Paul was unsteady on his feet, but at least he was moving.

Which meant it was time for Scottie to do the same. He backed up slowly, sloshing deeper into the river. As much as he didn't want to leave Craig, his only real hope was if the bear let him go. If it decided to be satisfied with the meal it already had. That thought almost did him in. Still, he kept moving. Backing away. If he could just put some distance between them, he could swim along the shoreline, find Paul and—

The bear ambled toward him, coming to the water's edge, its black eyes glassy.

A shriek came from the shoreline.

Paul.

A second bear stood in Paul's path.

Scottie stopped breathing. Not the cub he had expected. But another full-grown polar bear, this one with the scars of healed scratches crisscrossing its face.

What the actual hell was happening?

The first bear waded into the lake.

Heading for Scottie.

There was nothing more he could do to help Paul. He had to hope his friend still had more spray left in the can. That he could use it somehow to get away. Scottie dove under the water, swimming as fast as he could, fighting the sucking drag of his waders in the water. Over the sound of his own strokes, a loud splash came from behind him. And with it, he realized his mistake: polar bears spent half their lives in the water. As bad as things were on land, this would be so much worse.

He forced himself to go faster.

Stroke, stroke, breathe.

Stroke, stroke, breathe.

He could do this. He had to do this.

Had to get back to Michelle.

To his baby.

A vise clamped his leg. Pulling, tearing. White hot dots of pain blotted his vision as he fought to get free, and his head went under. His chest compressed, his pulse pounded in his ears. Another scorching burst of agony as something slammed into him — the hurting deeper, more brutal, more primal than anything he'd ever felt.

He screamed. And water filled his mouth, his lungs. He coughed it out, only to inhale more as he fought for the surface.

The bear pulled him closer. Claws and teeth tearing at his skin.

Something sharp seared into Scottie's stomach. Blood bloomed in the water around him. He twisted, trying to fight back. But he couldn't breathe, couldn't get free. He swung a fist at the bear's nose. Only his arm didn't move. It had gone loose, limp. His body no longer responding.

Another excruciating tear of flesh and muscle. The tang of copper spreading over his tongue. A flicker of Michelle's name through his mind. Then nothing but the black maw of the bear's open mouth looming above him.

CHAPTER 1

October 16, 2018

San Diego, California

Letty Duquesne wound her way through the ornate Spanish architecture of Balboa Park, dodging tourists and scanning the crowd. Even on a weekday, the place was packed. Families taking photos, school kids on their way to one of the twenty-plus museums spread throughout the park, and an assortment of street musicians playing everything from Mozart to Bon Jovi.

She dropped a few dollars in an upturned hat and aimed for the shade of an archway. As much as she wanted to pretend otherwise, her shift from the familiar comfort of working in academia to her current situation — a new job, in a new company, in a new city — hadn't been exactly smooth. No matter how committed she was to making the Jessa Duquesne Foundation a success, the past month she'd spent "starting over" was harder than she'd expected.

Lonelier.

Which was how she'd wound up on the friendship equivalent of a "first date."

Letty scanned the crowd again and, this time, spotted Gemma on the opposite side of the lily pond, waving to her from the foot of the Botanical Building.

The JDF's office manager and general jack-of-all-trades looked like Debbie Harry. She had a shock of what had to be home-dyed platinum-white hair, Doc Martens, and jeans that had been hacked off mid-calf.

Gemma pointed to a short stone bench, her eyebrows raised in a question — this good?

Letty gave her a thumbs-up and made her way through the crowd to where Gemma now sat cross-legged on the bench. "This is perfect." Letty smiled as she sat beside her. "Thanks for meeting me."

"Thanks for the invite." Gemma slid a silver packet from the pocket of her oversized blazer, her voice kissed with a South London accent. "I usually eat at my desk. But with everything that's been going on, I'm glad for the break. I'm knackered."

"I bet." Letty pulled a takeout salad from her bag and balanced the plastic clamshell on her lap. "Seems like getting Mark ready for tomorrow's presentation took a full-court press." The handful of people that made up the foundation's on-site staff had been in and out of his office all day, every day for the past week. Mark would be at his desk when she arrived in the morning and still there when she left each night, poring over binder after binder of data. Reviewing everything the foundation had been able to find about the rise in animal attacks, the increase in zoonotic diseases crossing over to the human population, and the myriad governmental responses… or failures to respond.

In a reasonable world, the volume of the data alone would've been enough to establish the need for greater action. The need for some centralized agency, like Jessa's foundation, to manage a response. But, of course, things didn't work that way. Not when half the congressional committee formed to look into the public's concerns were the same folks who claimed climate change was a hoax.

The thready notes of "Livin' on a Prayer" slipped through the courtyard, the street musician's violin shrill but on beat.

"You have no idea how mad it's been." Gemma ripped open the silver packet and pulled out a rainbow-sprinkled Pop-Tart. "Usually Mark's only in after hours. He's got to be at Stafford Oil during business hours, but lately he's at the foundation all the time.

And he's stressed as hell." She picked a sprinkle from the top of the pastry and popped it in her mouth. "At least Kathryn came to the rescue. I can't imagine how we would've gotten Mark ready without her helping to manage his Stafford Oil work load this week." Gemma chewed another bite and swallowed. "Even if having her here does set my teeth on edge."

"Really?" Letty forked through her salad, building the perfect bite of chicken, feta, and cucumber. "She seems nice enough." And the day Kathryn had arrived had been the only time Letty had seen Mark smile since she'd come to California.

"She's alright, I guess. Does so much for the JDF, she should be on payroll." Gemma shrugged, brushing crumbs from her jeans. "I just don't trust anyone that doesn't age."

Letty laugh-choked on a piece of lettuce. Kathryn's Upper East Side vibe was sort of intimidating. "Well, Botox or not, I'm glad she's gonna be there tomorrow to back him up." They had too much riding on what happened at that meeting for Mark to go it alone. There was only so much the foundation could do to identify what might be causing the changes they were seeing in the animal world without having access to real-time information about what was happening globally. As much good as they were doing handling any individual case, it wouldn't be enough to make a real difference unless they could see the trends and follow them back to the source.

Poor Mark had to know how much was riding on tomorrow's presentation, had to feel the weight of what failure would mean. Especially when the foundation's future would be decided by a bunch of political cronies. "I can't imagine how stressed he must be. I mean, who gets called to speak before a congressional committee?"

"He didn't exactly get a summons. He volunteered, so that's a little less scary. And he's there for the greater good. Maybe he'll get a nicer reception than they give their usual lot."

"True." The other CEOs who spoke before congressional committees were usually there to get a public reprimand. A slap on the wrist after they'd used the corporate structure to get away with one form of mass destruction or another. And those people were nothing like Mark. She felt an odd sense of pride in her once almost brother-in-law, now boss, even though she couldn't claim responsibility for all the work he'd done in Jessa's memory. For all the things he was still trying to do.

Letty picked her way through the salad. Where would he be now? On a plane? Probably halfway to DC, with his dark head bent over another binder. Wearing the glasses that made him look so much more serious than he did in her memories.

The ones she shouldn't be thinking about.

Gemma popped open an energy drink. "All we can do at this point is keep our fingers crossed and hope for the best."

"Yeah, for sure." Letty cleared her throat, forcing herself back to the present. To reality. "I'm glad we did this." She looked up at the palm trees swaying above them, then to the giant lath structure of the Botanical Building reflected in the pond. Built for a world's fair more than a hundred years before, it still stood proud and beautiful, giving them shade on a day too warm for October. "It's nice to be outside for a bit."

"Careful what you ask for." Gemma broke off another piece of pastry. "I'm surprised they didn't just skip orientation and send you out into the field already. We've been swamped all summer and now into the fall, every scientist on the team out on assignment since the doors opened. Seems like every other day we get a request from somewhere. Mountain lions turning the hiking trails in Oakland into a buffet. Or some crazy hyper-virulent bird flu popping up in the middle of Copenhagen. God knows what's next."

Letty shoved a bite of salad in her mouth, chewing it along with the guilt she'd been trying to ignore since she'd realized how understaffed the foundation was. A situation that was in some part — maybe a large part — her fault.

She'd been meant to start working with the foundation in August. But it had taken longer than she'd expected to end her lease, to close up her life at the university, to say goodbye to Bill and Priya. And, then, she hadn't wanted to miss Andrew's wedding. A smile flickered over her face. Renee had been beautiful at the ceremony, she and Andrew both glowing over Renee's baby bump.

Of course, she hadn't realized her delay would leave the foundation short a scientist. She cringed. It was not an ideal situation for them to be in as Mark prepared to offer up their services to the world.

Literally.

Gemma finished her Pop-Tart and took another deep swig from an eye-poppingly chartreuse can of caffeine. "You know, if Mark convinces the committee to let the foundation manage the country's national response, you may never see the inside of an office again."

Letty couldn't imagine anything better. She stabbed a cucumber with her fork. "I'd almost always rather be in the field." And a little space from Mark wouldn't be a bad thing either. He'd be back in a few days, and so would the awkward silences that cropped up anytime the two of them were alone together.

It wasn't that he was rude. He'd taken her to lunch when she first started, said all the right things — he was so glad she was there, she should let him know if she needed anything, maybe they could grab a coffee or he could help her get settled. But it was stilted, and no matter how nice he was when they ran into each other in the halls or at the office coffee pot, she could never think of what to say. She put her fork down with the cucumber still stuck to the tines. It was like the past clogged up her throat, wrapped her brain in cotton, and nothing but basic banalities would come out. If that.

He had eventually stopped trying.

Which was almost worse.

Gemma's phone rang from her purse. As she went digging for it, a huge brown bird with white markings swooped through the promenade. It narrowly missed a camera-laden tour group, the crowd ducking and screeching as it swept past.

A red-shouldered hawk.

Letty tracked the bird's ascent back into the sky as it rounded over the Botanical Building and came back for a second pass. What was it after? She scanned the ground for a mouse or chipmunk. Maybe a smaller bird? Hawks would eat most anything their size or smaller. Although it was odd for it to be hunting here, in a place so crowded with people.

"This is Gemma." Her new friend finally answered the call, her tone now formal and pure Queen's English, which meant the call must be important. Something for the foundation. "I'm sorry. I didn't quite hear that. Could you start again from the beginning?"

The hawk swept back across the pond, its trajectory lower as it headed toward the entrance to the Timken Museum. It landed on the handle of a baby carriage. The mother stood with her back turned to the stroller as she searched for something in a diaper bag.

Gemma lowered her voice. "What do you mean missing?"

Letty glanced back to Gemma. Whatever that was, it didn't sound good. She kept half her attention on Gemma, the rest on the bird.

The hawk leaned forward, as if trying to see past the cloth draped over the carriage to find what soft morsel might wait inside.

Letty's mouth went dry, and she clapped her hands, hoping to startle the bird into flight.

It ignored her.

The animal would have no reason to hurt a child. But if the past year had taught her anything, it was that she couldn't assume it would act predictably. Things were different now. Very different.

Letty shifted to the edge of her seat.

The bird turned, meeting Letty's gaze. Its eyes reflected a flat, predatory black.

"Shoo." She stood, clapping her hands again in its direction and moving closer. "Excuse me?" She called out to the mother, who was still busy digging through the baby's bag.

The hawk kneaded its claws against the stroller's handle.

"You're not going to believe this." Gemma turned her way.

Letty didn't break eye contact with the bird. "Hang on." She strode toward the carriage, the bird not moving an inch. A few other tourists turned to look, but no one moved to help.

The mother plucked a pacifier from the bag and turned. A shriek tore out of her, and she threw herself toward the carriage. The bird took off in a flutter of indignant feathers, and a wail came from inside the stroller as the mother hurried to wheel the child away.

Letty finally let go of a breath and turned back to Gemma, who seemed only now to have realized what had been happening with the hawk. They both watched as the bird disappeared over the roof of the museum.

Gemma refocused on Letty, and lines creased around her eyes. "Cody Crawford's gone missing."

"Crawford?" Letty tried to place the name. "That's the large mammal guy, right?"

"Yeah. That's him. He's been up in Alaska working on our polar bear case. Seems he went out to the incident site and got lost in the woods." She cringed, whether from worry or as an acknowledgment of how bad that sounded, Letty couldn't tell.

Gemma dropped the phone back into her purse. "Search and Rescue's out looking now, but they say it doesn't look good. No sign of him."

Letty sat on the bench, watching the sky for any sign of the hawk.

The idea that Crawford might just "get lost" in the woods didn't sound right. She'd spent an hour after work one night browsing the bios for the foundation's other scientists, mostly out of a perverse desire to know how she stacked up. From what she remembered,

Crawford was an experienced field researcher like her, mostly working with large carnivores. He would have known not to go out to the site alone. And, even if he had, he wouldn't just wander off and not be able to find his way back. When you spent your life working in one unknown wilderness after another, navigation was part of the basic skill package.

Letty closed the lid on her salad, her appetite gone.

If Crawford was missing, chances were good he wasn't coming back.

CHAPTER 2

Somewhere above St. Louis, Missouri

Turbulence shimmied down the jet as Mark rubbed both hands over his face, two days' worth of stubble scratching against his palms. He'd planned to fly commercial, not wanting to use the company's Gulfstream for foundation business. But his Aunt Kath had been right. The last thing they needed tonight was an audience. He looked across the jet's center aisle. "What do you mean missing?"

Aunt Kath pulled a cardigan from the travel bag she'd dumped in the empty seat beside her. "The seaplane pilot dropped him off at Brooks River at nine Monday morning. Came back to pick him up at noon, as they'd agreed, and Crawford was gone. No sign of him." She draped the sweater over her shoulders and picked up her coffee cup, wrapping her hands around it. "No luck on the sat phone, and his cell goes straight to voicemail. The pilot called the park service, who looped in Fish and Game and the local police. They've all been out looking, but, so far, no one's found a trace of him. Or the polar bears the survivor reported."

An image flashed in his mind of Crawford's body, broken and bloody, cached somewhere in the woods. A bear's meal saved for later. Mark's stomach twisted. "Shit."

"I know." Kath said, her voice soft. She looked away and sipped her coffee. "He may still turn up. Could've gone out and twisted an ankle, the phone batteries gone dead."

"Yeah, maybe." Although that seemed unlikely. Part of him wanted to tell their pilot to turn around and take him to where Crawford had disappeared. He wanted to join the search himself. To keep looking until they'd found the man, one way or the other. They had only met a handful of times since Crawford had been hired, and those interactions had been minimal. A handshake hello, a quick welcome to the team. But Crawford was one of their people, and Mark couldn't help but feel responsible. It was his foundation that had sent Crawford into the field to begin with, which meant it was his responsibility to make sure Crawford came home safe.

He made himself take a breath. There were already people out looking, people trained to do just that. And he couldn't miss the presentation tomorrow, no matter how much he wanted to make sure Crawford was okay. His hand drifted to his chest, finding the rings he wore on a long chain, tucked safely beneath his shirt. His and Jessa's wedding bands were always with him. Their weight against his skin a constant reminder of why he was doing what he was doing.

Too much was at stake for him not to. Not just for the foundation but for the world. If the time he'd spent preparing for this hearing had convinced him of anything, it was that the scope and scale of the problem they faced was worse than what anymore realized. And it went far beyond any normal aberration or trend. The world was shifting, changing in seismic, fundamental ways that would be disastrous if left unchecked.

The sandwich he had forced down in the airport before they left San Diego turned to lead in his stomach. If they couldn't study the phenomenon, collect real and complete data, they'd never know why animal attacks were on the rise or why zoonotic diseases now crossed virtually unchecked into the human population. Worse, they'd have no chance of stopping it.

Still.

How could he be flying to the opposite end of the country and still feel he'd done everything within his power to bring Crawford home? Didn't he owe it to everyone he sent into the field to make sure they came back?

Aunt Kath held her coffee cup out to the flight attendant, who refilled it from a shining silver carafe. Kath took a contemplative sip, waiting until the fresh-faced young man returned to the plane's kitchen before she spoke. "Crawford's disappearance shouldn't be a problem tomorrow. Right now, the story's only been picked up by the local press. No reason to think any hint of it will hit the news in DC. And, even if it does, we can easily have the PR team handle it."

"I'm not worried about the press." He stared out an oval window into the night sky. Not a star in sight. The darkness unbroken except for the clouds they flew through, the jet's reflected wing light turning them an unnatural red. "I'm worried about Crawford. This is the first time we've lost someone in the field."

"Of course you're worried about him," she said. "We all are."

Nothing about the man's disappearance made sense. The JDF was there at the invitation of the Alaska Department of Fish and Game, working hand in hand with the National Park Service. Any site examination should have been done with a team of experienced, well-armed locals. There was no reason for Crawford to be investigating a bear attack without their support, especially when the animals responsible were still at large. Mark shifted in his seat, the soft ivory leather creaking as he moved. "Should we check in again with Search and Rescue?"

Kath shook her head. "They'll let us know as soon as there's any sign of him." She made a small frown, probably thinking the same thing he was. The longer they went without finding Crawford, the less likely it was they'd find him alive. She cleared her throat. "I'm sure they're doing everything they can."

He didn't doubt that, but it didn't make the lack of answers any less frustrating. He stared back out at the bleak, starless sky. He couldn't handle another death on his conscience. His hand drifted back to his chest, only this time, he pressed down, indenting the rings into his skin.

Crawford wouldn't have been in those woods if Mark hadn't sent him. Wouldn't be missing. Maybe dead, his body rotting away somewhere.

Like Jessa's. Her body lost to the sea.

No way to lay either of them to rest.

No place for loved ones to go to say goodbye. To feel close to them again.

Just gone.

The back of his throat burned.

And what about the polar bears who'd attacked those fishermen? Bears who had already shown a willingness to attack people. Still on the loose, the authorities no closer to figuring out how they'd gotten so far south or what had led them to attack.

What if Crawford's disappearance delayed the investigation so much that other people were attacked?

That other people died?

He swallowed hard, his throat so tight it hurt. The hum of the jet's engines changed pitch, growing louder in his ears.

"Stop, Mark." Aunt Kath's voice broke into his thoughts.

He looked over at her, watching him, her gaze fixed on the hand he still held pressed to his sternum. He made himself let go. It wasn't the first time she'd caught him doing it, not by a long shot. But she'd never said a word about it before.

"Stop what?" He could still feel the impression of the wedding bands where he'd pressed them into his skin. He'd probably have a bruise. Not that he cared.

"Blaming yourself." She gave him a small, sad smile. Her mouth twisting down the same way his father's had. So much about the way his father and aunt looked was the same, even if their personalities couldn't have been more different. Him, the center of every room, forever working some business contact or political connection. As ruthless as he was successful. Her, a constant, quiet calm, usually standing bemused in a corner. She was one of the best people he knew, sometimes prickly but fiercely loyal. And, as a kid, Mark had always felt most comfortable beside her, watching his father work his toxic magic from a distance.

Who would have ever thought the two of them would wind up at the helm of Stafford Oil together? Not just that, but running a foundation at the same time. Two introverts forced into the limelight.

"I'm not," he said, even though he was sure she knew that's all he'd been doing since Jessa died. "I'm just trying to get my head wrapped around everything before we walk into that meeting tomorrow." He cleared his throat, digging for anything that might allow a change in topic. "Did we get confirmation that our materials arrived at the hotel?"

Her eyebrows quirked up, and he cringed. She wasn't his assistant. "Sorry, I—"

She waved him off. "Everything's there. Your office manager emailed us both. The rooms are ready, and a car is set to pick you up tomorrow morning at eight."

"Good, good." He closed his eyes and let his head fall back against the headrest, pretending he was trying to sleep. Even if it was the last thing he felt able to do. He should've pulled a sketch pad from his travel bag before he let the attendant stow it. He could have lost himself in the freedom of the blank page, given himself a place to go where his thoughts wouldn't follow.

"Mark?"

He cracked an eye. His aunt was still watching him, concern on her face. That couldn't be good. He lifted his head. "Yeah?"

"There's something else." She shifted in her seat. "I wasn't sure I wanted to say anything, not with everything else on your plate. But it's getting to the point that, if I don't bring it up, it feels like I'm keeping it from you." She looked away.

He sat up straight, his attention now completely on her. "I know you wouldn't do that."

Another sad smile. "I'm hearing more grumbling from Reid Schaefer and his cohort. You know they've been unhappy since you decided to have Stafford Oil endow the foundation. They feel its mission is *contrary to the company's interests*," she said the words with implied air quotes, "and they're getting noisy about it."

"Fucking hell." If anything, between the tax write-off and the good PR, providing funding for the JDF was a net benefit for Stafford Oil. Not that he was surprised Reid was claiming otherwise. Reid had been angling for a seat at the head of Stafford Oil's table as long as Mark could remember. Nipping at his heels, questioning his every choice. Mark clenched his jaw, heat creeping up his neck. It was one thing to make a power play within the company, but to do it now, with the foundation's future at stake… that crossed a line.

Kath shot him a worried look. "Worse, I'm afraid Reid's getting traction with the board. You've been out of the office so much lately. And you appearing before the committee tomorrow seems like a public confirmation of their claim that you're too focused on your passion project and not enough on the company's bottom line."

His hands tightened into fists in his lap. He'd tried his damnedest to do both but… Reid wasn't entirely wrong. When he started the JDF, he hadn't had any real idea of the amount of time it would take. He had imagined, once he got it up and running, he would be acting in a more advisory role, not being there every day like he had been lately. "I know I haven't been as present at Stafford Oil lately, but I've been careful not to let anything fall through the cracks. And I'll be back full time soon enough. I just need to get the foundation on solid footing first."

"I know. I've had a front row seat to how much you've been burning the candle at both ends. But with this year's rate of production, the price per barrel at only fifty-four dollars, and contracts down thirty percent…" She shrugged. "We're primed to take our first annual loss in the history of the company, and you know the board isn't going to take that lightly."

Mark closed his eyes, his mouth going dry. She wasn't wrong. Never mind that the same numbers were true for every oil and gas company industry wide, or that Stafford Oil had been touting its commitment to environmentally sustainable business practices long before Mark took the helm. All he'd done was make those claims true.

Still, if he didn't turn things around fast, heads would roll.

And his would be the first.

CHAPTER 3

October 17, 2018
San Diego, California
Sunlight streamed in through Letty's window. She had a full cup of coffee, plenty of space to spread out, and top-of-the-line tech — everything she could need to work at her absolute best. But none of it seemed to matter today. Letty flipped through the pages of yet another incident report, trying to ignore the "vroom" of the imaginary vacuum cleaner running back and forth outside her closed office door. Gemma's five-year-old son, Noah, had been at it for the better part of half an hour, and he didn't show any signs of tiring.

She had noise-cancelling headphones buried somewhere in her mountain of still unpacked boxes at home, but she hadn't had any luck finding them. Letty cupped her hands over her ears instead and forced herself to focus on the file in front of her: An elderly man on an early morning walk through the Singapore Botanic Gardens had been attacked by a family of otters, bitten repeatedly, and nearly bled to death before a jogger came to his rescue.

Odd? Yes. But did that mean the attack was outside the realm of normal animal behavior? Not necessarily. Otters often found their way into populated areas. And a family of otters could mean pups, which could explain the adult otters' aggressive behavior. She checked the reported time of the incident, approximately 5:45 a.m.

Another series of "vrooms" from the hallway. Gemma's muted voice, the thud of little running feet, and then, finally, quiet.

Thank God.

Letty stared out the window. Outside, a snarl of interstates crisscrossed one over another, but her mind's eye found her across the world, in a wooded, waterfront park on a small, tropical island off the tip of the Malay Peninsula. The sun wouldn't have been up before six, and in the predawn darkness, the otters could easily have confused the man with a predator. If he'd come upon them suddenly…

She shifted the report to the bottom of her stack. She'd need to do a little more work, confirm the details, check to see if there had been other incidents with the same group of animals. But, for once, it looked like there might be a simple explanation.

She reached for the next file but found her hand on the computer's mouse instead. It wouldn't hurt to check the news one more time. There had to be something about Mark's presentation to the committee, eventually. She clicked through the news sites she thought most likely to cover the hearing, CSPAN, a few of the blogs posted by environmental groups who'd been tracking the foundation's work so far. She scanned each landing page before she clicked to the next.

None of them had anything relevant.

She clicked over to the joint committee's website but didn't really expect to find anything new. It took months, sometimes years, for the government to post footage of congressional committee meetings. And predictably, the site had nothing up yet. She grumbled out half a curse and, mostly as a Hail Mary, clicked over to CNN.

A new headline flashed onto her screen, "Is the Natural World on the Edge of Collapse?" A photo under it showed Mark grim-faced and ignoring the cameras as he strode down a wide, carpeted hallway.

"Holy shit." The foundation wasn't just getting press. They were major news. She clicked on the article, breath trapped in her lungs as she skimmed down the page. A brief summary of some of the more well-known recent disasters — the die-off of honey bees along the west coast, the spike in treatment-resistant bovine tuberculosis, the violent alligator attacks that had shut down Orlando's biggest theme parks. A quote from Texas senator Tom Hilliard followed. "These events are tragic but unrelated. Any attempt to draw a connection between them is fear-mongering at best. Our hearts go out to…" Letty read past the empty thoughts and prayers, skimming until she spotted Mark's name.

"Mark Stafford, CEO of Stafford Oil & Gas and head of the Jessa Duquesne Foundation, arrived at the capitol today. Many on the Hill expected him to deliver impassioned remarks regarding the need for a greater and more coordinated government response to what he has previously called 'an unprecedented threat to the balance of nature.' Stafford's own fiancé was killed when— " Letty skipped down another paragraph. She didn't need the reporter to tell her why Mark was there.

Didn't need another reminder of how her sister had died.

Her chest constricted with a dull, bruised pain. She forced herself to ignore it and kept reading. "Stafford arrived to a room packed with press, members of the public, and representatives from a wide variety of special interest groups. But minutes before the meeting was set to begin, congressional aides cleared the room, pointing only to unspecified national security concerns and refusing further comment as to why the meeting had been closed."

Letty leaned back in her chair. What part of Mark's presentation could touch on issues of national security? No doubt the threats the foundation sought to address were of the utmost importance to the nation. Really, to the world.

But national security sounded like a different sort of threat.

She tapped her nails against the desk. What was she not seeing?

Another "vroom" echoed through the office.

Letty put her hands over her ears and went back to the article, where another image had been inset into the text. A photo showed members of the public filing out of the meeting room. Behind them, the joint committee looked on from behind a long conference table on a raised dais. One of the faces stood out. Senator Hilliard. The same man quoted earlier in the article. The one who'd already gone on record disputing what Mark was there to establish, who'd offered platitudes instead of action.

As usual.

Son of a—

A knock sounded from her door.

"Come in." She called out, taking her hands from her ears.

The door swung open to reveal Gemma, who had Noah hanging from one arm. The little boy had surfer blonde hair, the remains of what looked like strawberries smeared around his mouth, and eyes only for his mother. He looked up at Gemma with pure adoration.

Gemma tucked the boy against her side and took in the files stacked around Letty's computer. "I need to ask for your help with something."

Letty looked to Noah, then back at Gemma. "I'm not much of a babysitter."

"Not that kind of help." Gemma laughed and planted a kiss on the top of her son's shaggy head before whispering in his ear. "Would you go clean under mummy's desk? I saw some hedgehog-sized dust balls under there."

Noah slid from Gemma's arms, grinned at both of them, and "vroomed" down the hall.

"Sorry about the noise. Noah's usually at my ex's on Fridays, but Donny no-showed this morning." She closed her eyes and gave an irritated shake of her head. "I swear he's hoping I'll get the sack."

Letty scoffed. "Never gonna happen. This place would literally fall apart without you." Gemma not only managed the entire team's schedules, she made sure every new case was assigned to the right person. She saw to it the team had everything they needed to do their work and ran the office itself. Even down to replacing the IT guy, whose skill set had seemed to begin and end with telling anyone who had an issue to reboot their machines. "And why would he try to get you fired?"

Gemma shrugged. "Noah and I were only able to stay in our flat after Donny left because the foundation pays twice what my last job did. And trying to find an affordable place in San Diego's even harder than trying to find a decent job." She toed one of her big black boots against the hardwood floor, like she was trying to decide whether to go on. "Donny's favorite tune is that I can't give Noah a 'stable' home. And, so far, the judge in our custody case loves to sing along. I've made some mistakes, in the past…" A flush crept up Gemma's face. She looked at Letty, then away. "Sorry, that's probably too much information."

Letty shook her head. She knew first hand what an unstable home looked like — her parents wouldn't have known stability if they'd tripped over it — and Gemma was nothing like that. Gemma might live on a diet of sugar and caffeine, but her son had come into the office with a bento box of yogurt, cut fruit, and veggies. "You've got nothing to be sorry for."

"Well, actually, about that…" Gemma cleared her throat, a grimace twisting her face. "We need you to go to Alaska."

Letty waited for what Gemma said to make sense. It didn't. "What?"

"The rest of the team is already out in the field. Crawford disappeared before he could even file a preliminary report on what he'd found on the polar bear attack." Another tap of her boot against the floor. "And the locals are still expecting our help."

Letty shook her head. "I don't think that's me. I'm a disease ecologist. I've traced different pathogens in everything from tadpoles to bobcats. But never bears. You need a large mammal specialist. Surely the local Fish and Game Department and the park service are better equipped for it than I am. At least until one of the other large mammal folks can get there." She didn't want to sound like she wasn't a team player, but it wouldn't do anyone any good for her to go make a mess of things. "Isn't the team handling the elk case supposed to be back at the end of this week?"

"That's what I told Mark when he suggested you go." Gemma leaned against the door frame. "But he said you were the best person for the job. And I think he's worried any further delay will make it impossible to track the—"

"Mark asked for me specifically?" For reasons she didn't want to look at too closely, that changed things. The last thing she wanted was to let Mark down. She owed it to him to do everything she could to help. She owed it to Jessa.

"Yeah, but he'll understand why you can't. You're only just now getting settled in. And it isn't fair to make your first on-site assignment something that's already a bit off in the deep end."

Letty nodded, even as she questioned her own thinking. The case wasn't just in the deep end because Crawford had vanished. It was more than that. He'd disappeared while the foundation's future was on a razor's edge. They couldn't be seen as unreliable. Not when Mark was asking for Congress to give them more authority. To trust them to handle even more of the government's response. This was their chance to do something important, to make a difference. To keep others from dying in a freak animal attack, the way Jessa had.

Letty cleared a tightness from her throat. "Did he say how it was going in DC?"

A line formed between Gemma's brows. "Not in so many words."

That didn't sound good. Letty leaned forward on the desk, her elbow knocking into the mouse, bringing the computer awake. The image of people filing out of the congressional meeting room reappeared. Hilliard still sat behind the conference table, his face an unreadable mask. A young senator from New York sat next to him, her hair slicked back in a no-nonsense bun. The fire of righteous indignation burned in her eyes as she watched the public led from the room.

Whoever'd decided to sit the two of them side by side had a real sense of humor. Half of every news cycle seemed dedicated to barbs one of them shot at the other. Hilliard, lamenting her "out of touch liberal elitist agenda" and her, laying blame on him and the rest of the Republican party for everything from gun violence to the rising national poverty level.

It was pretty clear, even from that one image, the committee's battle lines were already being drawn. But it was impossible to say which of them would sway the vote.

What if the foundation's failure to properly handle the bear attack in Alaska was what decided it? She couldn't let that happen. Couldn't fail Mark again.

"Tell him I'll do it."

CHAPTER 4

Washington D.C.

Mark turned a corner, then another. Each endless, unfamiliar hallway looked the same as the last. Long swaths of Burgundy wallpaper broken only by bland oil paintings depicting one patriotic scene or another. Small groups of people in dark suits stood clustered outside closed doors or in the occasional alcove, their heads bent together, their voices pitched low. Everything about them spoke to some great, serious purpose. Faces drawn, arms crossed.

Some gave him a polite hello, others ignored him altogether. But, without exception, a wake of whispers floated down the hall behind him.

"Yeah, that's him."

"What would his father have—"

"...board must be losing their shit."

Whether they were aides, lobbyists, or members of Congress — there for him or for something entirely unrelated — he couldn't tell and didn't care. He made another left and, this time, found the hallway blissfully empty. His footsteps made no sound, his progress consumed by the thick carpets beneath his feet.

Mark finally let himself exhale.

He'd spent all day under a microscope. Him on one side of a table, the entire congressional committee lined up on the other. Like he was a meal not quite big enough to go around, everyone angling to get a piece before all the good parts were all gone. He hated crowds under the best of circumstances, much less when they were staring at him. No one like him belonged at the helm of a multinational corporation. He would rather be anywhere other than the spotlight.

But then, he'd never been given a choice.

He was there because his father had wanted it that way. And even from beyond the grave, Conrad Stafford always got what he wanted. It'd been that way Mark's entire life. His father shoving something down his throat, his mother coaxing him to swallow it. Or at least, she had until she'd decided Gin and Tonics were better company.

Mark dropped onto an upholstered bench in a shallow alcove and checked his watch, 3:50. Ten minutes until he'd need to be back before the committee, ready to answer more questions. He rolled his neck, the muscles in his shoulders protesting like the strings of a guitar tuned too tight. He should be going over his notes, looking back through the binder where he'd organized the foundation's action plans and proposals.

But he couldn't stop thinking about his conversation with Gemma that morning.

He let his head fall back on the wall behind him. When he'd asked her to see if Letty would take over for Crawford, it had seemed to make so much sense. He needed someone solid on the ground. Letty was brilliant, and he couldn't think of anyone he trusted more when it came to making sure the foundation was a success, to making sure they did absolutely everything they could to honor Jessa's memory. She was just as invested in what they were doing as he was. Maybe even more.

But then, hours later, as he'd been trying to focus on the committee's repetitive, inane questions, it had occurred to him — taking over for Crawford might be dangerous.

That prospect had taken his train of thought out at the knees. He'd had to ask the senator from Massachusetts to repeat her question. It was only because he had over-prepared so thoroughly that he'd managed to recover and stay on script.

Even now, the worry plagued him.

The last person he'd sent to Katmai hadn't come home.

Mark rolled his neck again, rubbing at one of the knots in his shoulder.

What if Letty didn't come back?

He shook off the thought. She would hate it if she knew he was thinking that way.

She was a grown woman, a scientist at the top of her field. Someone who knew more about surviving in the wilderness than he could ever hope to. She didn't need him to protect her, wouldn't want him to try.

God, she hardly tolerated him.

He looked down at his wingtips.

Not that he blamed her.

The memory came back, like it always did. The moment he had realized Jessa had been gone too long. The cold shock of the water when he'd jumped in. The fire of the jellyfish tentacles as they'd reached up to pull him down into the black depths of the water beneath. Fighting against them, against the pain, even as he knew Jessa must be down there, somewhere. So close and yet… gone.

As beyond his reach as if she'd disappeared completely. Consumed by the sea.

He pressed a hand to his chest, to the rings, to where they lay over the worst of the scarring, hidden by his tailored shirt and jacket. But always there. It didn't hurt anymore, at least not physically. Letty had lost her only sister because he hadn't been there when Jessa needed him. Hadn't realized anything was wrong until it was too late. Until Jessa was already gone, and there was nothing he could—

A murmur of voices came from the end of the hall.

Two men rounded the corner and stopped, not seeming to notice he was there. They talked with their heads close together.

Senator Hilliard, who'd sat in the meeting all morning without asking a single question. His face like he'd just sucked a lemon. The second man, Mark recognized but couldn't place. Salt and pepper hair, parted sharp enough to cut glass, his face long and drooping. Heavy cheeks pooled near his chin. The man ran a hand down his tie and tapped the end, tilting his head toward the senator as if to leave no doubt the man had his rapt attention.

That gesture.

Mark had seen it before.

The droop-faced man had been at his house, or rather, Mark's parents' house. For cocktail parties, schmoozing with his mother, and in closed-door meetings with his father.

Senator Hilliard was deep in conversation with an oil and gas lobbyist. A man Mark would have seen as an ally in any other setting.

But here, today?

It couldn't mean anything good.

CHAPTER 5

October 18, 2018

San Diego, California

Letty fanned her shirt against her chest, but it did nothing to cool her clammy skin. She pulled her rolling bag around the end of a long row of seats and dropped into the only one not already taken. She had expected the airport to be empty so early. But even at a quarter-to-six, it was like an anthill in full swarm. Travelers clogged every space, haphazard and red-faced, yelling at trailing children or struggling under the weight of overstuffed carry-ons.

She wasn't a great flier on a good day, and the frenzied I'm-gonna-miss-my-flight vibe in the security line had been contagious. By the time she had collected her shoes and bag, she'd careened through the airport in a near panic, luggage in tow, to what — of course — wound up being the last gate on the terminal.

Only to find she had twenty minutes to spare.

Not enough time to go back for a cup of coffee, but at least a chance to sit down and look over her case file before they boarded.

She pulled the folder from her bag, careful to keep her elbows tucked so she wouldn't hit the men to either side of her. Both had manspread well into the aisle and casually draped themselves over not just their armrests but hers. One chattered into a Bluetooth earpiece. The other peered down at his phone, scrolling through NASDAQ reports.

She glanced away, not wanting to get caught looking. Even if the stock-junkie did have his phone propped more or less on her knee.

She settled the file in her lap and flipped it open, tuning out the clamor around her.

As usual, the file Gemma had prepared was organized and thorough. Every thing they knew so far, in one, portable place. She flipped through materials gathered from the local authorities, skimming past preliminary reports from the National Park Service, the Alaska Department of Fish and Game, and the Alaska Department of Public Safety, to the statement given by the one surviving fisherman. This was why she was here.

Paul Reardon, a twenty-nine-year-old man from Anchorage, currently lay recovering in a Bristol Bay hospital from unspecified injuries resulting from a bear attack. When interviewed, he had reported that the attack had been perpetrated, not by one of the thousands of brown bears inhabiting the Katmai National Park, but by two adult polar bears.

Which made no sense.

Polar bears were notoriously solitary creatures. They rarely traveled in groups, unless it was a mother and cub. And the bears would've been way too far from the pack ice where they usually lived. A quick Google search told her the furthest south a polar bear had previously been spotted was on St. Lawrence Island, more than five hundred miles north of where Reardon and the other men were attacked.

But what conclusions could she really draw from that information?

Not much, given what was happening in the world.

What had always been the norm for animal behaviors wasn't something they could count on anymore. And as the balance of nature continued to tip, chances were they'd see more and more of this sort of thing. Animals in habitats where they didn't belong. The world forced to adjust, with catastrophic consequences for the people who didn't.

Still, if polar bears had traveled that far south, there had to be a reason.

And it was her job to find it.

She tapped her pen against the folder, making herself take a step back. Before she got to the "why" of the attack, she needed to consider whether this case could hinge more on the "if". Eyewitness accounts were notoriously unreliable, especially when the witness was under stress at the time of the event — victims often could remember only the gun, not their attacker. And Reardon's experience had been nothing if not stressful. He'd nearly lost his own life, had watched two friends brutally mauled to death.

Would it be any wonder if his memory was unreliable?

What she needed was a way to confirm Reardon's statement. She flipped back through the reports. The seaplane pilot who'd come to his rescue had seen neither bear. The sound of his approaching engine apparently scaring both animals off into the woods before he'd gotten close enough to see the carnage he was flying into.

She shuffled the pages again, stopping on a hand-sketched map of the incident site. It showed the relative distances between the river, the lake, and the areas where human remains had been discovered. A picture formed in her mind of what must've happened. What Reardon and the others must've experienced. An uneasy foreboding curled through her, and she shifted in her chair. Her knee bumping NASDAQ's.

She mumbled a "sorry" and pushed her anxiety away. She couldn't let herself worry about the still-missing bears, about what might happen when she was standing where those men had died. This was her job, and damned if she wasn't going to do it.

The more she studied the diagram, the less plausible it seemed that Reardon could've experienced what he did and confused brown bears for polar bears. He hadn't just been attacked himself, he'd had a clear view of the apparent attack sites for both other men.

She stared off toward the floor-to-ceiling window looking out over the tarmac. A group of teenage girls in painfully short shorts, ponytails, and matching t-shirts sat sprawled on the floor beneath it. By their collective height, she'd bet a college volleyball team. Through the glass behind them, a plane pulled slowly to the gate, the cloudy gray sky reflected in the cockpit windshield. Each cloud heavy and black-bottomed, ready to burst. Although she doubted they would. It rarely rained in San Diego, especially not this time of year.

Rain.

Crap.

She scrambled back to her phone, pulling up last week's weather reports for King Salmon, Alaska. She held her breath until the data finally loaded. It had been overcast the entire week, but the park had had very little actual rainfall. Which meant she could probably still get viable prints, if she got there before the weather turned. She scrolled down the weather app, checking the forecast for the next week: overcast, mostly cloudy, then rain. A 48% chance, 54% the next day. It got worse from there. The sooner she could get to the incident site, the better.

Before all her evidence washed away.

She tapped her pen on the folder again. She'd known cataloging prints would be one of her first steps on site. The differentiation between brown and polar bear prints now all the more important. But would she even know what to look for? Brown bears' prints were shaped differently than black bears, with their toes less arced and spaced more closely together. And while polar bears had evolved from grizzlies — the more inland cousin to the brown bears at Brooks River — their habitat would almost certainly have necessitated some notable evolution. Wouldn't it?

She should know the answer to that.

Crawford would.

But here she was, grasping around, trying to figure it out. Hating that her best bet — again — was to search the internet for an answer. She cursed her lack of relevant field experience for the thousandth time.

She needed to get her shit together. Now wasn't the time for self-doubt. She had packed all the field guides and research papers she'd been able to find. She would read each page of it, and by tomorrow, she'd know every damn thing there was to know about polar bears. Starting with prints and any other sign she could look for. There was bound to be some distinction she could identify. She'd guess size, if nothing else. Polar bears were marine mammals, after all, sometimes spending full days swimming without ever touching land. Chances were, their paws would be larger, more suited to water than—

A text dinged from her phone.

She dug it out to find a message waiting from Gemma: "Need you to pop into Puddlejump. Pick up files and whatnot."

Letty looked down at the message, trying to make sense of it. Gemma knew she was getting on a plane; she'd booked the ticket. And what the hell was a Puddlejump?

She rang Gemma's number and cupped a hand over her other ear, trying to block out the Bluetooth guy's conversation next to her. "You want me to do what?"

"Just pop by Crawford's hotel whenever you get in tonight and collect whatever you can find." Gemma said, her raised voice competing with the whir of the foundation's copy machine.

Letty grimaced, looking back out to the tarmac, where fat drops of rain spotted the concrete. The idea of walking into a missing man's hotel room to rummage around in his things sounded like a terrible idea. Worse than a terrible idea. "I don't think the hotel's gonna let me in."

Another loud clunk of paper, then the pop of a three-hole punch. "They don't seem to know he's missing yet. How that's possible, I don't know. The locals still seem to be treating it as a missing person, more focused on the rescue efforts. But you shouldn't have any problem getting into the room. There's a key waiting for you at the front desk."

If there was ever a time when she could've done with Gemma being slightly less capable, this was it. "How did you manage that?"

"I booked the room for him. My name's on the reservation, so easy peasy. I emailed you the address." The snap of a three ring binder clamping into place, and Gemma gave a soft grunt of satisfaction. "I'd have put you up in the same place. It looked like the nicest of the hotels in town. But they were booked. And all the other places I found were fishing lodges."

Super.

A thick thunk came over the line, then a tap tap tap. A sound Letty recognized as Gemma straightening the edges of an incident report against the countertop the way she always did. "With any luck, Crawford's files on the polar bear attack will be there. Could give you some idea of what happened with those bears. Or at least a place to start."

Letty shifted her suitcase to let an elderly couple in matching "Somebody in California loves me" t-shirts pass through the aisle. Gemma wasn't wrong. Even if Letty were to cram data into her head the whole flight, she wouldn't be as prepared as Crawford. His insights could be game-changing. This was his field, after all, not hers.

A blaring, garbled voice came from overhead. "Alaska Airlines flight 579 to Portland is now ready for boarding. All first class passengers may now…"

Letty waited for the announcement to end. Even if she could get herself comfortable with the idea of digging through Crawford's things, by the time she finally got to Alaska, she wasn't going to want to do anything but check into her own hotel and fall over. Gemma had gotten her the best flights available, but travel from San Diego to Bristol Bay borough meant three flights. First to Portland, then Anchorage, a three hour layover, and finally on to King Salmon, Alaska. It would be twelve hours of travel time, and that was all in the unlikely event none of her flights were delayed or canceled. By the time she finally got there, she was going to need something stronger than coffee. And she definitely wasn't going to want to go play Nancy Drew.

The PA system quieted, then immediately blared to life again, making Letty jump. "Flight 579 to Portland now boarding zones 1 and 2."

"That's me." She stood, joining the long line of passengers snaking out into the airport's main corridor.

"Ah, okay." Gemma let out a yawn. "I'll let you go then."

"Why are you already in the office? It's barely six." Letty patted her pockets, looking for her boarding pass. "Tell me you don't always come in this early." If she did, that might explain how one person seemed to do the work of twelve.

"Nah, I can't sleep when Noah's at Donny's. Thought I might as well get going on all the work that's been piling up. Try to get things organized before Mark gets back." Another yawn and the crack of a can opening. Gemma always had a Red Bull within reach. "Let me know when you get to King Salmon and if there's anything I can do from here to help."

"Will do." Letty shifted forward with the line and rechecked each pocket. Still no boarding pass. She checked her wallet, but it wasn't there either.

"Listen, I know going over there tonight after you've just flown in isn't ideal, but we need to get in and collect everything while we can."

The gate agent smiled a hello as Letty reached the front of the line, now digging through the outside pocket of her suitcase. The freaking boarding pass had to be there somewhere. She mouthed a "sorry" to the agent and another to the growing line behind her.

"What do you mean?" Letty asked Gemma as she finally fished the pass from the bottom of her bag. She had been in such a rush after she'd made it through security, she must have shoved it in under her laptop by accident.

"Eventually, the police are going to call off the search efforts and collect Crawford's things. You'll want to be in and out before they do."

She had to be kidding. Letty sputtered. "What— "

"Safe flight." Gemma said, and the line went dead.

Letty stared at the phone.

What the fuck?

The gate agent plucked the boarding pass from her grip and scanned it. "Have a nice day."

That seemed highly unlikely.

Letty took a deep breath and rolled her bag down the jetway.

What the hell had she gotten herself into?

CHAPTER 6

King Salmon, Alaska

A gibbous moon shone down through craggy treetops. Its light filtered in gray and broken. Bright enough for Letty to get around but not enough to read by. She flipped on her cell phone's flashlight, shining it at the key she'd picked up from the hotel manager's desk. The plastic fob had a number five imprinted on one side and the image of a rainbow trout on the other.

For a place that supposedly wasn't a fishing camp, the trout motif had been not so subtly worked into every aspect of the Puddlejump Inn. Nets hung above the check-in desk, faded fish print pillows rested on rocking chairs outside the front office, and the path she'd taken to the cabins had a weathered fish-shaped sign identifying it as "Trout Lovers Lane."

She tucked the key in her pocket and turned the flashlight beam toward the nearest in a series of rough-cut wood buildings. A two reflected back in dull gold from the right of the cabin's door. Letty kept going, shivering inside her fleece. She should've taken the time to dig her coat out from her suitcase at the airport. But she'd fallen asleep just long enough on the last leg of her flight to wake truly exhausted. Too tired to do anything but drag herself to the rental car counter and blindly follow the navigation system to the address Gemma had given her.

The worst of it was, even once she'd collected Crawford's files and found her way to her own hotel, she still had hours of work ahead of her to prepare for tomorrow. No way around it. She was looking at a long night. The prospect hung heavy on her bones and itched behind her eyes.

She shined her flashlight on the next cabin, found a number 4, and kept moving.

She wouldn't normally mind the work. She loved it, really. But she had to be at the marina by seven tomorrow to catch the seaplane. The pilot had been very clear — if they weren't in the air by eight, they weren't going.

The forecast called for rain. Not just a light sprinkle, but a storm strong enough to wash away critical aspects of the scene. A storm that could strand them in Katmai if they weren't back in the air before it hit. Letty sped up, crunching her way down the gravel path until she finally spotted cabin five. Like the others, it had peeling mud-brown paint, a shallow front porch, and a welcome mat printed with yet another fish.

No sign of life. Not that she expected it.

She went up onto the porch and peered into the cabin's over-sized picture window, half-hoping to find Crawford napping inside. The flashlight beam reflected back at her from the backside of a blackout curtain, which was probably standard on every room this far north. There were times of year when nightfall wouldn't come until almost midnight.

She bent down, struggling to line the key up with the lock. God, what she wouldn't give for a key card she could just wave in front of the—

The door flew open, smashing into her forehead.

Pain burst above her eyebrow.

She stumbled back. "Sorry, oh my God," she said, apologizing by habit as she pressed a hand to her head. The ache radiated out, wrapping itself around her skull and making her eyes water. The hotel must have rented Crawford's room sooner than Gemma'd thought. And Letty had probably scared the new guest half-to-death.

"I didn't realize anyone was here." She blinked her vision clear.

A dark form surged from inside the cabin, hooded and oddly shaped. The person's body too bulky somehow, the stomach distended.

What the fuck?

Letty backed away, but the person was moving too fast. Coming right at her.

She stumbled back, her heel slipping off the edge of the porch. She grabbed for the porch rail and missed. The nearest post a breath out of reach.

The world blurred as she fell backward, off the edge of the porch, and onto the rocky ground below. She landed with a thud that clacked her teeth together and whooshed the air from her lungs. Letty tasted blood and gasped in a breath. Whatever was coming, she needed to get the hell out of there, and—

The figure loomed over her.

The person's face hidden in the shadow of a hood. Still. Watching.

She shifted to get an elbow underneath her, pushing up. She'd been out of her mind to come here. At night, alone. Letty shoved herself backward. Anything to put distance between herself and whoever that was.

Another blur of motion and pain bloomed in her side; her attacker's foot connecting with her ribs. She curled away. Damp leaves pressed into the side of her face. She choked in a breath that smelled of decay and shrieked.

"Help!" She crossed her arms over her head, and waited for another blow.

Footsteps crunched over gravel, growing quieter as pain thumped in her head and kept time from the spot where her attacker's foot had found the bottom of her ribcage.

She lifted her head, risking a glance. The darkness around her stood empty except for the beam of her flashlight where she'd dropped it. A single beacon of light pointed directly up at the porch ceiling. Corner cobwebs glinted in the beam. Letty let a breath leak out, the clench in her stomach releasing.

A man's voice from behind her. "You alright?"

She yelped, pushing herself up. The pain in her head and ribs amplified at the movement. She ignored it, scrambling back.

An old man with wispy gray hair in a checkered shirt and long johns stood on the porch of the cabin across from Crawford's. He held his hands up, palms out, like he was trying to calm a spooked animal. "Something happen?" He glanced toward the other cabins where a handful of guests emerged onto their front stoops, all of them men. Everyone in plaid but her.

She pressed a hand to the throb on her forehead, where a lump was already forming. Then shifted around to check her side. She reached under her shirt, the skin tender where she'd been kicked and warm to the touch. She prodded it gently and hissed at a flash of pain. A bruise for sure, but no pain when she breathed. Which probably meant no cracked ribs, thank God. "Yeah, I... Somebody attacked me. They were in the room, they..." She pulled down the hem of her shirt. "I think I might've interrupted a burglary."

"Well, shit." The man disappeared into his cabin, then came back out with a cell phone in his hand. The screen lit his face an eerie green as he chicken-pecked in what she hoped was 911.

None of the hotel's other guests moved or offered help. They stood under porch lights or silhouetted in the lamp glow from the open doors behind them, staring. All except for the figure in the farthest cabin. A man-shaped form stood in the dark, featureless except for the glowing tip of a cigarette. She'd probably woken the entire hotel. And they'd come out only to find her there alone, no sign of any cause for the disruption.

None of them seemed happy about it.

Even the man who had said he would call for help had a pinched, distrustful look on his face. He held the phone tight to his ear, his voice too low for her to hear what he was saying.

She got to her feet, wincing as she righted herself, the pain only slightly more uncomfortable than the men's stares. Her gaze drifted back to the figure in the last cabin, whose cigarette made another lazy arc to his mouth.

Letty retrieved her cell phone from the porch, never losing sight of the other guests from the corner of her eye. Any one of them could pose a threat. Her heart pounded in her ears. Every beat hammering the thought home.

What if her attacker wasn't done?

．　．　．

Letty peeled back an edge of the blackout curtain, peering out toward the other cabins. The night had grown darker since she'd come inside, the moon nothing but a dull spot of light behind the clouds. Most of the porches now stood empty. The guests probably back in their beds. Her heart still thudded out of control, but at least away from prying eyes, she could breathe.

She let the heavy curtain fall back into place, releasing a waft of stale cigarettes and cheap fast food. Had she overreacted, scuttling inside to hide? She forced out another breath. Maybe. Chances were, her attacker was long gone. Any half-competent criminal would have to know lingering might result in being questioned by the police once they arrived.

Still, she felt safer behind a door she could lock.

Dozens of pieces of paper littered the floor, a file probably overturned in the burglar's haste. But nothing else seemed out of place. The bed had been made; the bathroom looked untouched. No towels lay discarded in the floor. No tube of toothpaste waited by the sink. The place could've been any low-end, roadside motel. Bed, dresser, television, ratty brown carpet. Not even a closet, just a folding stand where a suitcase might sit.

If Crawford's luggage had been there, it was gone now. No sign remained of his field gear, cell phone, or laptop.

An image of her attacker flashed to mind. The silhouette distorted against the night sky. She had no sense for the person's height or weight, not when the only real look she'd gotten had been as she lay cowering on the ground. Her breath caught again at the memory. The only thing she could recall for certain was that they'd looked misshapen.

Like they'd held something pressed to their chest.

Probably some of Crawford's things. That's why they'd looked so distorted, why they had kicked her, then run away.

They had what they'd come for.

Letty peered down at the nearest page on the floor. It had a familiar letterhead. The same one from the incident report in the case file Gemma had constructed for her.

Was it possible the one thing left behind was what she needed? That seemed a little too lucky. But then, what use would a burglar have for a bunch of research notes? She bent down for a closer look, her ribs aching with the movement. The document definitely looked familiar. Hope fluttered in her belly. She reached for the paper and hesitated. She was standing in a crime scene. Technically, the papers on the floor could be evidence.

Still…

The burglar clearly hadn't been interested in the papers. Whatever he'd taken, he had left them behind. And if the notes Crawford had made before he disappeared were hidden somewhere in the mess covering the cabin's floor, didn't she owe it to the men who had died to use it? After all, it wasn't going to do anyone any good in an evidence locker. And gathering whatever she could was the reason she had come to this cabin in the first place.

She flipped over another page.

This document she recognized for sure. It was the same diagram she'd reviewed in the San Diego airport. Letty allowed herself a smile.

Bingo.

A siren wailed outside. Letty sprang up, cursing another burst of pain in her ribs as she edged the curtain aside and peeked out. The hotel manager — a squat man with scruffy blonde hair curling out from under a knit beanie — had now joined the man who'd called for help. He turned her way, then stopped as her good Samaritan said something else. Probably talking about the crazy lady who had woken the entire hotel then gone back inside without a word.

Which, now that she thought about it, did make her look a little nuts. She cringed as she eyed the papers. Still, she'd come this far. And with the delay dealing with the police would cause, if she didn't at least try to use Crawford's documents, there was no way she would be ready in time for her site visit tomorrow.

She scooped up the paper by her foot.

It was exactly what she had thought. A page from the same report she'd been reviewing on the plane. The beat of her heart grew steady in her chest. Somewhere in the mess, there could be an insight she might need to do her job. Notes Crawford had made on the file, annotations, research he'd added. Maybe the key to figuring out what had happened to the men killed at Katmai.

A key she wouldn't find without them.

The squawk of a two-way radio came from outside.

She glanced around the window shade. Two policemen stood with the other men. Were there no women in Alaska? One of the officers looked in her direction, his expression flat as he spoke to the man who'd called for help. The man shrugged and shook his head.

That doesn't look good.

They were looking toward the cabin as if preparing to deal with a problem. Letty looked down at the papers, and back up at the cops. If she was going to do something, she needed to do it now. She rubbed the knot on her forehead.

She'd come all this way, been assaulted and beaten… she couldn't leave empty-handed.

She wouldn't. She was going to be on that plane to Katmai and ready to do her job tomorrow, no matter what she had to do to make that happen.

Letty snatched up documents from the floor, pressing them to her chest as she hurried around the room, her heart pounding in her ears.

Voices came from outside, then another siren. An ambulance?

She collected the last few pages and scanned the floor, grabbing a slip of paper half-hidden under the edge of the coverlet. This one was different from the others, smaller, a note more than a document. Worn at the edges, tattered with age or handling. A letter.

More male voices, coming closer fast.

Letty looked up to the door, a flash of cold panic breaking across the back of her neck. What was she doing? She couldn't just take evidence from a crime scene.

Except now, even if she left the papers where she'd found them, her fingerprints would be all over them.

Boots thunked on the porch outside.

Shit.

Letty shoved the papers into her waistband and tugged her fleece over the top.

CHAPTER 7

October 19, 2018
Washington, D.C.

"What do you mean attacked?" Mark jerked up in bed, an echo of fear chasing the last vestige of sleep away. This was his fault. He had known the bears were still on the loose, and he'd sent Letty to Katmai anyway. He rubbed at his face. How could he have been so careless? So reckless with Letty's life. "Is she okay?"

"Just a bump on the head, some bruises," Gemma said, and even over the phone, her voice sounded rough with lack of sleep. "The guy got away, but—"

"Wait, what?" He fumbled for the lamp on the side table and clicked it on, blinking as his eyes adjusted to the sudden brightness. "Someone attacked her?"

"The police think she interrupted a burglary at Crawford's hotel. All of his gear was gone, which makes sense he would have had his field gear with him when he disappeared. But not the rest, the laptop and whatnot. Letty said the attacker was carrying something. She couldn't see what though. Didn't get a good look at the wanker."

How had he never considered that the gear she and Crawford both carried was worth thousands of dollars? He pinched the bridge of his nose, squeezing his eyes shut. He'd outfitted every scientist at the foundation with emergency gear, satellite phones, multi-spectral cameras, and electronics specially designed to withstand the elements. Of course it could make them a target.

Especially in the off-the-grid places his people wound up, where locals would know the difference between a two thousand dollar sat phone and an off-the-rack Garmin. And Crawford wouldn't have carried all of that into the field. He would have left anything he didn't need behind in his room.

Shit.

His phone buzzed in his hand, and he glanced down, praying to see Letty's name.

Aunt Kath: "Call me as soon as you're up."

He ignored the message. A rehash of yesterday's presentation to the committee could wait. "Is she at the hospital now?" Mark checked the bedside clock, 4:40 a.m. Which meant it was almost one in the morning for Letty.

"She didn't go. The EMTs checked her out, said to come in if there were any signs of a concussion. I told her not to be daft. But she just wanted to get to her hotel. Get some rest."

He hated the idea of her at some remote Alaskan hotel alone. What if she did have a concussion? He ripped back the covers, and the sketch pad that he'd been working in before he'd gone to bed tumbled to the floor. Mark got to his feet, not bothering to pick it up. What if she fell asleep and didn't wake up? He paced back and forth, his footsteps marring the careful pattern left by a maid's vacuum on the rug. There wasn't a damn thing he could do about it from here. And why the hell hadn't she called him?

He crossed his arms over his chest. "Have you booked her a flight home?"

A long pause.

"She says she's staying."

"She what?" Even as he asked the question, he knew he shouldn't be surprised. Of course Letty would stay to finish the job. She always put work first. He rubbed a palm against his eye. He usually admired that about her. But right now, he hated it.

"She's heading out to the incident site in the morning. I'll get an update from her after that and let you know what's next. Also, we've got Ines coming in from Hong Kong tomorrow, and the Santiago team says they'll submit their final report to the Chilean ministry of health this week. Oh, and…"

He stopped listening. Why did it bother him so much that Letty hadn't called? He stared out at the lights of DC twinkling beyond his hotel window as irritation crawled up his neck in a hot blush. Part of him knew why — things between them had been strained ever since she'd come to work for the foundation. And that was his fault. She was the same person she had always been, but when she'd shown up for work, he had been aware of her in a way he never had before. Painfully aware. The easy comfort that had always lived between them was gone, replaced by a feeling he couldn't let himself acknowledge. And he wouldn't let himself disrespect Jessa's memory, or Letty, by giving it a name.

No wonder she avoided him like he was some multi-level marketer trying to sell her armpit-scented essential oils. She could probably tell he was being weird.

His phone buzzed again, and he jerked it away from his ear. Another message from Aunt Kath: "Board called a meeting."

He stared at the message. Why would they call a meeting now? Nothing about that made sense, and it was the last thing any of them needed, not when—

"Boss?" Gemma asked. "You still there?"

"Sorry. Yes, I'm here. Why don't you go get some sleep? I'll check in tomorrow." He barely heard her goodbye before hanging up and typing a response to Aunt Kath's text. "Any idea what the meeting's about?"

Dots danced underneath his message. Stopped, as if she'd changed her mind about how or whether to reply, then danced again. He'd never known Kath to be at a loss for words, and the longer it took for her to respond, the worse he knew it would be when she did.

Finally, another text. "It's ridiculous." Then two more, one immediately after the other. "Something about a breach of your fiduciary duty." And, "I'll handle it."

Oh, God.

He tossed his phone onto the bed, a tightness in his chest like an impenetrable knot. Kath would do everything she could to protect him. He had no doubt about that. She'd been doing it for Mark's father his entire life. But there were things she didn't know. The deals he'd made sure didn't go through, the ones he'd done without board approval, knowing they would never give it. The documents he'd falsified to keep it all hidden… that would be the part that got him. Mark ran his hands through his hair, his fingers catching on tangles born from yet another restless night's sleep. Once the truth came to light, his career was over. And that would be the least of it.

Some things even Kath couldn't fix.

CHAPTER 8

King Salmon, Alaska

Letty dumped water into the in-room coffee machine and yawned until her jaw cracked. God, she was tired. She hadn't finished giving her statement to the police until well after midnight. It had been one in the morning before she'd gotten to her hotel and probably three or four by the time she'd shut out the lights. She felt every minute of the sleep she hadn't gotten. She killed two ibuprofen with the last of the water in her bottle and snapped a coffee pod into the machine.

As nervous as she'd been talking with the police — Crawford's papers crinkling under her clothes with every breath — it had gone better than she could've hoped. The officer had raised an eyebrow when she'd asked if he thought the burglary and Crawford's disappearance could be connected, which seemed odd that he wouldn't have already have made the connection. But he'd promised to pass his report on to the officers assigned to the missing persons case, and there wasn't much she could do about it beyond that. She pulled the pod out to check that she hadn't accidentally grabbed decaf, smacked the lid shut, and hit "brew." The harder part had been concealing the documents from the EMTs. Only her claim of a nervous stomach, and a hurried trip to the bathroom with her bag, had saved her.

While the machine spit and groaned its way through making a cup of coffee, she tucked everything she needed for the day into the backpack she would carry to the incident site. None of Crawford's papers made the cut. She yanked the zipper closed, exhaling sharply through her nose. What a waste of time and stress taking them had been. She had pored through every page before going to bed last night and found nothing. Crawford's copy of the file was as unmarked as Letty's set had been when Gemma had first handed it over. Which made no sense.

She had covered her own copy of the file with scrawled questions to ask, possible explanations, or avenues to pursue. And she'd supplemented those notes with a mammoth to-do list. Crawford would've done the same. Any field scientist would.

The coffee machine made a final groan, the last bit of caffeine sputtering out into her cup.

Or was that a false assumption? Maybe Crawford didn't work that way. Maybe he made notes separately or dictated them. He could've had the notes that mattered on him, when he'd disappeared. She grabbed the coffee. That would make sense. After all, wasn't she doing the same thing? Packing up the notes that mattered to take with her to the scene?

Letty took a sip and cringed. How could it both be too weak and so bitter at the same time? She dumped in a sweetener and two creamers before tasting it again. Still awful, but at least drinkable now. She made one more pass through Crawford's documents, stopping at the only page that hadn't been included in the file Gemma had given her.

The handwritten note she'd pulled from beneath Crawford's bed didn't seem related to the case at all. Letty had shifted it to the bottom of the stack the night before, quickly deciding it was something private. An unsent personal letter that had accidentally gotten mixed in with the other papers.

But now, she shifted it to the top of the stack, curiosity getting the better of her.

Darling,

My bright flower. You have been the best thing in my life these past years. I am so sorry I can't be the man you need. If there were any path forward that made sense, I would take it. But I am too much of a coward.

Know that I will love you both always.

He'd signed the note with a scrawled letter "C." Whoever he'd meant the letter for, Crawford hadn't had the chance to deliver it before he'd disappeared. Or maybe he hadn't had the nerve. The note was well worn, as if it had been handled a lot. She read it again, then stopped, lowering the page.

Could this be a suicide note?

Crawford wouldn't be the first person to do something drastic when a love affair went wrong. And if that was true, if the note might help explain his disappearance, then she had taken something relevant to the police's investigations after all. A stone of guilt sunk to the bottom of her stomach.

She took another sip of coffee and shoved her feet into the hiking boots she'd been issued by the foundation. What could she do about the note now? She couldn't give it to the authorities without admitting she'd taken Crawford's documents in the first place. Which would be tampering with evidence. And if they thought she'd done that, what else might they think she'd been involved in? The burglary, his disappearance…

She stilled, one boot half-tied. The laces now limp in her hands.

No. She'd only flown into town the day before, so they would be able to confirm pretty quickly she'd had nothing to do with that. And anyway, that was crazy. There was no reason to think Crawford's disappearance was anything more than a tragic accident.

But could the fall-out from her taking the documents undermine the work she still needed to do for the foundation?

Maybe.

That was a risk she couldn't take. Letty finished lacing her boots and checked her watch. Already half past six. She had to be at the marina in thirty minutes, and she had no real idea how to get where she was going. Whatever the note was, it could wait.

Letty gulped down the rest of the coffee, gathered her gear, and swept out of the motel room. The sun wouldn't be up for hours, but the parking lot was well lit. She made sure the door was fully closed and locked, then jogged down a set of cracked concrete stairs littered with straw wrappers and stuck gum. Every step made her body ache worse, but she ignored it. The pain reliever would kick in soon, and then she could give her entire focus to what she had come to Alaska to do.

An icy wind blew her hair around her face and pushed through the few anemic trees dotting the parking lot. It smelled like rain.

Shit.

She eyed the still night black sky. No sign of storm clouds, which was something. She yanked the coat's zipper up to her throat and veered across the parking lot toward her rental. She just needed the weather to hold a little longer, and maybe she'd manage to pull this thing off.

Letty popped the trunk and dropped her gear inside, wincing again at the sharp jab of pain in her ribs. You had to be a real fucker to kick somebody when they were down like that. With any luck, the burglar would find that out the hard way. In prison, once the police caught them. Or through good old-fashioned karma.

She closed the trunk and squinted through the back window glass. The front windshield looked wrong, the view of the road beyond it splintered into a thousand pieces.

"What the—?" She rounded the front of the rental. Her windshield had been shattered. A spiderweb of glass crackling out from the spot directly in front of the driver's seat. "Shit, shit, shit."

She checked the ground for a fallen limb and looked underneath the car for a kid's baseball. But found neither, and that didn't really make sense anyway. There were no trees in this part of the lot, and she'd parked facing the main road. A dense forest thick with pines and tangled brush crowded on the other side. It wasn't a place kids were likely to play.

Had she paid for the extra insurance on the rental car? She'd been so tired, she'd just done whatever was easiest, hadn't read the legalese or bothered to consider what her own insurance might not cover. The foundation paid well, but still… She crossed her arms over her chest, rubbing the chill from her arms. She didn't have time to deal with it now. She'd have to squint through the cracks and hope she didn't get pulled over.

At least the car was still drivable. She looked back at the windshield. The shattered glass didn't look like it'd been hit with a baseball. It looked like someone had swung a bat at the spot where her face would've been. She rubbed harder at her arms, trying to knead back in some warmth. But the chill had already spread to the back of her neck, leaving a thin layer of ice under her skin.

A small piece of paper fluttered under the windshield wiper. An apology or a phone number left by whoever'd hit her? She tugged the page from under the wiper.

Two words in bold black print, "GO HOME."

CHAPTER 9

Letty stepped out of the seaplane, bracing herself on a strut under the wing as she watched the woods for Ranger Brenner's return. After what had happened to the fishermen here, and then to Crawford, she wasn't going anywhere until she got an "all clear."

Even half-beached on the lakeshore, the aircraft rocked unsteady under her feet. Choppy waves slapped against the plane's floats. The water the same malicious gray it had been in the photographs of the incident site in her file. Behind a rocky beach littered with fallen logs and neon orange markers, the forest waited, dark and dense. A single dirt path broke the tree line, but she could only see a few feet into the shadows. Letty pulled her bag from the cabin and adjusted her feet on the float's well-worn tread. Her stomach churned, and not just from the nausea-inducing flight.

You've got this.

Crawford's notes might have been useless, but she'd been through the file so many times, she knew it inside out. She'd read every page of relevant scientific literature she could get her hands on. She was as ready as she was going to get.

The only thing she could do now was hope it would be enough.

Ranger Brenner appeared at the trailhead, a shotgun resting comfortably on his shoulder. "We're good to go." Her escort had thirty years of service with the state park service under his belt and a face that looked like he'd spent every day of it in inclement weather. But he'd shown up half an hour early to meet her at the marina, answered all of her questions with the straight-forward pragmatism of someone accustomed to working on a well-oiled team, and had been so polite she'd wondered if he might actually be Canadian.

Their pilot was a different story.

"Great." She clambered down onto the beach, ignoring the grumbling coming from the cockpit. Other than a back-handed compliment about her "at least having the good sense not to come out here alone, like the other one," Ned Harley had been muttering complaints since she'd boarded — the weather wasn't going to hold, the trip wasn't worth making if they were just going to have to turn around and come home, and didn't they have anything better to do?

She rolled her eyes. Like hell she was going to miss the chance to assess the incident site before the rain destroyed it. Besides, she'd driven to the airfield this morning covered in bumps and bruises, on no sleep, with a shattered windshield and a not-at-all subtle threat in her pocket. One she hadn't reported to the police for fear she'd miss their flight if she got stuck back at the station giving another statement. If she could manage all that, Harley could handle working on a day he'd apparently planned to take off. Knowing Mark, he would be well paid for it.

Letty made her way up the beach, winding around logs too big to step over. The closer she got to the forest, the colder she became. The air held a chilly damp and seeped into her bones, having no apparent regard for all the layers she'd worn to ward it off.

Brenner gestured to the knapsack she held looped over one arm. "Can I help you with that, ma'am?"

"I've got it." The pack might be heavy, but she was well accustomed to carrying the weight of her gear on her back. She swung the bag over her shoulder. "Thank you, though." She took a minute to scan the tree line, her stomach sour, the aftertaste of her coffee-in-lieu-of-breakfast lingering in her mouth. Even with Brenner's assurance that there was no sign of bears nearby, walking where those fisherman had died made it hard not to feel like something lurked in those woods. She fidgeted with the strap of her backpack then glanced up at Brenner, who seemed to be waiting for her to give him direction.

She shoved her hands in her pockets, the slip of paper she'd found under her windshield wiper crinkling under her knuckles. She curled her hand into a fist, not wanting to touch it. "Why don't we start with you walking me through the scene?"

"Happy to." He led her to where the closest marker jutted from the ground. The small orange flag on top shuddered in the wind, like a bird caught in a trap. "This is where the first attack occurred." He pointed to a disturbed section of ground. Several large dark stains spattered the rocks and sand. The biggest of them like a comet with a tail, a pattern she recognized. Probably the killing blow, a paw swipe of a major artery, a sudden burst of blood loss. She swallowed past a sudden thickness in her throat.

"Craig Miller's body was recovered here... or, at least, some portion of it was." He shifted his finger further down the beach to a pile of branches marked with a second flag. A pattern of dark, diminishing drops led off in that direction, likely blood dripping from the bear's fur as it moved down shore. Brenner's voice stayed steady, even as the lines deepened around his eyes and mouth. "Other portions of the body were recovered there, where the bears seem to have cached the remainder of both Murkowski and Miller's bodies for later consumption." Which told her the bears had returned to the scene a second time. After Paul Reardon had been rescued but before the other bodies were recovered.

And everything else Brenner said tracked exactly with what she'd read in the file. But, still, standing here, where Mr. Miller had lost his life, the true horror of what those men had been through seemed almost surreal. Being attacked by not one but two towering masses of muscle, claws, and teeth that could stalk and devour a person as easily as it might pluck a seal from the sea. Animals who would attack a human being the same way it would another bear — teeth to teeth. It wouldn't just lash out...

It would go for your face.

She couldn't imagine anything more horrifying.

Letty cleared her throat, ignoring the burn in her stomach, trying like hell to keep her voice professional. "And the other flags?"

"The ones just past the plane indicate where Mr. Reardon was attacked. Guy got dang lucky their ride home showed up when it did. Scared the bears away, so help could get to him. If the plane hadn't arrived just then, we'd be looking at three bodies instead of two." Brenner let out a heavy breath. "The other flags are where we've marked the bears' tracks, as best we could. Follow me." He turned, striding back toward the trailhead. "Best set of them is in the soft mud near the riverbank."

She followed him down a winding trail through dense forest, the wind now abusing the trees. Her hand closed around the note in her pocket. She should've thrown it away. She had enough to worry about. The bears. The assignment she wasn't entirely sure she could pull off. The enormity of what was riding on her success… She didn't need a reminder that someone wanted her gone on top of all that.

Having the note with her now felt like a bad luck talisman.

Brenner spoke up to be heard over the wind, running through the same basic set of facts she'd gleaned from the file: The fishing spot the men had chosen didn't intersect with any known bear paths. They'd carried bear spray. They'd been fishing catch and release, and they'd carried no food with them. They'd done nothing to unduly attract predators.

She focused on the path under her feet as she listened, careful to avoid the roots that clawed up as if to trip her. Dozens of footprints marked the earth. Some of them probably belonged to the men who'd been attacked. Most looked newer, likely left behind by all the agencies who'd been on the ground before she'd arrived — the Alaska Department of Fish and Game, the state troopers, the National Park Service.

She'd had the vague idea last night that she might be able to use the bears' tracks along with the fishermen's to get a better idea of what'd happened here. But any story they might've told had been trampled beyond recognition.

Not that she could talk. She glanced back at her own trail of footprints in the dirt, and a drop of rain plopped onto the back of her neck.

Shit.

She wiped the wet away, yanking back several layers of sleeves to check her watch: 11:20. It was too early for the rain to start. Not that it seemed to care. Another fat drop splatted into the dirt by her feet. She tugged her sleeves back into place. The forecast had said they'd have hours yet. She sighed through her nose and quickened her pace, following Brenner to the river's edge. Two more orange flags fluttered in the wind.

He shifted the shotgun against his shoulder and pointed where the bears' tracks led into the water. "From what we can tell, the animals high-tailed it through the woods when the seaplane arrived and went straight for the river. But we haven't been able to find any sign of where they came out."

As if the bears didn't want to be followed.

She shook off the thought. These were bears, not criminal masterminds. They weren't concerned with hiding their tracks, just filling their bellies.

Rain dotted the river's surface, slow and steady now. Harley's voice echoed through the forest, too muffled for her to make out his words. He was probably yelling at them that it was time to go, but she couldn't tell for sure, and she wasn't sad about it.

She raised the hood of her parka, pulled off the backpack, and dug around inside until she found her camera. "I think I'll walk around a bit. See what else I can see."

"Yes, ma'am." He tipped his hat. "I'll be here if you need me." Brenner made his way back to the mouth of the trail, still scanning the forest. Above the trees, the sky had grown darker, the morning now dim enough to look like dusk.

Having Brenner on the lookout should've made her feel better, but somehow, his hyper-alert focus on the woods around him made her feel less safe. She'd feel a lot better if he was playing solitaire on his phone while he waited. But the bears were still out there, and they both knew it.

Letty took a deep breath and made herself focus. She had work to do.

She knelt down, taking a closer look at the bears' tracks. Two distinct sets, both adult. One slightly larger than the other. Both led in the same direction toward the water. And thanks to last night's research binge, she had no doubt they'd been made by polar bears. These prints had brush marks — a subtle smudging caused by the hair covering their paws that would not be present in brown bears.

She pulled out a measuring tape. Tracks from the larger bear's rear paws measured more than thirteen inches long. "Jesus." She muttered under her breath.

The bear wasn't just big, he was massive. Each paw bigger than her head. She tried hard not to think of what it would feel like to come face to face with an animal that size.

Especially not when her job might mean doing just that.

She shivered, the chill only half caused by the day's still dropping temperature. She didn't have time to worry about that now. She measured the other bear's prints and marked the dimensions of both sets in her field notebook.

She'd hoped to find that one of them had been a juvenile. That wouldn't explain why they were so far south, but it would at least answer the question of why they were together. A mother bear often migrated with her cubs. But neither set of prints was anywhere near small enough for that. She put her measuring tape and notebook back in her bag.

She was looking at the tracks of two adult bears — both likely male, given the size. There had to be some explanation for it.

She got back to her feet, did a complete canvas of the area, and photographed all the prints she could find. Then she followed Brenner back down the trail, tracing her own footsteps. Her new boots hadn't had time for the tread to get worn, and they'd left a perfect geometric pattern in the dirt.

What the—

One of her prints faced the wrong way.

Two paces in front of her foot. A perfect matching print headed back toward the lake.

No, not her print. Crawford's.

Holy shit.

He'd have been wearing the same foundation issued boots she was. It shouldn't have been a surprise to her that she'd come upon his prints. She obviously knew he'd been here, but still, it caught her off-guard. She spun around, apologizing to a startled Brenner, before following Crawford's tracks back by the river, then again through the woods to the incident site. Crawford had taken the same basic path she had. Like hers, his footprints led to the water's edge and stopped.

No prints led back away from the shoreline.

But why? When he'd come back to the water's edge, there had been no plane to board. No boat waiting. He'd been at the site alone. Dropped off by Harley's partner and then never seen again.

It wasn't like he could just disappear into thin air.

So where had he gone?

A sharp knocking came from the water.

Inside the seaplane, Harley wrapped his knuckles on the windshield again and gestured toward the black clouds now covering most of the sky. He scowled out at her, his mouth forming words she was still glad she couldn't hear. Not that she'd be able to avoid an earful during the ride back to the marina.

She held up a pointer finger in a quick "one minute" gesture and refocused on Crawford's prints. The note she'd found under Crawford's bed flashed to mind.

"I can't be the man you need."

"We should be in the air already." Harley yelled from the plane. Apparently tired of waiting, he now hung halfway out of the passenger-side door. He glared at her, a deep crease between his brows.

She gave him a thumbs-up that only deepened his scowl. Her mind still focused on the note.

"If there were any path forward that made sense, I would take it. But I am too much of a coward."

The words lodged in her head.

What if Crawford hadn't gotten lost?

What if Crawford never left?

She winced at the thought but forced herself to keep moving. The rain pounded against her hood and around her feet, already blurring the edges of Crawford's prints. She took another quick series of photos. She'd planned to rephotograph the entire area, to spend time following each set of tracks she could still see, but there was no time for any of that now. Not as the raindrops fell faster and heavier, beating a sharp staccato on the surface of the lake. She took a few more shots of Crawford's tracks, stepping to put her own boot beside his print for scale. Then jogged back to the plane with Brenner on her heels.

She climbed on board as the plane sputtered to life, Harley still grousing from the cockpit. "Better strap in, this is gonna be one gnarly ride back."

Letty ignored him, staring out at the lake's angry black water as she tightened her safety belt and wiped rain from her face. Even before the downpour had started, she had barely been able to see more than a few feet under the surface.

God knew what might wait underneath.

CHAPTER 10

Cumberland County, Kentucky

Oil wells bobbed along the horizon, like giant metal birds coaxing oil from parched earth. A relentless pull and drag, pull and drag under the blazing afternoon sun.

October in Kentucky was usually Mark's favorite time to visit, mild and in the mid-sixties. Not this year. He wiped sweat from his forehead and followed Jimmy Mahathy around the side of a worn, burnt-orange well. The pumping unit sat frozen in place, its head resting against cracked dirt.

"Your daddy and I drilled this one together. She hit at just over sixteen hundred feet, not a drop of water in the flow." Jimmy rested a soft hand on the gear box. As though he was saying goodbye to a well-loved horse he needed to put down.

Another bead of sweat trickled down the back of Mark's neck, and he pulled at his shirt collar, trying to circulate some air. "She tapped out?" Jimmy's reference to Mark's dad wasn't an accident. Jimmy was a lifelong gambler with a poker face to match. If he was taking the conversation in that direction, he had a reason. Whether it was meant to put Mark at ease or to come around to the fact that his father wouldn't approve of what Mark had done, there was no way to know.

At least not until Jimmy wanted there to be.

"I reckon' she is." Jimmy pulled off a work glove and smacked it against the leg of his Levi's, dust blooming off. "But you didn't come all the way out here in the middle of a heat wave to listen to me talk family history." He eyed Mark from under a weathered John Deere cap, his eyes bright blue and shrewd.

Whatever Jimmy had to say, he thought Mark needed to be ready to hear it. Mark looked away, his mouth going dry. The field stretched off into the distance, all brown grass and rusting barbed wire fence. As much as he wanted to pretend nothing was wrong, they both knew this wasn't a social visit.

Sometimes it was better to just rip off the band-aid. Mark met Jimmy's gaze. "I guess you heard about the board calling a special meeting."

"Notice went out yesterday." Jimmy pulled off his other glove and pursed his lips. He started toward a dirty F-150 parked on the edge of the field.

Mark followed. Like his father before him, Mark had elected not to sit on the company's board, wanting to focus his attention on other aspects of running the company. This was the first time he regretted it. "I was hoping you might know what's going on." Jimmy wouldn't be aligned with Reid Schaefer. The two almost always fell on opposite ends of the board's old guard versus new blood voting blocks, but nothing happened on the board without Jimmy knowing.

Jimmy didn't so much as blink. He settled into the driver's seat and leaned over, swinging the passenger door open. "Hop on in." He tilted his head toward Mark's now filthy loafers. "You're not exactly in walking shoes."

Mark had packed for DC boardrooms, not a half-mile hike from Jimmy's house to what remained of the oil wells scattering his lower pasture. He climbed in and closed the door behind him. "Appreciate it."

The inside of the truck was stifling. The windshield amplified the sun until he felt like a beetle trapped under a child's magnifying glass. Mark shifted on the bench seat, his shirt sticking to the skin under his arms and across the small of his back. Jimmy rolled down his window but still said nothing, his silence making the truck's oppressive heat even heavier.

Mark's phone chimed from his pocket. "Sorry." Normally, he'd have turned the ringer off before he got there. Jimmy wasn't a fan of the "cell phone generation." But right now, Mark couldn't afford to be out of touch.

"G'head." Jimmy started the truck, and the A/C blew hot air in Mark's face.

He dug the phone out. If there was any chance it was Letty, he didn't want to miss her. He still only knew what little Gemma had been able to tell him.

Another message from Aunt Kath: "Wheels up in an hour."

He ran a hand through his hair. Of course it wasn't Letty.

He shoved the phone back in his pocket without responding. The pressure of a time clock wasn't going to help. It was hard enough to get anything out of Jimmy under the best of circumstances. His godfather had negotiated some of the most lucrative deals in Stafford Oil's history — including the right to continue operating his own private wells despite being on the company's board — always with a good old-boy grin. He leaned heavy on other people's tendency to underestimate a man who looked like he'd gotten his education from a tractor supply catalog.

It was a mistake they only ever made once.

The truck bumped over deep ruts in the road, the Ford's struts long since worn out. Jimmy seemed not to notice, one elbow leaned out the driver's side window, the sun glinting off the oyster shell buttons on his western shirt. "Saw you on the TV yesterday." He drove through a pothole, the truck bouncing both of them in their seats. "Hope you took a good long shower after you got done."

Mark raised his eyebrows. "Sorry?"

"Nothing but filthy vipers in that pit." Jimmy navigated around another rut. "Course, there're snakes in the grass nearer to home, too."

What did that mean? Mark watched the man out of the corner of his eye. His weathered face was as familiar as Mark's own father's. Jimmy had been in his life almost as long. He'd never been the warm and fuzzy type, but, unlike Mark's dad, he was always there. Palming him a fifty at his first communion or taking him out for a steak dinner when Dad missed his birthdays or high school graduation. His father too busy glad-handing or skiing the Alps with one of his girlfriends to bother with something as insignificant as celebrating the milestones of his only son's life. Jimmy wasn't a soft place to land exactly. But he had always been someone Mark could count on.

Today his expression was tight, grim. His jaw clenched, a slight purse to his lips. He looked pissed.

But at who? Him?

Or the people trying to take over control of the company?

Because this conversation could go two very different ways.

Mark found the rings under his shirt, pressing them against his chest. "That's why I'm here."

"Mmmm-hm." Jimmy glanced over at Mark, the look on his face telegraphing the rest of the answer. Something worse than anger glinted in those sharp blue eyes.

Disappointment.

Mark forced himself to keep a neutral face.

He knows.

CHAPTER 11

Bristol Bay, Alaska

Letty stepped out of Harley's dock-side office, letting the door fall closed behind her. The handful of seaplanes moored along the dock sat still and empty. Bruised purple-gray clouds hung above them and reflected back in the marina's mirror flat water. Only Harley's now-muffled bitching broke the silence.

How Brenner put up with the crusty old pilot, she had no idea. But he seemed as immune to Harley's attitude as he was unfazed by the spin cycle their trip home had been. The storm had lashed the plane for at least the first hour. The wind and rain a relentless torrent. Each gust rocking them like it was an angry child trying to break a toy.

Her stomach might never recover. Brenner, on the other hand, had dug out a tuna and onion sandwich from a soft-sided cooler as soon as they'd stepped inside Harley's office.

She'd nearly barfed on the floor.

At least, out on the dock, it smelled more like brine than dead fish. A marginal improvement. She chewed two antacids from the bottle she kept at the bottom of her bag, crossed her arms on the dock's wooden rail, and rested her forehead on top. She needed a few hours to regroup, to go through the pictures she'd taken at the incident site, to decide what her next steps should be.

And not just about the bear attack.

What was she going to do about Crawford?

Between the note she'd found and the footprints disappearing at the lake's edge... the idea that he'd died by suicide seemed all too possible.

If he was dead, if his body was somewhere at the bottom of the lake... Didn't she owe it to him to tell someone? Didn't she owe it to his family — to whoever he'd intended to send that letter — to let the authorities go look?

A loud whine came from the horizon.

She lifted her head. A seaplane on approach to the marina, coming in from the south. She squinted at the aircraft. Something about it looked off, blurry. The plane veered left, and a dark shape ghosted after it.

What the hell?

Another veer, this time to the right, and another black smear across the sky.

Birds.

Too small to be waterfowl. Mourning doves? They often caused bird strikes, but they didn't usually migrate this far north.

The birds flew in a cluster around the plane. Not a migrating flock caught in the aircraft's flight path. A swarm of tiny black bodies beating themselves against the plane. Letty pressed a hand to her mouth.

A snarling pop echoed across the marina, and smoke poured from one of the plane's engines.

Oh my God.

One or more of the birds had flown into the propeller.

The office door smacked open behind her, and Letty jumped as the plane banked hard to the right, aiming for the bay. The birds still pelting themselves against the fuselage. Others threw their bodies against the windshield, as if trying to break the glass to get to the pilot inside.

Harley charged out onto the deck, coming to stand beside her. "What in God's name?" He stared up at the plane, his jaw clenched. He probably knew the pilot.

She held her breath. The plane continued its approach, coming in fast. Too fast.

Heading straight for them.

She took two steps back, not that it would matter. If the plane couldn't stop in time, they were all going up in a ball of fire.

The plane banked again, circling away, then back toward the marina. This time on a path that wouldn't collide with the dock where she stood. Thank God. But the birds still writhed in an angry mass around it, even as the plane came in for a landing.

Harley gripped the deck's rail, his knuckles white. "C'mon, Rusty. You can do it."

The plane hit the water hard, wobbled, bounced, then settled. The impact couldn't have been pleasant for anyone inside, but the plane stayed intact. And the birds shot off into the sky. She let herself breathe as the seaplane taxied toward a dock.

Bird strikes weren't uncommon. It happened more than ten thousand times each year. Most, like today, were during take off or landing, but this had been different. Not an accidental crossing of paths — this had been an attack. She made a note to get the details from the pilot so she could send a report in to the JDF; at a minimum, she needed to confirm what type of birds they had been. This was exactly the kind of thing the JDF was trying to track.

She followed as Harley took the steps down to the dock two at a time, striding toward where the plane had come to a stop. Blood smeared the outside of the windshield, and behind it, the pilot's face was a pure, stricken white. But he looked unhurt, thank God.

A buzzing came from Letty's pocket. She pulled it out to silence it and spotted the number. Kathryn Stafford. Letty blinked at the display, cursed herself for connecting the phone to the marina's Wi-Fi, and considered sending the call to voicemail. Why would Kathryn be calling?

Letty sucked in a breath and held it. Whatever Kathryn wanted, Mark's aunt wasn't someone you ignored. Letty connected the call

BROOKE L. FRENCH 67

as she watched Harley help the pilot from his plane. She tried to sound calm, but her voice came out as a croak. "Hello?"

"Good afternoon, Dr. Duquesne." Unlike Letty, Kathryn spoke with perfect elocution. She sounded like boarding schools and sailing lessons. Like money. "Mark said he hadn't been able to reach you. I thought I would check in and make sure you were all right. To see if there was anything we could do to help from here."

Letty cringed. She had seen Mark's missed calls but hadn't had the guts to return them. "I'm sorry I wasn't able to get back to you sooner. Things have been a little... hectic."

On the dock, Harley embraced the pilot. The two men turned to face the bay, both gesturing out toward where the birds had disappeared into the distance. She wanted to be down there listening to what the pilot had to say, but hanging up on Kathryn now didn't seem like an option.

"Gemma told us what happened." Kathryn made a soft tsk'ing sound. "Are you okay?"

"Just a few bumps and bruises." And a threat. And a smashed windshield. And maybe a dead colleague at the bottom of a lake. Letty's hand tightened on the phone.

"I am so sorry for what you went through." Kathryn paused. "I thought it might make things easier for you to ship Dr. Crawford's things back to the office. You can just send them to my attention, and I'll take care of it all. That'll at least keep you from having to haul so much around with you."

Kathryn obviously hadn't heard that Crawford's gear had apparently been stolen in the attack, but telling her that would also mean admitting that his files hadn't, or lying by omission, which made her really uncomfortable. The files were useless, but Kathryn wouldn't know that. And if Letty told her she had them, it would mean admitting she'd taken what was probably evidence from a crime scene. Letty winced. Still, Kathryn was being so nice about everything, it made not telling her borderline impossible.

"Dr. Duquesne? Did I lose you?"

"No," Letty cleared her throat, watching as Harley and the other pilot inspected the damage done to his plane. "Sorry. Still here."

"Okay, good. The sooner we get everything, the sooner we can figure out what our next steps should be. I understand the other large mammal specialist is due back soon. I'm sure he can pick things up where you've left them."

Where I've left them?

Letty's face warmed. She hadn't left anything.

And why would Kathryn think she had? She'd obviously called at Mark's behest. He must have decided the case was too much for her after all. An impression she probably hadn't helped by ducking his calls. But it still felt like crap. She'd only been there a day, and she wasn't done yet. She—

"Gemma didn't share your travel plans with me, but if there's anything I can do to make the trip home easier, I'd be happy to." Kathryn continued. "I could have my driver pick you up when you land?"

Letty tamped down her frustration. The woman was trying so hard to help. It wasn't Kathryn's fault if Mark had lost faith in her. "Actually, I'd like to continue my work here." She hadn't had time to even consider what that might look like, given how little time she'd been able to spend on site. But she at least wanted the opportunity to figure it out.

Kathryn didn't respond.

Letty cleared her throat and filled the silence. "I visited Katmai this morning. I haven't had a chance to go through my notes or the photos I took yet. But what I was able to glean from the scene before the weather became an issue is consistent with the statement given by the survivor, and I'd like to see where the evidence takes me."

"Do you think an additional trip to the site would provide more useful data?"

"No." Letty closed her eyes. The storm that had come through likely made any further study of the incident site pointless. And the chances the smattering of photographs she'd taken would produce a viable lead were slim. At best. She pulled her hands up into her sleeves and tucked an arm around her body.

"Are there resources available to you there that wouldn't be available to you in San Diego?"

As much as she wanted to say there were... "No, not that I can think of." Not with the evidence at the scene washed away and no trace of the bears for her to follow.

Letty sagged against the dock's rail. Kathryn was right. For more reasons than she realized. It made sense for Letty to work from the home office, especially if that meant she could do it with the help of someone who actually had experience working with bears. It also made more sense to assess her data from the safety of her office, rather than the hotel where her windshield had been smashed.

Where whoever had done it obviously knew to find her.

Going back to San Diego was the right thing to do. Even if it felt like giving up. She could gather whatever evidence she could find from the bird strike. Blood samples from the windshield, maybe a carcass from the engine, if she was lucky. And have it shipped out to the lab before she left.

"All right." Kathryn said. "It's up to you, of course. But, if it were me, I think I'd come home."

Letty sighed. "Yeah, okay. That makes sense. I—"

"Ma'am?" Brenner's voice from behind her.

Letty turned.

He stepped outside and settled his hat on his head. The shotgun back on its perch against his shoulder. "I think we've got one of the bears."

.   .   .

Letty jumped down from Brenner's SUV, tossing her backpack on as she stepped out into the gloom of late afternoon. The same eerie stillness that had hung over the marina before the bird strike had followed them a dozen miles north, down an endless dirt road, to what felt like nowhere. A tiny cabin stubbornly refusing to be consumed by the forest around it. Only the roof's front peak and a chimney remained visible through a dark, suffocating layer of leaves and branches. Splintered furniture scattered the front porch, and raw gouges scored the wood to either side of the front door. Claw marks.

Even without caution tape, it looked like a crime scene.

Letty rubbed a chill from her arms as Brenner came to stand beside her.

"Remains should be this way." He gestured beyond a pile of firewood, heaped like discarded bones. "The Trooper I spoke to said we'd find what's left of the bear in a clearing to the East."

Letty followed him around the side of the cabin, her attention sharp on the forest around them. There'd been no report of the second bear, but that didn't mean it wasn't in the area. With the trees pressing in from all sides, it was impossible to tell if anything might be hiding there, just out of sight. She held her breath, listening for the crack of branches or the crush of leaves underfoot.

Only their own footfalls broke the silence as she and Brenner wound around the cabin to the promised clearing. At its center, a bear's carcass lay sprawled at the foot of a small, metal swing set. Her gaze flicked away, the gore of the remains too much all at once. Pink tassels hung from both of the swing's seats, the white paint worn from the chain links where a child would've held on. The ground beneath bore two scarred ovals, scraped clean by dragging feet. According to Brenner, the little girl it belonged to had gone inside for a grilled cheese only moments before the bear found this place. What might have happened if she hadn't?

She shivered against the thought, forcing her mind back to the task at hand as she circled the polar bear's body. It lay on its right side, the left front and rear legs splayed back so that the carcass lay opened, gruesome and bloody. The step of skinning the animal had been foregone, as would be typical in a field necropsy. That much she knew from her work with any number of other mammals. Here, the focus would've been on the bear's intestinal contents and the evidence found on the exterior of the body.

"Where's the girl now? Her family?" Letty asked.

"Back at the station in town. We'll need to make sure this location is secure before they return."

She nodded, turning her attention back to the remains. A foul stench hung in the air, a potent mix of blood, intestinal fluid, and the gas that would've been released when cutting into the stomach. The bear had been lying under the swings long enough that steam no longer came from the body cavity, but not so long that scavengers had gotten at the remains.

That was a blessing. Evidence was easier to collect when it hadn't been eaten.

She pulled a pen and notebook from her bag, jotting down details. The bear was around nine and a half feet, head to foot. Emaciated, male, and in poor physical condition even before the gunshot wounds that'd killed it. Which she could've predicted. Sickly male bears were the most likely to attack. She circled the carcass again, careful not to step in the gruesome mix of blood and intestinal fluid covering the ground. She stopped at the animal's head. A small white disk protruded from its ear.

"Can I touch this?" Letty looked to Brenner for confirmation. Behind him, a row of half-dressed Barbies looked back from one of the cabin's ground floor windows.

That's not creepy at all.

He nodded. "Fish and Game says it's all yours. Necropsy's done. They've got fur samples, dental impressions, scrapings from the bears claws and between its teeth. They'll do a full analysis, check for the fishermen's DNA on the fur, check the bear's DNA against the saliva found on their remains, compare the impressions with the men's wound patterns…" His Adam's apple bobbed. "I'm confident we'll find a match."

Letty inspected the disk. A GPS tag. Less reliable than the collars used on female bears, but more apt to stay in place. Male bears' necks were so thick in relation to their heads, the collars would slip right off. An ear tag, although still notoriously hard to keep in place, would've been the best bet to track this bear. If she could figure out who had placed the device and get them to share their data, it could give her vital information on how the bear got so far south.

Fingers crossed.

She tucked her notebook away, snapped several pictures of the ear tag, and, with a silent hallelujah for the miracle of still having cell service so far out in the middle of nowhere, she texted them to Gemma with a note: "Would you check this with the USFW and USGS? See if they know of anyone's research subjects going AWOL?" The two agencies managed polar bear research in Alaska, and she'd spent an unreasonable amount of time on both their websites as part of her preparations for the trip. If anyone could point her to the right researcher, the U.S. Fish and Wildlife Service or the U.S. Geological Survey would be the ones to do it.

A tiny thumb appeared on top of the text message, and Letty hummed her approval. Having Gemma on board was like cloning herself. She could get twice the work done in half the time.

She eyed the bear. Scratch marks crisscrossed its nose, which was consistent with Reardon's description of the bear that attacked him. But they also weren't unusual on an older male bear who'd likely spent years fighting over food or mates, so not definitive.

"Anything interesting in the stomach contents?" Their victims' remains would've been gone within twenty-four hours of the attack, but the contents of the bear's stomach could still tell them where the bear had been in the meantime. Berries that only grew in certain places, trash that could indicate the animal had been sticking closer to inhabited areas, or God forbid, if there were additional victims they hadn't yet discovered, other human remains. She grimaced at the thought.

Brenner held out his cell phone, an image of a gold ring on the screen. "They recovered this."

The phone showed an image of a simple metal band, two strands woven together. One yellow gold, one rose. She'd seen it described in her case file. "Craig Miller's?"

"We're waiting on final confirmation from his wife, but yes. I'm confident it is." Brenner put his phone away.

Letty nodded and looked away. Those men had been husbands, fathers, sons, and brothers. Somewhere there were families who felt the loss of Miller and Murkowski like aching cavities. People whose lives would forever be severed into two parts — the time before, when they had the people they loved, and the after. She knew the feeling all too well.

She still picked up her phone to send a text or had some thought she couldn't wait to share with her sister... only to remember Jessa was gone. And she was never coming back. Letty circled the remains again, trying to swallow past a throat gone tight. Trying to hold focus on what she was there to do.

It wasn't really a surprise to find the ring. Predatory carnivores normally went for their prey's abdomen — the body's organs were, after all, the most nutritious parts — but that didn't hold true when the prey was human. Then predators went for those areas not covered by clothing. Which meant damage was often centered around the victim's head, neck... and hands.

She knelt down for a closer look. The animal's fur was filthy, matted. A white cotton string trailed down from a wound in the animal's neck. "Is that?"

"A tampon." Brenner said.

She squinted up at him, waiting for a punchline.

"Standard procedure when they take down a bear suspected of an attack. Plugs the wound, keeps the animal's blood from mixing with any human blood that might remain on the fur." Brenner gestured toward the stained fur. "Makes a DNA match easier if the animal's doesn't mix with the victims'."

"Makes sense." Letty got to her feet. What she wouldn't give to have been a fly on the wall the first time that tactic was proposed to the burly group she imagined the Alaska Department of Fish and Game to be.

She moved carefully through the rest of the site, scanning the ground for tracks or other evidence. Brenner trailed behind her, his gun still at the ready, his attention focused on the dense, unyielding forest around them. The rain had left the ground soft and pliable, a perfect medium for the bear's prints. One set. No sign of a second animal. The tracks led from the forest to the cabin, then back into the clearing where the bear's body now rested. She took photographs of all the relevant areas, tracing the bear's path backward, trying to determine as best she could where he'd come from. She followed along until the prints disappeared in an area too rocky for her find his trail.

The only thing certain was that the animal had been coming from the south when he'd found the cabin. That was no surprise. All signs pointed to this bear being in Katmai the week before. Still, Letty kept looking, ignoring the grumbling coming from her stomach. She hadn't had time to truly dig into the first site. She wasn't going to miss her chance to glean everything possible here. If that meant another missed meal, so be it. Letty traced back over her steps until the sun dipped so far beyond the horizon she'd all but lost her light, and Brenner's stomach rumbled loud enough for her to hear it, too.

Her phone dinged as she followed him back to the truck.

A message from Gemma. "USGS says your bear was tagged by an outfit doing work in Sallow Bay. Emailing details now."

Bingo.

Letty stretched the kinks from her back. It'd been a long day, but so worth it. This was the break she'd needed. With the GPS data, she could trace the bears' migration, maybe even identify what had driven them all the way to Katmai. She pulled up a map on her phone. Sallow Bay was on the far northeastern shore of Alaska. The town sat on a tiny inlet off the Beaufort Sea in an area so remote it was virtually unreachable except by air. She tapped her phone against her palm and stared off into the darkening snarl of the woods.

How could this bear be from the Beaufort area?

Ranger Brenner had spent the drive over from the marina telling her everything he knew about Alaska's polar bear population. Starting with the fact that it was essentially divided in two. The Beaufort bears usually followed the ice-pack edge as it retreated in the warmer months and advanced as the weather cooled. Their migration patterns were stable, predictable. She'd assumed they were dealing instead with the western Chukchi and Bering population. Not just because those bears lived several hundred miles closer to where the attack occurred, but because western bears migrated so much further. The home range for Beaufort bears was half that of their western counterparts.

So it was highly unusual to think this bear had come all the way from Sallow Bay to Katmai. She put her phone away, waiting for Brenner to unlock the SUV so she could climb in. Something niggled at the back of her mind.

Sallow Bay.

The name was familiar.

Had she seen it in the file?

No.

Letty pressed her eyes closed against the truth.

She'd seen it on the news. "Save Sallow Bay" had been the rallying cry for protesters objecting to the expansion of oil and gas exploration off the northeast coast of Alaska. It had been a few years ago now, but how many times had she seen the same video clip playing on TV? Enough that the image had stuck in her mind. Demonstrators with homemade signs trudging back and forth in the Houston heat, a grim line of police holding them back.

The towering glass structure of Stafford Oil's headquarters looming behind them.

CHAPTER 12

October 21, 2018
Sallow Bay, Alaska
Letty pulled at the strings under her chin, tightening her hood around her face. To her left, a solid expanse of unbroken ice disappeared into the distance. Called fast ice, because it was fastened to the land, it extended dozens of miles into the Arctic Ocean. Which was odd. Landfast ice shouldn't be set up in this region for another couple of months, especially not with the rate climate change was heating the Arctic. She had expected the coast to look more like what she found to her right, where seawater chopped hostile and gray against the half-frozen shore. In the far distance, she could just make out the silhouette of Stafford Oil's drilling rig. All its details blurred by snow and ice.

She tucked a loose strand of hair under her hood and sucked in air so cold it burned in her lungs. This place couldn't be any more different than the lush, green outdoor spaces she'd spent her life loving. Not a single tree grew anywhere. It felt wrong. She felt wrong. Not meant for this barren, frozen wasteland, where both the ice and sky were bleached of any color or vitality. The landscape was as alien as if she'd stepped out onto the surface of some desolate, far away planet.

Alone and out of place.

An icy flake landed on her cheek, and she brushed it away, turning back toward town. Or what there was of it. A marina, the airport, a tiny clinic and a smattering of local businesses. The rest of the town's lifeblood she couldn't see from there. Each of the oil companies working in the area had their own private campuses outside of town, where most of the locals commuted for work every day. Sallow Bay was ten, maybe fifteen square miles of civilization carved out of one of the most inhospitable places on Earth. Once an Inuit village, it now revolved around the money that could be made from the oil and gas industry. Above a collection of short, blocky buildings, the tail of the plane that had dropped her off slid across the horizon. Like a shark, visible only by its fin.

One tiny plane came in and out of Sallow Bay each day, staying only long enough to unload its cargo before departing again. It lifted off, banking out over the small marina on the other end of town before escaping back toward home, leaving her behind. She wrapped her arms around her middle, as much for comfort as to hold in what little warmth her body had managed to retain.

Snap out of it, Duquesne.

She double-checked the address, but she didn't really need confirmation she was in the right spot. The chopper waiting beside the facility would have been hard to miss. She had seen one like it before, in pictures from a research project her mentor, Bill, had done as a grad student in Manitoba. The Bell 407 helicopter was sleek, gray, and coated in ice. Beyond it, Arctic Transport shared a central garage with the Sallow Bay Research Facility. The combined structure was twice the size of any other building in town and a strictly modern affair. Mainly steel, it stood in stark contrast to the near uniform square wooden boxes of the other structures.

"Hiya." A rough voice came from behind her.

She turned to find a small man with a broad, open face and smiling eyes approaching from the building's open hangar. He wobbled slightly as he walked, as if he'd recently had a hip replaced or needed to.

Letty held out a hand. "Mr. Quinnayuak?"

The man's gloved hand closed around hers, his grip surprisingly strong for a man his size. "Call me Charlie."

"Nice to meet you, Charlie." She smiled as she opened and closed her fingers, still recovering from his vise grip. "Letty Duquesne."

He turned back toward the garage and waved for her to follow. "Let's get you a cup of something warm." They passed through an oversized garage. Tools hung from every surface, and machine parts covered the floor. Several snowmobiles lay in various stages of deconstruction or repair, and on the far side of the space sat a massive Hagglund snowcat. The tank-like vehicle had an articulated front and rear cab, supported by thick rubber treads. A rear hatch had been propped open, and a heavy-set woman with spiky gray hair stood at the top of a ladder, leaning over the opening with some sort of tool in her hand. She didn't look up as Letty passed.

Charlie held open an interior door. "How was your flight?"

"Not bad." Except for the twenty-three hour layover she'd spent in Anchorage. Most of it, eating middling airport sandwiches or asleep in a hard plastic chair at her departure gate. She'd need a three-day nap and maybe a neck brace by the time she got home. But if she could get out to the bears' stomping grounds, get some feel for why they'd broken their usual migratory patterns, she'd deal with most anything. "I'm anxious to get out on the ice now that I'm here."

Charlie's face tightened in an expression she couldn't read as she followed him into a small office. What must have been years of notices and receipts covered the walls. The paper overlapping, the edges curled. She tried not to gawk. "I understand you were the guide for a group of researchers from the Polar Bear Research Fund." She checked her notes for the names of the scientists who had tagged her bear. "Dr. Patel and Dr. Salinas?" She hadn't spoken to either of them directly yet, but Gemma had forwarded all their data to her via email. Which had told her two very important things. First, the tagged bear had been perfectly healthy a year ago when the tag was applied. And, second, Letty now had detailed information about the bear's migration patterns over the time it'd been tracked. Once she got on the pack ice, she knew exactly where to go.

"That's right. They were focused on an area about two hours north. All sorts of dens up there. Couple of good size leads. Lots of seals." A phone rang behind the desk, and Charlie held up a finger, leaning over to grab the receiver. "Arctic Transport." His face softened as he turned away. "Hello, honey."

Letty took a sip of the coffee and grimaced. It tasted like a wet sock, but it was warm. She wrapped her hands around the cup and stared out a small window looking over ridges of banked snow, while she waited for Charlie to finish his call. If the weather allowed, they could get out on the pack ice tomorrow and try to figure out what the hell had caused those bears to stray so far. Polar bears usually had fidelity to certain regions, traveling in the same areas from season to season. Which clearly hadn't been the case here.

The question was, why? Russian poachers had a long history of killing polar bears for their hides. And, because it was an illegal trade, there was no way to quantify what that impact might actually be. Other than completely fucked up, which it definitely was. But that seemed less likely than a more pedestrian cause, like a reduction in the bears' prey population.

And, of course, climate change was a contender for that. Every summer when the ice melted, more and more bears came onto land looking for food. Could that be happening in the fall, too? The fast ice attached to the Sallow Bay shoreline seemed plentiful enough. But she wouldn't know the condition of the pack ice, where her polar bears had lived, until she could get out there.

She pulled off her hood, a trickle of wet snow finding its way between her ponytail and the fleece she wore under her jacket. Letty shivered against the icy finger trailing down her spine.

Charlie had said the area where they were headed had good-size leads, the large fractures in the ice giving the bears access to seals and other prey beneath the water, but the size of the seal population could've changed. If the bears didn't have enough to eat, that would drive them to find an area where they did. If she had to bet what would've motivated the bears to go so very far from where they were accustomed to hunting, that would be it.

She looked back out the window, where fat snowflakes hung in the air, as if suspended in a held breath. She hoped to God something she found out on the ice tomorrow proved her right. Because if she was wrong, if the bears had migrated south due to chemical contamination in the food chain or an increase in industrial activity… it would be all that much more plausible to put the blame on Stafford Oil's shoulders.

The chances it was actually the culprit seemed slim. Habitat disruption could have a thousand different sources. And even if it was incidental to oil and gas exploration, Stafford Oil was hardly the only company trying to extract the billions of barrels of oil trapped beneath the bay. But the idea that Stafford Oil held responsibility for those fishermen's deaths would have an unparalleled appeal to a media market salivating for its next corporate villain. Mark had been all over the news since he'd appeared before the Congressional committee, arguing for the need for immediate action to understand and address the unsettling changes they were seeing in animals world-wide. This could make for a spectacular fall from grace. The media would eat it up.

Everyone who had opposed the foundation or, worse, argued nothing was wrong with nature to begin with — idiots like Senator Hilliard — would jump at the chance to cry foul. To argue Mark's true purpose was to hide his own company's misdeeds.

Fuck.

It wasn't that she had any particular love for oil companies in general, but she couldn't let that happen. With the authority Mark had asked Congress to give it, the foundation would be humanity's best chance at figuring out why the balance of nature had gone so off-kilter. Not to mention one uniform source for data collection and assessment. That was maybe the most important part. The world would finally have a complete global picture of what was happening. Which was, so far as she could see, their best chance to turn things around. A chance they could easily lose if the foundation was discredited before they got that authority.

And God knew when that was coming. The committee could make a decision next week or next year. Her mouth went dry. How long could things keep going as they were before whatever was wrong went too far to fix?

How long until nature became so imbalanced, there was no going back?

"Sorry, that was my daughter." Charlie hung up, pulling her back from her thoughts. "I'm happy to take you out there." He looked away and rubbed a hand over the back of his neck. "But I'm afraid I can't do it as soon as we'd planned."

She glanced outside. The day still drooped overcast and gray. She'd known weather could be a problem, but the last check she'd done of the graphical forecast of the area, or GFA, had looked promising. A new GFA was released every four hours, displaying the clouds, weather, icing, wind turbulence, and freezing levels. Two hours ago, the GFA had shown a clear flight window for the next twelve hours, but maybe conditions were expected to worsen after that?

A seed of worry planted in her gut. "Okay." She cleared her throat, willing the seed not to grow. As anxious as she was to get out on the pack ice, a short delay wouldn't be so bad. She'd have time to regroup, take a proper shower, get some actual rest. Maybe even eat something that didn't come from a vending machine. "When do you think we'll get our next window?"

He shook his head. "Weather's not the problem. Your bird got stranded over in Barrow last night, and the pilot with it. Simple enough fix, but we're waiting on a part. My chopper here is booked for the next two weeks solid." He shrugged. "I'm sorry, Dr. Duquesne. I tried to reach you to let you know, but I think you were in the air when I called." He wobbled out from behind his desk, remorse creasing his already lined face. "I checked with a friend in Prudhoe. Good guy, great pilot. He could probably have you in the air in five or six days, a week tops."

"A week?" Her irritation spiked, but it wouldn't do any good to take it out on him. She blew out a slow breath, trying to think through her options. Sallow Bay was too small to offer any other transport services, which meant Charlie, and his contacts, were the only game in town.

Charlie's phone rang again and with a grimace of apology to her, he answered it. "Arctic Transport."

She turned away. Could she stay here a week? She had only been in Sallow Bay an hour, and she already itched to be anywhere else. Even knowing this strange, frozen world teemed with its own sort of life, it didn't feel that way. It felt empty. Desolate… dead.

Worse, what could happen in that amount of time? They hadn't had any more attacks. Thank God. But how long would that remain true? Her mouth wasn't just dry now, it felt like the bottom of a dustbin. The second bear was still on the loose, still a danger to anyone it might come across. And both Gemma and Ranger Brenner had passed on several not-yet-verified reports of other polar bears spotted well south of where they should be. Whatever was going on, it wasn't over. She made herself take a sip of the sock-water coffee.

And then there was the fact that she had asked Brenner to notify the local authorities of the Katmai bears' connection to Sallow Bay before she left King Salmon. That meant passing the details to at least four different agencies — the National Park Service, the Alaska Department of Fish and Game, the State Troopers, and Kodiak National Wildlife Refuge. It wouldn't take long for that information to find its way into the wrong hands.

The clock was ticking, every second taking them closer to disaster. And there was nothing she could do but wait.

And watch it happen.

. . .

Letty checked her watch. Not even six o'clock, and the world outside the bar's front window was already black, save the greenish glow of a neon sign. The grimy glass flickered with Technicolor graphics. A reflection of the TV behind her replaying the NHL's season opener. Capitals versus Bruins. Which made her think of her best friend, Priya — who despite playing no sports and having no connection to Boston — was a diehard Bruins fan. Letty cracked a weak smile. God, she wished Priya was here. Everything would seem so much less daunting if she wasn't alone. If she had someone to hash through the facts of the case with, to commiserate the absolute shit luck it took for those bears to have come from Sallow Bay of all places.

Not that she begrudged her friend's radio silence. Priya's dissertation was due early next year, and she'd gone into full sequestration to get a draft ready. In her shoes, Letty would have done the exact same thing.

Still, the possibility of waiting out the next week with nothing but worry for company, knowing every second that crept by could bring a catastrophic news alert or a frantic call from Gemma. It could mean the press had connected the Katmai attack to Sallow Bay... to Stafford Oil... Or, worse, that in the time she was delayed, there was another attack. More reports kept coming in of polar bear sightings near Katmai and far beyond. They weren't yet verified, but...

The whole thing made her crave a friendly face. And a drink.

She tapped a peeling coaster against the counter, staring at the bartender's back. The sole server had been locked in conversation with a hang-faced man at the far end of the bar since Letty had arrived, and she couldn't be the only one getting thirsty. She glanced around. Several groups of men slouched over the tables behind her, a few in Stafford Oil sweatshirts. Most of the others wore the logos of Stafford's competitors. They kept their voices low, gnarled hands wrapped around mostly empty glasses of beer or whiskey. All seemed deep in conversation, except the three seated at the table closest to the door. They wore matching Northrop Grumman hats, and the biggest of the trio, a muscle-bound tank of a man, glared at her from under its bill. The look on his face fell somewhere between appreciation and menace. Of the two emotions, the latter made her far less uncomfortable. Were there not actually any other women in Alaska? Letty turned back around, looking at the rows of liquor bottles covering the wall behind the bar but not seeing any of them.

Northrop Grumman meant defense contractors, although she vaguely recalled reading somewhere that their activities in the Arctic had more to do with research and development of products and materials for use in extreme climates than anything military. But the man staring at her like she was on the menu was probably still armed. She tore at the edge of the coaster, trying to ignore the press of the man's gaze on the back of her neck. Her hotel was a three block walk, and she'd be making it alone in the dark.

"Hey, Odele!" A man yelled from directly behind her.

Letty jumped in her seat, a hand pressed to her chest where her heart raced out of control. She turned to the man standing just over her right shoulder. Tall, square-jawed, and handsome as hell, wearing a bright orange jacket and a camera, hanging from a strap around his neck. "Didn't mean to startle you." He gave her an apologetic smile as he gestured to the bar stool beside hers. "May I?"

"Sure." She shifted her stool to make room, her heart still finding its normal rhythm as she looked up to find the spiky haired woman from Charlie's shop, now waiting to take her drink order. The mechanic had swapped her overalls for a dingy polo shirt with

"Odele" embroidered over one heavy breast. Letty hadn't recognized her from behind.

The woman seemed less than pleased to have her conversation interrupted for something as inconvenient as doing her job. "What'll you have?"

"Can I get a Jameson, neat. And…" The man turned to Letty. "Whatever she'd like." His words came out smooth and practiced. He'd no doubt said them before. Probably to scores of enthusiastic takers, given his looks.

"Oh no, you don't have to—"

"Please," he cut in. "I almost made you jump out of your seat. Let me make it up to you."

She hesitated. Taking the drink would necessitate at least a few minutes of small talk after, so she didn't seem rude. Normally, she'd rather just buy her own drink and keep her own company. But at the moment, being alone seemed like less of a good thing than usual. "Okay, thanks…" She pointed to one of the IPAs in a row of taps between her and Odele. "I'll take the Bitter Monk."

The bartender made a noise that could have been tacit approval. Or, more likely, gas. Then set about pouring their drinks.

Letty turned to the man beside her. "I'm Letty Duquesne."

A flicker of what looked like recognition crossed his face, but then it was gone. Maybe it hadn't been there to begin with. He held out a hand. "Adam Wan." They shook, and his fingers closed over hers, calloused and warm against her cold skin.

"Nice to meet you." He smiled, the skin crinkling around his eyes, his teeth white and straight, a bright contrast against his tanned skin. He looked like he'd walked out of a REI ad. Unlike everyone else she'd seen — including herself — he managed to make the five or six layers of clothes they all wore look rugged and intentional. She glanced down at herself. She looked like she'd snowballed through a rummage sale, picking up random layers of fleece and Gore-Tex as she rolled.

The bartender smacked a pint onto the bar in front of Letty, foam sloshing over the rim. Then poured Adam's drink, left it by his elbow, and stomped off.

"Don't mind Odele." Adam took a sip of his whiskey. "First time I came up here, it took two weeks before she said hello. She warms up eventually."

That didn't seem likely. Letty glanced down the bar to where Odele and her friend had fallen back into conversation, heads tilted together, their eyes darting over to where Adam and Letty sat talking.

"So what d'you do, Letty?" Adam turned his glass in his hand.

"I'm a researcher." She took a sip of the beer, which was the perfect balance of bitterness and citrus, trying to decide how much more she should say. It didn't make sense for her to give details to a man who, for all she knew, worked for the local news. He certainly looked good enough to be on TV. "Polar bears." She took another drink. "You?"

"Same." He twitched a smile, then nodded down at the camera. "Well, I'm here for the bears, anyway. I'm a wildlife photographer. Second stint in Sallow Bay. This time shooting for Nat Geo, although I haven't had much luck yet on this trip. Plenty of shots of seals out on the fast ice, walruses, some birds, but no bears." He pulled two menus from a holder on the counter and passed one her way. "When I saw you, I thought you might be the new scientist working with Charlie."

She stopped, her hand frozen halfway to the menu. "Sorry?"

He gave her another full-wattage smile. "That came out creepier than I intended." He rubbed a hand over the back of his neck, looking up at her from under long dark lashes. "I'm working with him, too. We're supposed to head out onto the pack ice day after tomorrow. Hoping to have better luck finding bears there." Adam put the menu on the bar in front of her. "Charlie told me what happened with your bird when I stopped by earlier today… That's a tough break."

"Yeah, it is." This town really was tiny. She looked down at the bar's meager offerings but couldn't focus. It wasn't Adam's fault her own trip had been delayed. That she was stuck, waiting and desperate. He wasn't taking her helicopter, no matter how much it felt like it. She took a deep swallow of her beer.

Adam watched her drink. "You know, if you're looking to get out on the pack ice, we're headed the same way. I've got the chopper for one more week before the next guy takes it. And I'd be glad to share my ride with you. It's just me and Charlie going out. We've got space."

She put down the pint. He couldn't be serious. "Really?" She straightened in her seat, the possibilities flinging around her mind like pinballs. They'd need to clear it with Charlie. He'd be losing the fee the foundation would have paid for a separate flight, which might have been why he hadn't raised the possibility of them sharing a ride. And what would Adam's employer think of subsidizing her research trip? And— "Are you sure?"

"Absolutely. Truth be told, I'd be glad for the company. I've been spending every day in an observation pod I have out on the fast ice. It's not bad, almost big enough for me to actually stand up in it." He grimaced. "But so far, I haven't seen a single bear. Nat Geo isn't paying to me take cute seal pics. Might be good to look further north. Charlie says he knows where to go."

Two roughnecks at the opposite end of the bar broke into raucous laughter, and Adam lifted the camera, as if by habit, capturing a volley of shots. The two clinking glasses, throwing back whatever was in them, then giving each other the kind of back smacking half-hugs men tended to do. Adam checked the image with a satisfied hum then let the camera hang from its strap again and turned back to her. "If I go back out on the ice without breaking the monotony soon, I'm going to start responding when I talk to myself." He grinned at her as he got up from his seat. "Be right back. If Odele comes by while I'm gone, would you order me a burger and another round?" At her nod, he headed off toward the restrooms in the back corner of the bar.

She watched him go. His ass filled out his pants in the best possible way.

She forced herself to look away. Maybe the dry spell she'd had since Pete had gone on a little too long. She was now apparently at the "ogling near-strangers" stage of sex deprivation.

A warmth spread from her stomach up her chest: a mix of the IPA she'd drunk too fast on an empty stomach, the eyeful making his way to the back of the bar, and the dawning possibility that she could get out onto the pack ice after all.

She took another swallow of beer. She'd needed this. Needed a stroke of good luck, when everything else seemed to be going against her. So many crazy things happening, she had begun to feel like she was cursed.

Not just Pete. Or Crawford going missing, or the bears coming all the way from Sallow Bay. But the burglar in Crawford's room. The attack outside his room. And the note on her car...

GO HOME.

She drank the last of her beer, trying to wash down her worries. She had done her best not to think about the note since she'd flown out of King Salmon, leaving the problem of the damaged rental car and whoever had done it far behind. Part of her hated the idea that the person who had smashed her windshield might think their threat had worked. She turned her now empty glass in her hand. She hadn't left because of the note. She'd gone because the case dictated it. She needed to be in Sallow Bay to finish her investigation.

But what if whoever left the note didn't think she had gone far enough?

She stopped spinning the glass. She hadn't gone home. She'd come here. And she hadn't missed the threat behind that smashed windshield, the implication that, if she didn't do what she was told, the consequences would be violent. She waved to get Odele's attention, pointing down at her and Adam's empty glasses. The bartender/mechanic gave a curt nod and went back to her conversation, making no move toward refills.

Letty hadn't been the only one on the plane that brought her to Sallow Bay. Her attacker could very well have been on it, too, and she'd be none the wiser. She had been so focused on her notes, on preparing for what was to come, she had hardly looked at the other dozen or so people who had filled the remaining seats. They could be here now, somewhere in the crowd behind her. She fought the urge to turn around and scan the other patrons' faces again.

No way around it, someone violent wanted her gone.

The bright burst of excitement she'd had when Adam offered to let her ride along onto the ice pack dimmed, eclipsed by a darker realization.

Whoever it was wanted her to disappear.

The same way Crawford had.

CHAPTER 13

Houston, Texas
October 22, 2018
Mark sat next to Aunt Kath at the head of an over-sized conference table. The same one he'd played under as a toddler and done his calculus homework on in high school. The oil painting of the Alamo his mother had chosen decades ago hung above an antique sideboard on the far wall, and the room smelled of coffee and furniture polish. Like it always had. Normally, this room made him feel like he had a home court advantage, but not today. Not when it was his own company he was up against.

The members of Stafford Oil's board filled the other seats around the table. Most wore dark Brooks Brothers suits, conservative haircuts, and silk ties. Only Aunt Kath and Jimmy broke the dress code. Her, in an ivory sheath dress, and him, in Wrangler jeans and a pressed western shirt. Mark's godfather helped himself to a second donut from the tray in the center of the table. A cruller. The old-fashioned ones Jimmy usually preferred were gone already.

Mark knew the rest of the faces around the table, where their kids went to school, who was a scratch golfer, and who had the audacity to cheer for Baylor instead of UT. But only Kath and Jimmy met his gaze.

The miserable mix of shame and indignation he'd been struggling with all morning was only tolerable because they were there to support him.

At least, they were for now.

Mark stared at the sticky mess of congealed icing Jimmy's donut had left on the platter, his stomach turning. By the time this meeting was over, there was a chance neither his aunt nor his godfather would be speaking to him anymore.

Reid Schaefer, resident thorn in Mark's side and President of the Board, rapped his knuckles against the table. "Okay, let's go ahead and get started." He ran through the corporate formalities, then cleared his throat and swept his gaze over the room. "As you know, today's meeting was called to address recent allegations of corporate misconduct. Late in the evening on October 18th, I received an anonymous tip, accusing Mark Stafford of self-dealing."

Self-dealing?

Mark leaned back in his chair as murmurs skittered around the room, muffled by the white noise in his head. What the hell was Reid talking about? Mark had crossed lines, yes. Bent the rules, maybe even broken them. But he'd never done anything that would amount to self-dealing. The bad choices he had made had nothing to do with profit. If that was what they'd called him in for, there was a chance this would all go away. The vise around his lungs loosened enough for him to take an almost full breath. "That's ridiculous."

He glanced at Kath, whose face remained as calm and unlined as ever, a perfect mask of incredulity. She'd know the idea was ludicrous. Everyone there should have. They knew the family he'd come from. If there was anything Mark wasn't motivated by, it was money. He'd grown up with more of it than he could ever spend, and his father had made sure that would be true for Mark's children's children as well. If he ever had any.

Mark tried to catch Jimmy's eye, but his godfather's gaze was locked on Reid. Jimmy's face the same mask Mark had seen him wear to countless poker tables, corporate squabbles, and courtroom brawls. Unreadable and not to be fucked with.

Reid had the decency to look uncomfortable. He shifted in his seat, shuffling the papers stacked in front of him. "I'm sure when we get to the bottom of the allegation, we'll find there to be a perfectly reasonable explanation. But that doesn't change our obligation to take any alleged breach of fiduciary duty seriously."

Kath gave Mark's hand a quick pat under the table. A silent reassurance of what she'd told him before they walked into company headquarters this morning: He just had to keep his cool, and let her deal with it. Mark took in another breath. Maybe she'd been right. Maybe the anonymous tip was baseless after all, and she could make it go away. Like she'd dealt with so many other family problems over the years.

Kath rested her elbows on the table. "No one is suggesting we ignore the allegation, just that this seems like an overreaction, not to mention a substantial waste of company resources." She gave a short shrug, her words measured and reasonable. "I mean, think of all the time and money wasted for all of us to just walk away from the important work we would otherwise be doing to come in here at the drop of a hat. Just because of some random, unsubstantiated tip."

"I'm not sure we can call this unsubstantiated." Reid raised a hand, gesturing for his secretary to come forward from where she'd been waiting by the door.

She slid a thick folder onto the table to Reid's right.

"We haven't had a chance to go through it all yet, but the tip was accompanied by a rather large number of supporting documents." Reid tapped his hand on the top of the file.

Another murmur of voices rounded the room. Mark stared at the file, as if the force of his gaze could somehow tell him what was in it. Anything supporting an allegation of self-dealing would involve his financial records or possibly his emails. Either way, they would have to have come from Mark's own office. How would anyone get access to it? And, even if they had, it would be some mistake, something being read the wrong way... or something falsified. He bristled.

Who would hate him enough to do that?

"It would have been courteous to share whatever that is in advance of today's meeting." Kath looked down her nose at Reid. "I assume copies will at least now be provided to the board for review." She sat back in her chair. "It seems only fair we should all be able to judge the basis of the tipster's claim for ourselves. And the quicker we can go through it, the quicker we can clear Mark's name and get back to business."

Reid lifted the file, and let it fall back to the table with an authoritative thunk. "We have a moral, ethical, and legal responsibility to investigate any alleged breach of fiduciary duty, especially one against Stafford's CEO." He paused, allowing time for sounds of agreement to circulate the room. "This is even more the case here, when Mr. Stafford has put himself so squarely in the public eye."

Even the faces that had seemed sympathetic to Mark when the meeting started tightened at Reid's mention of the press. The other board members tolerated Mark's work with the foundation, but he was under no delusions — that would last only so long as it didn't impact Stafford Oil's reputation or bottom line. And, if news of the allegations against him leaked, it could tarnish both.

Kath crossed her arms over her chest. "I'm not suggesting that we don't take the tip seriously, merely that we're allowed access and the opportunity to assess the documents purported to—"

Reid raised a hand, cutting Kath off. "You'll have it. But given the severity of the allegations and Mr. Stafford's very public profile, an internal review is simply not enough. There'd be no truly objective assessment of what may or may not have taken place."

Mark cleared his throat, ignoring a warning look from Kath, who'd all but sworn him to silence before they walked in. "What are you suggesting, Reid?"

"I propose the appointment of an independent investigator, who can assess not only the documents provided by the tipster, but the underlying transactions and activities."

Larry Glick, one of Reid's usual supporters, spoke up from his left. "We could use the same guys who did the spring audit last year. They were thorough, and Owen Lockwood's got a stellar reputation. Leaves no stone left unturned, and—"

"This is outrageous." Kath's words shook with anger.

Mark's gaze snapped to his aunt, whose face flushed an agitated red. She never lost her calm, ever. And the only reason he could think for her to be that upset was if some part of her believed he was actually guilty of lining his pockets, as they'd said. That, more than anything, hurt.

Kath put both hands flat on the table. "It's nothing but a witch hunt. Time this board could be spending building our business, rather than tearing down the people who are dedicated to ensuring its success. I know, with an internal investigation, Mark doesn't have a legal right to see the documents in advance, but it would certainly aid in his ability to explain what's surely an innocent mistake or misunderstanding." A flush crept up her throat, the color a bright contrast against the fine, pale fabric of her dress. "At minimum, the board should be allowed to review these alleged supporting documents before we—"

Reid cut in. "Mark will be given copies in due time. And there's no sense in circulating documents which purport to show corporate malfeasance to any more people than is absolutely necessary, especially before they've been properly vetted. If this all turns out to be a hoax or a mistake — as I'm sure it will — doing so could do irreparable and unnecessary harm to Mark's reputation. I'm sure you can see why Larry's suggestion that an independent investigator be appointed bears real consideration."

Kath leaned in, as if getting ready to launch another argument. Mark stopped her, putting his hand on her arm. "Let them do what they need to do." Reid's henchman could paw through his banking records all they wanted. They wouldn't find anything amiss there. And maybe he'd manage to regain her and Jimmy's respect.

Reid nodded. "How about we put it to a vote?"

Kath sputtered another objection, as Reid pushed forward. "I'd like to make a motion to hire Owen Lockwood as an independent investigator to look into allegations of misconduct by current CEO Mark Stafford, and to relieve Mark of his position pending the outcome of that investigation."

The white noise descended again. Mark gripped the edge of the table, fighting the urge to walk out or tell them all to go fuck themselves.

They didn't just want an investigation. They wanted him out.

He forced his face to stay neutral, even as his mind spun out of control. How could he have been so stupid?

Of course that's what was going on. It's what Reid had wanted since Mark had taken the helm from his father. Larry Glick's voice came from Mark's left. "I second the motion."

Hands went up around the table, one after the next.

Until only his and Kath's weren't raised.

Jimmy finally met his gaze, his hand lifted. His eyes hard.

CHAPTER 14

Sallow Bay, Alaska

Light teased the edges of the horizon, a subtle glow along the seam of sky and ice. Letty shifted on her feet, boots squelching in the snow. The sun wouldn't be up for another hour, and what pale, anemic light seeped into the night sky brought no warmth with it. She shivered as she rapped her knuckles against the facility's door for a third time and checked her watch, 9:30. Right when Gemma had told her to be there.

The two scientists Gemma had contracted with to help Letty with her research were supposed to have been there waiting, ready to get her prepared for an afternoon out on the pack ice. She leaned her ear toward the door and listened for anyone moving around in the facility. A snowmobile whined from the opposite side of town. A dog in a nearby house gave a sharp series of barks. But no sounds came from inside.

Fuck it.

Letty tried the door, and the handle turned easily in her grip. "Hello?" She called out as she nudged the door open. Letting herself in might not make the best first impression, but at least she wouldn't freeze to death waiting for them to show up.

She stepped into a small mudroom. Outerwear in an array of sizes and colors covered the wall opposite the door, and several pairs of battered snow boots sat cradled in a waterproof tray underneath. "Dr. Becker? Dr. Adeyemi?" Freezing wind gusted through the open door behind her, and Letty reached back to pull it closed.

With the door shut, the place had a decidedly empty feel. The air thick with quiet. Which did not make her feel any more comfortable walking in uninvited.

She rubbed her arms against the lingering chill. "Anyone here?" Letty stepped deeper into the facility. Originally constructed by the National Oceanic and Atmospheric Association as part of the efforts to track the effect of climate change in the Arctic, the facility had expanded over the years into a space for scientific collaboration. It now housed a constantly shifting cast of Arctic scientists from different universities or NGOs, with an equally broad range of specialties. Which made it a perfect place for the foundation's purposes. The mudroom opened onto a large common area with a basic galley kitchen on her left. Through an oversized glass door to her right, a lab gleamed with stainless steel and glass. Everything set up for work but no one there.

Where the hell are they?

A large window on the far wall offered a view of the shoreline, ragged and craggy with ice. Everything cast in bruised shades of blue and gray, the sea chopping violently against the shore. Somewhere out there, Stafford Oil's drilling rig mined the ground beneath the shallow, half-frozen water. But it was too far out for her to see it from here, with the weather the way it was.

Letty set her bag on a deep red sectional sofa in the center of the room and clicked on a lamp on the side table. That at least chased some of the shadows away. The facility had a worn, lived in feel, like a space used to being filled with people. A battered foosball table, a flat screen tv, a series of towering bookshelves packed well beyond capacity with research manuals, board games, paperbacks, and at least a dozen assorted binders. Everything that might help keep visiting scientists sane during the long, cold winters when the world outside would be dark for months at a time.

She peered down a hallway at the back of the room, but it was too shadowed for her to tell what might be back there. Probably the living quarters. As tempted as she was to go poke around, it wasn't worth the risk of getting caught doing it. Letty dug out her phone, connected to the facility's Wi-Fi, and dialed Gemma. "Hey, they know I'm coming, right?"

"Course they do. I confirmed arrangements with Dr. Becker yesterday. She seemed well pleased to stay on. Her last grant just ended, so the timing worked out perfectly. She and Dr. Adeyemi should be able to provide you with lab support and any gear you may not already have. I just emailed you the details on another polar bear sighting. This one seems less credible than the others, though. It's from all the way over on the Canadian border, sort of near Fairbanks."

Letty peeled off her parka. Gemma was right to question the report. Even with the abnormal range of their missing bear's migration, that would be a long way for it to have travelled since the last sighting. "Thank you, I'll take a look at it as soon as I can."

"No problem. Oh, and the samples you sent over from the bird strike in King Salmon came in. Lab's working on them now."

"That's good." She paused as she hung her coat in the mudroom, trying to decide whether to circle back to the rest of what they'd discussed the night before. Gemma hadn't exactly seemed convinced by what Letty'd had to say when she'd called from the hotel — that Crawford's body might be floating in a lake in Katmai. That she'd accidentally concealed evidence of it when she'd taken the strange note from his room. And, maybe even more than that, that she couldn't shake the feeling something else was going on.

Something bigger. Something dangerous.

"Have you given any more thought to what I said last night about Crawford?" Letty dropped her snow boots next to the others.

A pause, long enough to become uncomfortable. "Yeah."

"And?" Letty padded back to the common room in her sock feet, dropping onto the sofa.

Gemma sighed. "And I think you're reading too much into it all. Maybe Crawford's footsteps led to the water because he waded out to take a water sample, or maybe someone picked him up in a boat. Or let's say you're right, and he did top himself in the lake, I can't imagine the body's still there. Not with all the animals about."

Letty shuddered. The idea that Crawford's remains might be in some creature's belly wasn't a comfortable one. "What about the rest? How do you explain the note on my windshield?"

"Maybe you parked in somebody's favorite spot. Or the burglar you interrupted wanted to make sure you thought twice about cooperating with the police, if the asshole wound up in a line up or whatever."

Which would mean the attacker had followed her back to her hotel. She cringed. "You're not making me feel better."

"All I'm saying is that there's probably a rational explanation for what's happened, and there's no reason to think you're in any danger now. From what you told me about Sallow Bay, there's not much of anywhere to hide. You'd see anyone sneaking up on you a mile away. And you've got enough on your plate without worrying about that, too."

Letty started to argue but couldn't fault Gemma's logic.

Gemma took advantage of her pause. "Look, leave Crawford with me. I sifted through his employee file and his desk last night after we talked. Mark and Kathryn are still MIA, so I was able to take my time about it. I didn't find anything to indicate he was struggling before he disappeared. All his cases were up to date and handled without incident. Nothing weird on his background check." A can popped open on Gemma's end of the line. "I'll keep digging around, though. Maybe see what I can find out about him online."

Letty's brows rose at that. She didn't know exactly what Gemma had been involved in before she came to the foundation.

But in Letty's short time at the JDF, she'd already picked up enough from water cooler gossip to know Gemma's computer skills fell somewhere on the far side of legal. If anyone could find answers, it'd be her.

A door slammed from the front of the building, and Letty got to her feet. "Okay, alright. That sounds good. Thanks, Gem."

Letty disconnected the call as voices came from the mudroom, followed by the thud of boots dropping to the floor.

A tall woman with ice blonde hair walked into the common room, her cheeks still pink from the cold, a bright turquoise scarf wound around her neck. "Ah, I was afraid we were late. You must be Dr. Duquesne. I'm Hilde Becker." She smiled as she unwound the scarf, turning to gesture with her other hand toward the man who'd slid with near silence into the room behind her. He was even taller than his colleague, long-limbed and lean, like a distance runner. "And this is Dr. Musa Adeyemi."

He gave her a shy smile that transformed an otherwise skeletal face into something open and warm. "Welcome to Sallow Bay." The soft African lilt in his voice made a sharp contrast to Hilde's hard-edged Germanic accent.

"I apologize that we were not here to welcome you when you arrived. I woke up with a taste for pancakes but not for making them. The diner is usually quick but not today. Big group in from Northrup, taking up all the seats." She rolled her eyes, then smiled as she crossed the distance in two long strides, holding out her hand. "I understand you're in need of some lab support, equipment, and perhaps a more comfortable place to stay?"

Letty hadn't considered the possibility of staying at the facility, but being able to work around the clock, having access to the lab and its resources at any time of day… Letty shook Hilde's hand. "That would be lovely, thank you."

"Let me fetch you a key." Musa hurried down the hall.

"I'm glad you let yourself inside to get warm. We don't usually leave the door unsecured, what with all the equipment we have on site." She gestured toward the lab. "But Musa thought it best, just in case. You'll find most of Sallow Bay leaves their doors unlocked." Hilde folded herself to sit cross-legged in a sagging upholstered chair opposite the couch. She was a large woman, at least six feet tall and muscular, with skin still tan despite the fact she'd probably spent the entire time she had been working in Sallow Bay covering every inch of it against the cold. She twisted a chunky turquoise ring around her finger, a flicker of some expression Letty couldn't name crossing her features.

"That's... very quaint." And not at all consistent with her impression of the town so far. The haggard Alaskan town didn't exactly give off a drop-by-anytime sort of vibe.

Whatever Letty'd seen on Hilde's face a moment before deepened into a grimace. "I wouldn't call it that." She tilted her head toward the window.

Letty followed her gaze. A single caribou stood on an icy outcropping. The early morning light casting its huge body in heavy shades of gray, like it was carved from stone. The angles too sharp, its ribs a jagged iron ripple along the animal's flank.

Dark shadows hid the caribou's eyes, but it seemed to be staring right back at her.

Letty looked away, trying not to show it'd spooked her.

Hilde continued. "It didn't feel right to just go back to Fairbanks with things the way they are here. But with our grant at its end, I didn't see much of a choice. At least, not until your Gemma called."

Letty furrowed her brow. "What do you mean 'the way things are here'?" That sounded like something beyond a few bears gone AWOL.

"You are here to find out what is wrong with them, yes?" Musa spoke from the hallway, a key card on a lanyard dangling from his hand. "With the animals?"

Of course, that was exactly what she'd been trying to do. She'd been trying to understand what was going wrong in the natural world since things had started to go so off-kilter, and especially

since Jessa's death. But that obviously wasn't what Musa meant —
he wasn't talking in generalities.

Hilde leaned forward. "I know your purpose in coming here
started with tracing the bears from that attack in Katmai, but…"
She gestured back toward the caribou, who hadn't moved in the
time they'd been speaking. "I assumed you would think this was
related."

"This?" Letty still had no real idea what "this" was beyond
some iteration of strange animal behavior. And she was starting to
think she might not like the answer.

Musa came to join Letty on the couch. He sat on the opposite
end, one leg crossed over the other, his hands folded neatly in his
lap. She'd have thought him to be perfectly composed, were it not
for his foot bouncing with nervous energy. "These past few
months, we've had an influx of animals coming into town. Sick,
emaciated, their eyes dull with hunger. Breaking into trash." He
shrugged, as if this was to be expected. "But also following anyone
who happened to be outside alone. Not groups, just those on their
own. Charlie tried to rig a detection system with some infrared
cameras, but the system's alarm seemed to be going off every night
and waking half the town. People got together and decided to just
keep their doors open instead. If you got caught outside alone and
one of the animals ever came too close, you'd have a safe place
to go."

Letty sat up straight. If animals were coming in off the ice, it
made sense the Katmai bears could've been among them. "You're
seeing bears? More than usual, I mean."

"Not as much in the last week or so, but yes, among other
things." Hilde looked back to the caribou, now painted in a brighter
shade of gray by the shifting morning light. In place of the shadows,
sunlight glinted off the black of his eyes. "Fox, caribou, bears, even
the birds. They seem to be heading South. And all of them,
they're… odd." She cleared her throat. "This is not what we were
here to study, you understand. My grant related to the changes in

sea-ice thickness, not whatever... this is. But it seems important we find out, yes? I had thought to go seek out more funding to come back to do that work. But then the foundation called and... here you are." She glanced at Musa who nodded his agreement.

Letty looked back out the window, where the caribou still waited, motionless. Its gaze pinned to them. Deep, black, and unbroken. Letty fought a tightness in her throat. Hilde was right, something about the creature was off. Not just that it looked sickly. Waves of menace rolled from it. Whatever was going on here wasn't just about the bears.

And what freaked her out most of all was, although they'd volunteered to help, neither Hilde nor Musa had offered any possible explanation. Like her, they were scientists. At the core of who they were, what they were, was the driving need to explain what seemed inexplicable. The mystery behind the animals' behavior should have had them both amped with the thrill of scientific exploration. But that wasn't what she felt from either of them. They both projected a clear undercurrent of fear.

Letty swallowed, her throat catching as the caribou finally moved.

It tilted its head. The gesture too slow, too smooth.

Like something unnatural. Or something possessed.

CHAPTER 15

Sallow Bay, Alaska

An armed escort was not something Letty had ever expected to need. Your average ecology department leaned more toward vegan leather and world peace. But in the Arctic, she was no longer an apex predator; a gun wasn't optional. She glanced up to where Charlie stood a few yards away, a shotgun resting on his arm. Like Brenner, he gave off the odd mix of absolute concentration and comfort while standing guard, even in what were, by no means, comfortable conditions. It was barely more than twenty degrees. The snow had finally stopped, but he'd been still so long, it had accumulated in ridges along his shoulders and stuck in his eyelashes. Charlie didn't seem to notice. His gaze never left the horizon.

Adam was somewhere out there, beyond what she could see. Hopefully having better luck getting the photographs he needed on this part of the ice than he had in his observation pod. If it weren't for him agreeing to let her fly out to the pack ice with him, she'd have been stuck back at the research facility, wearing a groove into the carpet. Instead, she was standing on the same ice where her bear had once walked. She couldn't help but be grateful.

Letty refocused on her work, raising the last of three replicate water samples from the hole she'd drilled into the pack ice. Any nerves she'd had about hiking out into the polar bears' home territory — especially after what Hilde and Musa had said about the animals' behavior — had worn off hours ago. She hadn't seen a single living thing since their helicopter had taken off from Sallow Bay. No seals, no walruses, no polar bears. Not even any prints or other sign they could've followed to find where the animals had gone. Letty scanned a cloudless expanse of brilliant, unbroken blue sky. As gorgeous as it was frigid and empty.

There should at least be birds.

She'd come out on the ice hoping to take biological samples from the local seal population. Their hair and tissue could be tested for signs of disease, toxins, or hydrocarbons, which she hoped like hell not to find. She wanted answers, yes. But calling Mark to tell him she'd found petroleum byproducts in the displaced bears' primary food source... it wasn't a conversation she wanted to have.

And, in any case, it was a borrowed worry. She couldn't test what she couldn't find.

At least she'd come prepared to take water samples as well. If she hadn't, today's trip would have been a complete waste. And that was time she didn't have to lose, not with Congress busy debating the foundation's future. If she had results before they did — whenever that might be — it was possible she could help sway their decision in the JDF's favor. She turned, scanning the sky over the pressure ridge towering behind her. The steep, hulking mass of sea ice fragments had formed where two floes converged, creating a crest at least ten feet high. It cast her in a shadow that dropped the ambient temperature even more.

She tugged her fleece gaiter up to cover her nose. The sky above the ridge still held nothing, and the longer she went without seeing a living creature, the more concerned she was about what the samples might show. She poured her sample into a vial, pulled a Sharpie from the chest pocket of her parka, and marked the container "LNW-3". Using the data pulled from their bear's GPS tag, she'd mapped the area the animal had most frequented, dividing it into quadrants. Northeast, northwest, southeast, and southwest. Then divided each of those into an upper and lower section. She slipped the last of three lower northwest samples into a small cooler, now heavy with the other specimens she'd taken that day.

She slid the lid of the cooler closed and got to her feet, her back protesting the movement. They'd been out on the ice for hours. She'd known it would take several days' work to hit all the quadrants but had hoped to at least get through half of them today. That hadn't happened. They'd spent the first half of their afternoon flying over the ice, looking for wildlife. Adam's gyroscopic camera mounted and panning empty ice. He'd grown more and more quiet the longer they'd gone without seeing anything and had disappeared behind the pressure ridge to see what he could scout on foot as soon as they'd landed. In the hours since, the cold had seeped through her layers and under her skin, leaving her half-frozen and exhausted. The thermos of coffee she'd left back in the helicopter sounded like heaven.

She stepped out of the shadows and into the sun, tilting her face toward what little warmth it offered. As it had lowered in the sky, the temperature had fallen with it. "Should we head back to the chopper? See if Adam's there?"

"Sounds good." Charlie finally shifted, the accumulated snow tumbling from his shoulders only to catch in the wind and blow away.

As if summoned by his name, Adam rounded the ridge, his jacket a bright slash of orange against the blinding white-on-white of the world around them. His face was healthy with the flush of exercise. His hood had fallen back, and ice crystals glistened in the midnight black of his hair. A different kind of heat kindled in the pit of Letty's stomach.

The corners of Adam's mouth lifted as their gaze met. His eyes flickered with the same amused connection they'd had when they met at the bar. She chewed her bottom lip, suddenly glad for the gaiter covering any blush that might betray her thoughts.

He tilted his head toward the hole she'd drilled in the ice. "Any luck?"

"Hope so." She lifted the cooler. "You?"

"Some decent landscapes." He shrugged, adjusting the camera strap which was, as always, slung around his neck. "It's usually pretty deserted this far out on the pack ice. Maybe just a polar bear or a ringed seal here or there." He looked out over the empty terrain, a line of worry drawn between his brows. "But today's so quiet, it's almost eerie."

"Ah, well." Charlie stomped circulation back into his feet and clapped his gloved hands together. "There's always tomorrow. Long as the weather holds."

"Yeah, I'm sure today was just a fluke." Adam nodded, but he didn't sound convinced. He fell quiet as they loaded the cooler, the power head auger, bit, and extenders onto the gear sled. She tucked the Kemmerer bottle she'd used for collection on top and made sure everything was strapped in place, her fingers growing stiff with cold. "All set."

Charlie grabbed the tow rope, and they settled into the silence as they trekked back to the helicopter. They'd landed roughly halfway between her two northernmost test sites, which meant a twenty or thirty-minute hike back to where they'd started. Normally she would have enjoyed it, but it'd been a long day, and she was bone tired. Newly fallen snow squeaked under their boots. A rising wind howled unchallenged over the ice. And with the monotony of their steps, Letty's mind drifted back to Crawford. His footsteps leading into the lake. The note she had found in his things.

His family still waiting by the phone...

That thought held on and wouldn't let go, making each of her strides heavier.

By the time they finally reached their ride, she'd all but lost feeling in her hands. She fumbled with her gear as she stowed it and then with her buckles as she strapped into her seat. Even the bliss of the hot coffee she and Adam shared, passing the thermos between them, did little to thaw the anxious chill in the air.

No matter what Charlie had said, they all had to be thinking the same thing.

There should have been animals on the pack ice.

When they'd chatted on the flight there, Charlie had all but guaranteed she'd see seals coming up for air through the small holes the animals made in the ice. Or that she'd find them gathered in one of the leads. Ringed seals often surfaced in these open areas of water between ice floes. They might spend most of their life swimming beneath the ice, but they still had to breathe every half hour or so.

Or so she'd thought.

There hadn't been any air holes. And the leads were nothing but empty ribbons of sea water carved through the ice. Like thin, bony fingers clawing across the snowscape.

She raised the thermos in Adam's direction as Charlie started up the helicopter.

Adam mouthed "I'm good" over the noise as they both hurried to put on their headsets. Not only did it let them talk, it helped muffle the beating of the rotors overhead. Even with the headsets on, the noise was still so loud she could feel it thumping in her chest and reverberating in her teeth.

Adam adjusted his mic and leaned toward Charlie, his voice crackling through her earphones. "Have we got enough fuel to swing past the observation pod on the way back?"

"You betcha." Charlie manipulated the controls, and the helicopter responded immediately, lifting forward and up before banking hard to the right. "I never set out on the ice without a full tank."

Letty finished the last of the coffee and tore into a granola bar she'd stuffed in her gear bag that morning, taking in the frozen world beneath her, as they travelled back over the pack ice. When they had first set out, the monotony of white on white had seemed suffocating in its sameness. But now she could see that it was anything but. The ice ranged in color from white to gray to blue. Almost turquoise in places. She tucked the second half of the bar away and wrapped her hands tighter around the thermos, watching as they approached open sea. The water was as beautiful as it would be deadly to anyone unfortunate enough to spend more than a couple of moments underneath its surface.

Maybe they hadn't seen any animals because the wildlife had fled the noise of the helicopter? Noise pollution was a well-documented cause of wildlife distress and relocation. Or maybe it was just that they'd looked at too small of a sample size. They'd seen a proportionately small part of the pack ice. And only for a few hours of the day. Maybe they'd just gotten unlucky and been looking at a time and place where the animals happened not to be?

To her right, Adam stared out his own window, tension lines around his eyes. A camera rested in his lap but, unlike on their trip there, it wasn't at the ready. He still had the lens cap in place. She alternated between watching him and the brutal half-frozen sea beneath them. He had less than week left to get what he needed. He had to be worried about not meeting his deadline. About going back to Nat Geo with nothing but a very expensive stack of what was basically b-roll. A tiny, unwelcome voice in the back of her mind piped up, reminding her that technically Adam was press. He was a photo-journalist. If he didn't get the story he had come to Sallow Bay for, he could easily offer up what he knew about Letty's investigation instead. Between the Katmai attack, the Stafford Oil connection, and the local animals' unusual behavior, it would make quite the scoop. The lumbering skeleton of a drilling rig appeared in the distance. A massive platform with a central tower, surrounded by cranes and metal scaffolding. Stafford Oil's logo emblazoned on the side. She looked back at Adam. Was she ridiculous for believing he wouldn't make her the story, if worse came to worst?

Maybe. But she just couldn't see him doing it. She touched his shoulder. "Sorry today didn't go as planned."

"It happens." Adam straightened and offered her a smile, but the tension lines didn't go away. He had put his neck on the line to share the helicopter with her, letting her choose what parts of the ice they went to. They were both looking for bears, but without her there, Adam would have relied on Charlie's expertise, not the data Letty pulled from the Katmai bear's tracker. Would Adam's employer think that was why he'd come back without the pictures they wanted? That he'd gotten distracted, or let her project take them off course, and that's why he'd failed to deliver? She looked back to Adam, hating that anyone might use his kindness against him. Hating that she let herself doubt him.

The only real solution was to keep going out on the ice until they both had what they needed. "We should check the GFA when we're back." It would tell them when they could safely try again. Weather in the Arctic was brutal on a good day but could be absolutely deadly if you didn't respect it. "Musa said they would have dinner ready around seven. You could join us, and we can look at it together." The words left her mouth before she'd realized what she was saying. They'd had dinner together last night, but that'd been because they were both already at the bar at dinnertime.

Now, she'd basically asked him out.

Adam's smile widened, a glint of mischief in his dark eyes as her face went warm, this time with no gaiter to cover the tell-tale pink no doubt crawling up her cheeks. Her brain scrambled for anything she could do to make what she'd said less awkward. Point out again that they wouldn't be alone. Or that it only made sense for them to work together to plan for tomorrow? And they had to eat, anyway. She was just being efficient — two birds, one stone. Nothing more to it than that.

Right.

"I'd like that." Adam gave her another heart-stopping smile and held her gaze until she had to either look away or die from embarrassment. Outside her window, snow drifts slanted across the ice.

"Oh my God." Adam said, his voice cracking.

She whipped back toward him, leaning over to follow his gaze where it was pinned out his window.

A bloody red smear slashed across the snow. Several feet wide and at least twice as long.

Letty stopped breathing. Whatever had been alive out here, it wasn't anymore.

Nothing bled that much and survived.

■   ■   ■

Letty scrunched her wet hair with a towel, tilting her head against her shoulder to keep the phone in place. "I'm so glad you called," she said, with what she hoped sounded like sincerity. She had seen the foundation's number and answered as she was stepping out of the shower, expecting it to be Gemma.

Kathryn Stafford hadn't been a happy surprise.

"Yes, well, I'm just now getting back to San Diego. Mark's a day behind me, and I'd hoped you might have an update on the Katmai case. Gemma and I are trying to make sure we have status reports on each of the JDF's open investigations ready when he arrives." The hiss and crack of a bottle opening came from Kathryn's end of the line, probably one of the bottles of Perrier Gemma kept stocked in the conference room mini-fridge. "Our last conversation ended rather abruptly, and I was... surprised to hear you were in Sallow Bay."

Damnit, Gemma.

Muted laughter and the clank of a pan against the stove came from down the hall as Letty hustled from the bathroom to her bunk room. It wasn't Gemma's fault. Not really. Part of Gemma's job was keeping everyone informed and on the same page, even if that did mean looping Kathryn in. It wasn't like Letty could hide where the GPS data had taken her. "Yeah, I'm sure you were."

She'd known she would have to report in. She had just hoped to have something more concrete than a list of worst-case scenarios when she did. "I'm sorry not to have updated you sooner. Things here progressed quickly." Letty closed the bedroom door, muffling the cheerful sounds of Adam and Hilde working on tonight's dinner. Knowing Adam, he was probably busy taking candid shots of the food. The man photographed everything.

"Not a problem," Kathryn said. "Why don't you just get me up to speed now?"

Letty rooted through her suitcase as she launched into an explanation of what had brought her to Sallow Bay, the strange behavior of local animals, and the inexplicable absence of wildlife on the pack ice. She plucked clean clothes from the now-jumbled pile of sweaters, socks, and underwear. "Dr. Becker is looking into the possibility of noise disturbance to the animals' habitat. And Dr. Adeyemi is analyzing our first set of water samples. Should know what micro-organisms are living in it anytime now. And I'll go back out to gather the rest of the samples we need from the pack ice as soon as the weather allows." Letty pulled a thick sweater over her head, pausing long enough to admire the now yellowing bruising around her ribs from where she'd been kicked. "After that, we'll take biological samples from animals on the pack ice." If she could find anything to sample. "And then from wildlife on the fast ice, which seems to be more populated."

Animals like the murdered polar bear they'd taken tissue samples from that afternoon. Discarded behind a snow bank near the giant smear of blood they'd seen from air. Her stomach twisted as she pulled on a pair of leggings. It wasn't just the gruesome image still burned into her brain that bothered her, but the thought that someone would kill such a magnificent creature for nothing but its fur. Its skin peeled away, the carcass a pink white mix of blood and fascia. Its head and chest left gaping by devastating bullet wounds.

All because the bear's pelt could be sold for thirty grand on the Russian black market. Letty yanked on a thick pair of socks.

"And what is it that you're expecting to find?" Kathryn asked.

Letty winced. She should've started with an explanation of what they were doing, not how they were doing it. "We're looking for anything that seems out of order. Contaminants, toxins, disease, any unusual noise disturbances that could cause the animals to flee their dens. It's all pretty exploratory at this point." She took a deep breath before she continued. This was going to be the hard bit. "Of course, part of that process will be seeking to eliminate petroleum byproducts as a possible cause. We have no reason to believe there's a connection right now, but—"

"But we have to address the possibility." Kathryn cut in, her voice as manicured as ever. It held no surprise or condemnation of Letty's recognition that Stafford Oil's own operations, or one of the other oil and gas operators, could be the culprit. Letty ran a brush through her hair. She knew from online sleuthing that Kathryn had gotten a PhD in geology from MIT before she joined the family business. It made sense she'd understand what Letty had to do. Kathryn might be a businesswoman now, but she'd started out a scientist.

Letty collected her wet towel from the floor and perched on the edge of her bunk. "We're doing a hydrocarbon analysis, but we won't know if any petroleum byproducts are present for several days. That testing isn't something Dr. Adeyemi — he's one of the two scientists Gemma hired to help us here on the ground — it isn't something Musa can do in the lab here, and there'd be an obvious conflict of interest in using any of the labs the oil companies themselves have on-site, so we're sending samples to an outside lab. It'll take a day for transit, then at least twenty-four more hours for them to turn the test around, even with it marked urgent."

"I see." A bottle clinked glass, probably Kathryn putting her water bottle down on the polished surface of the conference room table. "You'll let me know as soon as you hear?"

"Absolutely, as soon as I know anything. I've also asked our guide to connect me with some of the local subsistence fishermen, to see if they've noticed any changes in their catch. And the other scientist here, Dr. Becker, is looking into the possibility of noise pollution as a factor."

Which could also point to Stafford Oil's operations as a potential cause for the bears' unusual migration, but that couldn't be helped.

"Thank you, Letty. I appreciate your work and the update. I'm sure this will all wind up unconnected to anything Stafford Oil has done but, if we're wrong. If we have a problem… we'll deal with it." Kathryn sounded like she meant it.

Maybe Letty had underestimated Kathryn. She had been nothing but straight-forward and pragmatic since they'd met. "There's one more thing." Letty's gaze drifted to the overstuffed bag she'd brought with her from Katmai. "I have some concerns about Cody Crawford's disappearance."

Another clink of glass, this one sharper. "Tell me."

"I found something unusual in Crawford's documents." The ones Letty hadn't sent to Kathryn as she'd asked. The same documents she'd pocketed from a crime scene. Letty cringed. "Most of what I found were copies of the same incident file I already had. Nearly identical to what Gemma gave me before I left San Diego. But then I found a note…"

A long pause. "What kind of note?"

"I disregarded it at first. It seemed personal, but then, someone smashed in my rental car's windshield. Left a note telling me to go home. And then at the incident site in Katmai, I found Crawford's prints leading out into the water, and it made me think… what if he didn't just get lost in the woods? What if he killed himself? Or something worse happened? I think we should reach out to his family or maybe even the authorities to tell them we think it's a possibility. I just… I don't feel right leaving things like they are."

"That's…" Kathryn cleared her throat. "A lot."

Letty pressed her face into the towel. This was why she hadn't wanted to report in before she had actual answers. Saying everything out loud made her sound crazy.

Kathryn continued. "Did you include the note in the documents you mailed back to the foundation? I'm only just now getting through the backlog of what piled up while Mark's been away. I haven't had a chance to read everything."

Shit.

This conversation was going from bad to worse. She dropped the towel. There was no way around it now. "I haven't sent the documents yet." With the investigation and the last-minute travel, she hadn't had the chance. Or the desire to incriminate herself for taking them from a crime scene. "I will, though, I promise." She should have sent the documents the first time Kathryn asked. Especially since she really could have just scanned them in and emailed them, anyway. There was no good excuse for the fact that she hadn't.

A soft knock came from the door. Letty looked up. "Come in."

The door eased open. Musa stood in the frame with his hands clasped so tightly in front of him, his knuckles were white.

"Letty?" Kathryn asked. "Are you still there?"

"Yes, sorry about that." Letty hurried out the words. "Can I call you back?"

"Of course you can. Whenever's convenient." Kathryn said and rang off.

"What's going on?" Letty got to her feet, trying not to let Musa's expression freak her out. "Did you find something in the samples?"

"Nothing," Musa said, his voice taut.

Letty shook her head. She hadn't expected him to find anything useful, not yet. He'd had the samples for less than an hour. Barely enough time to put all of the samples under a microscope, let alone catalog everything in them. There must be something else to it. "What do you mean nothing?"

"There are zero living zooplankton in your samples. I looked at them all, several times." He wrung his hands together. "Everything in those samples is dead."

CHAPTER 16

October 23, 2018
San Diego, California
Dust motes floated in the morning sunlight filtering in through Mark's office window. Suspended in place, going nowhere. In the hallway, behind his closed door, Gemma laughed with the Sri Lanka team who'd arrived back at the foundation the night before. Everyone but him congregating in the hallway, debriefing, making lunch plans. Whatever it was people talked about when their lives hadn't just imploded. Mark went back to doom scrolling. His laptop panned headlines in a monotonous parade of bad news. Another mass shooting. The stock market lower than it had been for a decade. Bouts of unrest following famine in Sudan. Nothing about him being asked to step down as Stafford Oil's CEO or about the company's internal investigation.

The story could break any minute. Or not at all.

The uncertainty was driving him crazy. Everything coming down to whether Reid and his cronies prioritized money or power. Mark's temporary removal from his position as CEO was a lot more likely to become permanent if it became public. But that news would also tank Stafford Oil's stock price. The fact that a quiet investigation was better for the company, for the foundation, and for him… he'd bet that wouldn't even factor into their thinking.

"Bastards." Mark tightened his jaw and scrolled again, pausing at a story marked with a graphic content warning. A four-hundred-pound tiger at a safari park in Japan had attacked a handler he'd worked with for years, biting off her hand and then mortally wounding two zookeepers who attempted to come to her aid. All as a group of schoolchildren watched from an observation deck suspended above the carnage.

Jesus.

Mark closed his eyes, rubbing a tender patch of skin on the underside of his chin. He'd shaved with an old razor he found in the bottom of the medicine cabinet that morning, not caring if it hurt. He had needed to go through the motions of getting himself ready for the day. To prove to himself he was still in control. That he was still doing all the things he'd always done. He was still the person he'd always been.

Even though none of that was true.

He wasn't the same man he'd been before Jessa had been killed. Confident, arrogant, entitled. Blind to how many things could go so wrong so quickly. He squeezed his eyes tighter shut. Shit, it was worse than that. He wasn't even the same person he'd been last week. Not a CEO, not a man the board respected, that Jimmy respected.

He scratched at the razor burn, a sharp painful rasp against already irritated skin.

If news got out of what had happened… if people knew what he'd been accused of, or, even what he'd actually done, what would that mean for the JDF? For the plea he'd just made to Congress to let them manage a unified, global response to the crisis unfolding in the animal world? His hand drifted from his chin to his chest, finding the rings under his shirt. It would be exactly the excuse Hilliard and his cronies needed to say no. And more attacks, like the one at the zoo in Japan — like what happened to Jessa — would continue unchecked.

A soft knock came from the office door.

Fuck.

He straightened, closing the lid to his laptop. The last thing he wanted now was company. "Come in."

The door eased open, and Aunt Kath came in with a smile that held more worry than happiness. "There you are." She settled into one of the sleek leather chairs facing his desk. Unlike his office at Stafford Oil, which was all heavy wood and oil paintings — his mother's idea of corporate sophistication — he'd furnished the foundation's corner office himself. Nothing but clean lines and bold modern colors.

Kath folded her hands in her lap. "How are you holding up?"

"I'm fine," he said, even though he was sure she knew that wasn't true. He forced his face into a polite smile. "Just trying to get caught up on everything here."

Her gaze flicked over his empty desk, then to the laptop closed in front of him. Her brows lifted, and she leaned back, crossing her legs at the ankle. Her posture a clear message: she wasn't going anywhere until he spit it out.

Which half of him wanted to do anyway. He wasn't just embarrassed or worried. Deep down, he was pissed. "How could anyone think I'd steal from the company?" He tugged a hand through his hair. "It doesn't even make sense. My father might not have been dad of the year," or really much of a dad at all, "but he made sure mom and I would never run out of money, no matter how much we spent." And the coffers had only grown since Mark took over. His family's net worth would put some countries' GDP to shame. "The whole thing's ridiculous."

"You know as well as I do that having plenty of money doesn't stop anyone from wanting more. Most greedy people already have well beyond what they could ever need." Aunt Kath crossed her arms, a delicate gold bracelet sliding out from under the sleeve of her pale gray blazer. "The best thing we can do is expedite this idiotic investigation so it's over before it's begun. Get them the evidence they need to prove your innocence as quickly as we can. Try to minimize any damage to you or the foundation in the meantime."

He nodded again but couldn't muster an answer. It felt good to hear that Aunt Kath still believed in him. But the investigation was just as likely to destroy him as it was to save him. Of course, he couldn't say that any more than he could control what happened next. The ball was in the investigator's court. And from what he'd heard of Owen Lockwood, the man wouldn't stop until he knew everything there was to know.

"I've spoken with Lockwood, who seems all right enough. Or as all right as a hired henchman can be." She rolled her eyes in a decidedly not Aunt Kath-like gesture, which under any other circumstances, would have made Mark smile.

"I've told him he'll have our complete cooperation, and I've had my people begin gathering everything he requested. I thought I could spare you that, at least. Although, I'm sure they'll ask for more documents after they review the first round. And you'll still have to sit down for an interview with him at some point." She toyed with the bracelet, an odd look on her face. "You know, this could all turn out to be for the best."

That seemed… unlikely. He raised an eyebrow. "How?"

She paused before answering. "What if you were to step down?"

He sputtered, straightening in his chair. Why the hell would he—

She held up a hand. "Hear me out. You're pulled so thin, Mark. Between the company and the foundation. Your whole life, you've always been busy, driven, but with everything that's happened in the last few years, it's too much." She paused again, and even though she didn't say it, he knew what she meant by "everything that's happened." She meant Jessa.

Pain spiked through the center of his chest, and his hand drifted back to where their wedding rings lay tucked inside his shirt.

"Remember when you were younger? You always had a pencil in your hand. I'd see you lying in the grass under that old oak tree in the front yard, face buried in a sketch pad." She gave a soft laugh.

"Your dad used to hate when you'd bring your drawings to the dinner table." Her smile faded, her voice going serious again. "If you stepped down, this could all go away. You could go to art school, maybe someday fall in love again... have a life."

The burn of a thousand reasons she was wrong surged up his throat. But he couldn't get them out. Because she wasn't. At least not entirely. In the year and a half since Jessa died, he had found himself working late into the night, not distinguishing weekdays from weekends, taking no breaks or holidays. Work had become a way to avoid everything else. A place to bury his grief. Or at least, that'd been what it was until he'd formed the foundation. Until his work there had given him true purpose. Given him a real chance to make up for what he hadn't been able to do for Jessa. To save others the way he hadn't been able to save her. Every case an apology that he hadn't been there sooner, hadn't been strong enough to pull them both from the water. To save her from winding up dead at the bottom of the ocean.

He blinked back a stinging behind his eyes as Kath continued. "If you want to work, wouldn't it make more sense to spend your time here, rather than splitting your focus? I would make sure the endowment continued. Think of all the good you could do if you were to work at the foundation full time instead."

"I don't know," he said, even as the rightness of her words settled in his chest. He had never given less than his all to Stafford Oil. Or, at least, that had been true until recently. But, even before that, there was never any joy in it. He did it because he was supposed to, because people were relying on him, and it wasn't in him to let them down.

"Think about it, okay."

"I will." He choked out. "I promise."

"Good," she said, with a quick nod. "Now to business."

He gave her an appreciative smile. She knew him well enough to know he'd want the heart-to-heart portion of their conversation over as quickly as possible.

Kath launched into a quick update on all their open cases and pointed to a stack of binders on the floor he hadn't yet cracked open. "Gemma put all the details you need in there, or at least all the details you need to get started. I'm guessing you'll want to follow up with the folks we have in the field once you're up-to-date on where their investigations are now."

He bent down, shifting the binders from the floor to his desk. This was what he should've been doing all morning. He had people out on assignment who needed his support. People like Letty. And with Kath handling the Stafford Oil investigation for now, he was free to do the work that mattered. He should embrace it, like Aunt Kath suggested. He couldn't control what the board did or what Lockwood found. But he could sure as hell do what needed doing here in the meantime.

"Mark?" Kath toyed with her bracelet again, as though she was trying to decide whether to say whatever was on her mind.

Crap.

He'd thought amateur therapy hour was over. "Yeah?"

"I'm concerned about the Katmai investigation."

With everything happening, he hadn't checked in with Letty the way he'd planned to. His grip tightened on the binder. "Why? What's happened now?"

"Apparently, Dr. Duquesne traced the bears back to Sallow Bay. You'll find a progress report on her investigation in the second binder."

"Sallow Bay?" What were the chances of that?

"She's in the early stages of testing water samples there and what not. But so far, the results have been… unusual." Kath sat forward. "I don't want to raise an alarm prematurely. I'm sure she'll discover some perfectly reasonable explanation. But… Do you know what Dr. Duquesne was working on before she was hired by the foundation?"

Mark blinked at the sudden shift in her focus, digging the details from his memory. "She was working for the University of Georgia. On a rabies case in Chattanooga. Why?"

"She wasn't working for the university." The lines around Kath's mouth tightened.

That didn't make any sense. She'd definitely been at UGA before she'd come to work for him. He'd gone there to see her. To recruit her. "What do you mean?"

"She wasn't authorized to work the case. She forced her way into a local investigation. Then threatened to leak information to the press if they didn't let her pursue what she thought was a lead on the source animal. It wasn't, as it turned out, and... the whole thing ended with several people dead and her in the hospital."

He shook his head, unwilling or unable to accept what she was saying as true. None of that made sense. "That doesn't sound at all like something Letty'd do."

Kath's voice softened. "UGA fired her over it."

Heat crept up Mark's neck. How had he not known that? And why hadn't Letty told him?

The idiocy of that thought hit him the moment he had it. Letty hardly spoke to him at all anymore. Of course she wouldn't volunteer something personal. Something she probably found embarrassing. Even if, as her boss, he technically had every right to know.

"I found the details online." Kath went on. "Last night after I spoke with her."

The heat spread to his cheeks. He struggled to believe Letty would be anything less than professional, but he didn't doubt Kath had found what she said she did. Which meant he would have found it, too, if he'd bothered to look. But he hadn't, because it was Letty. All he remembered was that she had been part of the team who'd found the source of the outbreak.

Shit.

He would never have made a hiring decision without checking her credentials if it were anyone else. He cleared his throat but still couldn't formulate a response. Because even if Letty had done those things, his gut told him there had to be an explanation. She'd have had a reason for doing what she did, and—

"I like Dr. Duquesne, Mark. And I know she's Jessa's sister, and you want to give her the benefit of the doubt. But the foundation can't risk scandal right now. We can't have someone in charge of such a sensitive investigation who could run to the press at any moment." She took a deep breath and let it out. "I don't want to overstep. I know my role with the foundation is… informal. But I can't help worrying…"

She reached across the desk, her hand soft on his. "I think you need to let someone else take over."

CHAPTER 17

Sallow Bay, Alaska

Letty circled the snowmobile, careful not to get in Charlie's way as he attached her gear sled to the back. She gripped the sat phone under her jacket's hood, unwilling to expose her ears to the morning's freezing cold. A gust of wind blew in from the water, so hard she had to broaden her stance to brace against it. She cupped her hand over the receiver. "Thanks for doing this, Gemma. I know how busy you must be, especially with Mark and Kathryn both there today."

"No worries. They're still behind closed doors."

Probably getting Mark caught up on what had been happening while he was away. Which would necessarily include telling him where Letty was and what she'd found there. She hated that it would add to his stress, but at least she hadn't had to deliver the bad news herself.

The crinkle of a wrapper came over the line. No doubt Gemma opening her morning toaster pastry. "Thought I'd take the reprieve to give you an update. Not sure I'll be able to call tonight. Supposed to take Noah to a film." They usually talked closer to the end of the day, giving each other a catch up on everything that had happened since they'd talked the night before. Letty emailed in status reports, too, but, as always, some things were best said in a format that wasn't preserved forever.

"You're the best." Letty shifted back a few steps, again getting out of Charlie's way as he checked the emergency gear stashed in the hard plastic cases attached to the back of the snowmobile. "What've you found?"

"Zero activity on Crawford's social media since he disappeared. No surprise there. Looked into his background. Not much in the file we have in the office, but you'd be amazed what the internet'll tell you." Especially if — like Gemma — your capabilities went well beyond a basic Google search. After a pause, her voice came back, muffled by a mouth full of breakfast. "Crawford grew up in a rough part of Houston. Single mom. Got a scholarship to UC Boulder out of high school. Worked his way through undergrad at a couple of nearby ski resorts, doing avalanche-control. Then grad school. Finished with a PhD in Ecology. After that, what you can see from his resume pretty much covers it. He had positions with Columbia and Yale, both focusing on large carnivore ecology. Unmarried, no kids. Only a handful of friends on Facebook, which hardly count as friends, and what online activity he did have was minimal. Mainly cat memes."

Gemma cleared her throat before she went on. "I saved the worst for last... his mom died the week before he got hired on at the foundation. I found her obituary. Annemarie Crawford, died at 53. Cervical cancer. No other family listed. I think it was just the two of them."

Jesus.

She had worried about someone waiting at home for Crawford, not knowing where he'd gone. But to know that he'd gone out on assignment when he was still probably deep in the throes of grief. And apparently reeling from the end of whatever relationship he'd written about in the note she had found. The one she'd found that spoke of a love that couldn't be. It was all so... sad.

It put a painfully fine point on her own isolation. Letty shivered. With Jessa gone, Letty's friends so far away, and her parents absentee, as always. She couldn't remember feeling more alone, or more selfish. This wasn't about her.

Letty watched Odele refuel the helicopter, even though they couldn't use it. Not with the windstorm expected to hit Sallow Bay that morning.

Another crinkle over the phone line, and Gemma went on, her words muffled again. "Only thing of note, other than that, is a gap on his resume before he joined the JDF. No explanation noted in the file that I can find. I'd bet it's related to his mother's illness, but I could ask. Mark would know."

"No." Letty said, a little too forcefully, then softened her tone. "He's got enough on his plate. Let's leave it alone for now." The loss of Crawford's mother made suicide all the more plausible. On paper, it all added up. His mother's death, the note, Crawford's apparent social isolation, his footprints leading to the water's edge... But there was no way to know for sure. No way to prove anything. She canted her head back and forth, trying to reconcile herself with the fact that it could all just as easily be a matter of coincidence.

She could be drawing connections, coming to a conclusion where none was warranted, just like in Chattanooga. Despite the cold, a blush stole over her cheeks.

She couldn't do that again. Couldn't put herself or anyone else through it. Crawford had probably gotten lost in the woods, like everyone else seemed to think. She was getting distracted from the things she actually needed to worry about.

Gemma's voice came back over the line. "Letty? You still there?"

"Sorry, yeah."

"Okay, love. Any luck with the second round of testing?"

Letty released a breath, glad to be back on more comfortable ground. "Musa's back in the lab this morning, but I'm not sure what else he can do with this set of samples." Another gust of wind smacked Letty in the face, ice cold and unrepentant. She turned away, letting the squall press into her back. "There's not a damn thing in any of them."

"Which is weird, right?"

"Very." Letty wiped her nose on her sleeve and shifted on her feet, hoping the movement would circulate some warmth into her body. "I was up half the night trying to figure out why." Maybe her testing method wasn't sound? Or it could be when she pulled the samples or where. Maybe life under the ice has patchy distribution. Something with the phenology? Which would make sense. Natural phenomenon were often cyclical or seasonal.

Charlie reemerged from the garage, a shotgun in his hand and the same grimace on his face he'd had since she'd insisted on going out that morning, even after he'd told her another job meant he couldn't go out with her.

She understood his hesitation — going out on the ice alone was bad enough, doing it in a windstorm was borderline stupid — but it wasn't like she could just sit around all morning, waiting. She'd go nuts if she did. And with Musa busy in the lab, Hilde out reading noise levels along the shoreline, and Adam not returning her calls, it wasn't like she had many options for company. "It's really hard to say until I can get back out to take more samples, and the weather seems dead set on making sure that doesn't happen." Handling the snowmobile in this weather wouldn't be ideal; flying a helicopter would be impossible. She glanced over to where Odele was finishing up her refueling. Her face just as pinched as Charlie's. Although Letty doubted it was from any concern over Letty's safety.

Charlie strapped the gun behind the snowmobile's seat, where it would be in easy reach if she needed it. Which, God willing, she wouldn't. He stood back, arms crossed, apparently waiting for her to finish her call.

Letty took the hint. "Thanks again, Gem. I need to hop off. I'm loading up now to go out on the fast ice. See if I have any better luck finding any biological samples there."

"Be careful, love." Gemma said and disconnected the call.

Letty smiled at Charlie as she stowed the sat phone in her gear, trying to soften him up.

His expression stayed uncharacteristically sour. "Still don't think you going out alone is a good idea." She wouldn't either if there was any other choice. It was go it alone or don't go at all. And if they couldn't take the helicopter out to the pack ice, where her bears had lived, she could at least go take samples from the seals Adam had photographed out on the fast ice. It was too early to conclude that the animals missing from the pack ice were now there, too, but it was certainly a possibility. Animals migrating south could easily have wound up there.

"I'll be careful. I've got the sat phone and the gun. I promise I'll call if I have any trouble, and I won't go any further than the observation pod." Which wasn't much of a promise, the pod sat on the other side of the ice floe, less than half a mile from where the fast ice disintegrated into the sea.

Charlie grunted. "You'd be better off waiting until someone can go with you. Things have been off lately. The animals are... aggressive." Odele looked over from the garage bay, where she hovered stowing gear, shooting Charlie a disgruntled look.

"I promise not to take any unnecessary risks." Letty wasn't blind to the danger — she knew better than almost anyone the danger nature posed, especially now. The animals' stalking people around town. The weather worsening by the minute. The freezing water waiting beneath the ice, so cold she wouldn't survive five minutes if she fell in. But she'd never been afraid to do what needed doing before, and she wouldn't start now. Not when one of the Katmai bears was still missing, when another attack could happen at any moment. And the same thought rounded her mind that had been plaguing her all morning — what if that little girl had been playing on her swing set when the bear got there? What if the next little girl wasn't so lucky? She needed to go find answers, if not from the water, then from the animals she'd intended to start her testing with from the beginning.

She softened her voice. "There's a chance what I find today could tell us why those animals are behaving like they are. If we don't figure it out soon, someone's going to hurt."

He shook his head. "It's still not safe, and I don't like it." A ringing came from inside, and he shot her another worried glance before wobbling off toward the beckoning phone. His limp was even more pronounced now than when she'd first met him. Whatever was going on with his joints, living in a place this cold had to make it worse.

Letty climbed onto the snowmobile. It had been years since she'd driven one, but this model was almost identical to the Ski-Doo she'd used the winter her family spent in an RV park in Tahoe. Except this one wasn't held together by duct tape and prayers. Any hesitation she'd had about going out alone melted under the purpose propelling her forward. She never felt better than when she was in the field. Even here, where everything felt so foreign, she loved the thrill of being on the trail of something, of knowing—

"Lemme guess." Odele came closer, her steps heavy in the snow. She wiped her gloved hands down the front of her overalls, her jacket hanging unzipped and open. "You're gonna go out and find some tiny, endangered fish egg that's more important than the people here trying to scratch out a living." She squinted at Letty over the top of a pair of wraparound sunglasses. "That's what all you Greenpeace hippie types think, right? That the oil industry's to blame for everything wrong with the planet." She gave a dismissive snort.

The irony of the accusation was almost too much. Finding that kind of connection would be the absolute worst possible result Letty could think of. But she couldn't say that, not without giving credence to a far-worse narrative than the one Odele had in mind. Letty'd rather be seen as clueless liberal do-gooder than give anyone a reason to think her research was biased because of how it was funded. "I'm just trying to figure out what's happening. Nothing more than that." She kept her voice even, reaching for the snowmobile's ignition. The sooner she got out of this conversation, the better. "I don't have an agenda."

She cranked the snowmobile, and the engine roared to life.Loud enough, Letty almost didn't hear Odele's words as she turned away.

"I were you, I'd watch my back."

■　　■　　■

Not for the first time since she'd left Charlie's shop, Letty wished she had been able to reach Adam to invite him along. He wouldn't have been as excited as she was for all the seals she'd found; he'd been clear he had more than enough pictures of those. But the day had turned beautiful as the wind died down. The ice almost magical in the way it sparkled in the sun. And it was the first time since she had arrived in Alaska that she could really appreciate its beauty.

It made her want to share it with someone. She glanced down at the ringed seal laying unconscious at her feet. Preferably someone human.

From a distance, the seal had looked healthy. The animal's dark gray coat dotted with its distinctive lighter rings still gleamed in the sun. But, once she'd gotten closer, it was hard to miss the mucus that shone around its nose, or the fact that, behind half-closed lids, a film clouded the seal's eyes.

Letty checked her watch. Given the dose of tranquilizer she'd administered, the animal should wake at any moment. It had been an hour and a half. Long enough for Letty to take a biopsy of fat and tissue, snip samples of the animal's hair, hike to where she'd left the snowmobile, stow her tranq gun and specimens, then hike back to the jagged crevasse where she'd left the animal. Whether it was the unexpected success of the day or her finally acclimatizing to this new strangely beautiful place, every step of her trek had felt more sure — more natural — than the one before.

Now it was just a matter of waiting until the animal woke so she didn't leave it unconscious and helpless against predators. Letty took in a deep breath, the air fresh and clean. The sun shone bright over a clear, cobalt sky. The wind storm had taken all the clouds with it when it blew itself out. She couldn't even bring herself to be mad about missing time on the pack ice today. Not when her impromptu trip here had been such an overwhelming success.

By half-past three, she'd taken samples from nearly a dozen seals and walruses. Either the wildlife on the fast ice hadn't yet been effected by whatever had happened on the pack ice, or these animals were only in the early stages of it. All of them showed similar symptomatology to the seal. Once it woke, and Letty made it back to the snowmobile, she would return to the research facility with more than enough material for Musa and Hilde to work with. Material that could help her find the cause of the animals' sickness and, with any luck, clear Stafford Oil of any responsibility in the process.

She took in another breath, holding the frigid air in her lungs. It had taken her a while to get it, but now she saw the appeal of working in the Arctic. Saw why some researchers spent half their careers trying to land grants that would get them back out onto the ice. Every time a project ended, the "just one more time" mantra would start.

Out here, the isolation didn't feel painful. It was beautiful. Quiet. Peaceful. She really wished she could have reached Adam and asked him to come.

A ghost of movement flickered on the horizon.

She tented a hand over her eyes, looking out. A smudge of something yellow-white shifted in the distance. What the hell? Fear bristled across the back of her neck. She dug her binoculars out from where she'd had them tucked between her coat and fleece and pointed them toward whatever she'd seen.

A bear.

Moving fast across the ice.

Letty froze.

The animal powered forward at a dead run. Heading straight for her. Terror prickled over her skin. Hot and cold at once, her body responding to the threat on a cellular level before her mind could catch up.

Holy shit.

No way she'd get away in time, and where would she even go? Polar bears could scent a seal twenty miles away, and she was so much closer than that. Out in the open, she was lunch on legs. And if that wasn't bad enough, she had an unconscious seal at her feet. Like an appetizer.

She reached for the gun by her feet, hating the thought of using it. Not just because she didn't want to take a life, but because shooting the bear was just as likely to piss it off as to kill it. She would have had better luck with the tranq gun, if it wasn't back at the snowmobile. And loaded with darts calibrated for something a fraction of its size. With the gun she had, only a close range shot to the head or spine was going to put down a polar bear. Which would mean waiting until it was all but on top of her to fire. The thought of letting it get that close was beyond terrifying.

But she'd do it if she had to.

Adrenaline tremors quaked through her as she scooped up the shotgun. She fumbled with it, her fingers stiff with cold inside her gloves, but she finally cracked the barrel. Two shells waited inside.

Letty let out a deep breath, trying to will her body to stop shaking. She should have known Charlie wouldn't have sent her out onto the ice without making sure the gun would be ready to use if she needed it. She snapped the barrel closed, and the gun slipped, tumbling from her hands.

"No!" Letty shrieked as she grabbed for it. Her heart hammered in her throat as her fingers brushed the stock, tipping the shotgun even further away. It pitched end over end.

And landed in the crevasse with barely a splash.

"Fuck fuck fuck." She peered over the edge, blood pounding in her ears. Knowing what she'd see, even before she looked. The gun was gone. Swallowed by the flat, black surface of the sea.

A wave of panic washed over her. How could she have been so clumsy? So stupid?

She shook her head, trying to fling off the useless thoughts. No time for any of that now. She needed a plan. Making a run for the snowmobile would mean running toward the bear.

Not happening.

Which only left her one option. It was further away, but—

At her feet, the seal stirred.

Shit.

"I'm sorry." She choked out, hating that her greatest chance of survival might be the bear getting sidetracked by the seal. "I'm so fucking sorry."

She ran away from the bear at a dead sprint, every breath tinged with a sour tang of guilt. No matter that she didn't have a choice. The bear had closed half the distance and was coming fast. They could run three times faster than her, on a good day.

If she could just make it to Adam's observation pod, she would be okay. She'd seen it from the air on their way back from the pack ice and again this morning as she'd been collecting samples. She knew where to find it… She still had the sat phone. She could get inside and call for help.

Letty flew over the ice, eyes peeled for fractures or air holes where seals had dug their way to the surface. One misplaced step could send her plunging beneath the surface. Frozen and dead within minutes. Lost where no one would ever find her. She'd disappear into the sea.

Just like Jessa.

She couldn't let that happen. She wouldn't. Her breath tore from her lungs, her heart a hammer against her ribs. She pushed herself to go faster, flying over the ice, even as the snow grew thicker, slowing her steps. Like quicksand.

"Jesus." She huffed out. How much further was it? Yes, she'd seen Adam's observation pod from the air, had taken samples only a few dozen yards from it earlier that day. But now, as she raced past snow berms and ragged icy outcroppings, everything started to look the same.

What if she was going the wrong way? Sweat broke on her forehead and across her back. Her layers now too warm, too heavy, her body on the verge of overheating as she rounded a snowbank.

The pod finally came into view. A four by four foot metal and plexiglass box had never looked so much like salvation. Just big enough for her to crawl inside and pray.

Thank God.

A little further. Just a little further.

She fought through the snow, her legs aching, her lungs burning.

If she could just get there…

Letty stumbled the last few feet, ripped open the hatch, and fell inside. Her breath ragged, her heart pounding. So winded, every gulp of air hurt as it sawed through her chest.

She scrambled back to her feet and slammed the hatch closed.

Stars dotted her vision.

Breathe.

She forced air into lungs starved for oxygen as she fastened the latches holding the hatch closed. Then pressed on both to make sure, beyond any question, they were fully and completely locked. Once she'd smashed them hard enough to leave indentions in her palms, she doubled over, letting her breath catch up.

Jesus. Mary. And Joseph.

She had made it. The pod was meant to keep bears out; it had been designed for that sole purpose. To give Adam protection if the bears he was there to photograph got too close. She'd be safe inside. She had to be.

Over the pounding in her ears, she listened. The world outside had gone dead silent, icy and unforgiving. Out here, a simple mistake could kill you. And she'd made more than one.

She couldn't see beyond the snowbank, couldn't tell how close the bear was. Or if it was still there at all. She tried not to think of the seal.

She clawed through the pockets of her jacket, ripping the sat phone out and powering it on. There was no 911 this far out on the ice. She was technically miles out in the Arctic Ocean, even if the ice made it feel like land. She'd have to find her own help.

She ripped off her gloves, dropping them to the floor as she struggled to make her shaking fingers work the phone's keys. She hit the first preset number. "Come on, Charlie."

The phone rang loud in her ear.

She kept her gaze glued to the snowbank. Praying the bear would give up and go away. But that was stupid, and she knew it. Unlike brown or black bears, polar bears saw people as nothing more than food. Prey to be stalked and eaten.

Another ring.

The bear burst into view, huffing from exertion. Almost a thousand pounds of hungry, muscled predator. Armed with claws and teeth. Close enough for her to see the wet of its nose, and the gleam of hunger in its coal black eyes. It slowed, its gaze meeting hers. An adult male, even bigger than the one she'd examined in Katmai.

Holy shit.

Letty's grip on the phone tightened enough to hurt. It rang a third time, a fourth.

The bear prowled closer.

Charlie's voice. Chipper, helpful. "You've reached Arctic Transport. If you're hearing this message, we're either out on the ice or…"

Fuuuuuuuuuuuuck.

His voicemail beeped in her ear. "Charlie, it's Letty. I'm in Adam's observation pod. There's a bear here. I need help. I don't have the gun." Her words caught in her throat. Her breath still coming fast and hard. He'd warned her, and she'd plowed ahead. Like a dumbass. She forced her breathing to slow so she could get the rest out. "I'm so sorry I didn't listen to you. Please send help."

The bear circled the pod, leaning forward. Scenting the air.

Scenting her.

She shrank back against the far wall of the pod, her skin clammy under her layers. All she wanted to do was curl into a ball, shut her eyes, and pretend none of this was real.

But nothing had ever been more real. She'd never been more present, more aware. More afraid. She forced in a breath.

There was only one way she was getting out of this alive. She hit the second preset number on the sat phone.

Musa or Hilde would be at the facility. One of them always was. And especially today, with Hilde's data starting to come in from the noise sensors she'd placed on the ice, they'd be there. They had to be.

The bear pawed at the pod, its claws a clacking scrape across the glass.

Like fucking Freddie Krueger.

Another ring.

The bear pressed its face to the glass, sniffing at the joints. Moving around the pod's exterior until it stopped at the hatch. With his sense of smell, he could no doubt tell that was the weakest point. He'd know it was where he needed to apply pressure. Like opening a clam.

A third ring.

Come on, come on.

The bear lifted onto his hind legs, his full height towering over her.

And there was absolutely nothing she could do about it. She curled into herself, clutching the phone like the lifeline it was.

Voicemail.

Letty sobbed out her frustration as the bear dropped its weight onto the pod. The entire structure jerking beneath him, rocking Letty back and forth.

"Help!" She screamed, even though there was no one there to hear her. No one who could help. She wrapped her arms around herself. She eyed the ramshackle bolts holding each section of plexiglass together. Some didn't even fit flush, a section of open air left gaping in between. Nothing between her and the bear's teeth. She looked away.

She couldn't think about that. Couldn't consider what would happen if the animal forced his way inside. The facility's automated voicemail beeped in her ear. "Musa, Hilde. It's Letty. I'm trapped in Adam Wan's observation pod on the pack ice." The animal raised onto its back legs again, this time resting its front paws on the top edge of the pod, rocking it again. Back and forth. Back and forth. The plexiglass creaking as it bowed under his weight.

Letty choked out the words. "Send help. Please." She crouched, holding onto one of the pod's metal supports so she didn't fall.

The rocking stopped as the bear angled its jaw into one of the open spaces between plexiglass and support, biting at the glass. Razor-sharp canines testing every possible entry point.

Letty stared into its gaping black maw, past huge yellow teeth and, finally, abandoned what was left of her calm. She screamed, the pod rattling and bowing around her, rocking back and forth under the bear's assault.

She closed her eyes, her body shaking, and forced herself to take in a breath. The bear would have to give up, eventually. He'd wander off, looking elsewhere for food that was easier to get to, wouldn't he?

The pod jerked again, and Letty stumbled, falling against the glass.

Even if the bear did go away, what was she going to do? Leave the safety of the pod and hike all the way back to the snowmobile?

She'd have two miles of wide open ice to cover. Nowhere to hide, no way to protect herself.

No way was she doing that.

She hit redial and prayed.

CHAPTER 18

Beyond the snowcat's broad windshield, the scattered outline of downtown Sallow Bay sketched along the horizon. Close enough to see but still twenty minutes away. Unlike the snowmobile they towed behind them, the massive tank Letty rode in now hadn't been built for speed. It lumbered along. Slow, steady, and so loud she had to raise her voice to talk.

"Thank you, again." She clutched Adam's thermos of coffee between her knees. She had been shaking too hard when he picked her up to undo the top and still was. She'd spent an hour eye-to-eye with the bear before the snowcat's heavy rumble finally chased it away. And her body seemed stuck in a fight-or-flight response. Every muscle tight, her teeth chattering together. "I feel awful that, after all that looking, the first time we find a living polar bear, it turned out like this." Her unprepared to take samples or even keep herself safe. Him arriving moments too late to get the pictures he needed. Not that he had seemed concerned with that when he'd finally gotten to her. He had been too busy checking her for injuries and hustling her into the snowcat. "I know I've already said it a dozen times, but really. I don't know what I would have done if you hadn't answered the phone."

"I'm just glad Charlie let me take the snowcat out. And that I saw your call coming in at all. My ringer's usually off when I'm working." Adam glanced over at her, his dark eyes worried. He looked back at the icy landscape in front of them that, for the moment, sufficed as a road. "I'm surprised he let you go alone. Charlie's not usually so reckless."

"I think that honor belongs to me." Letty fidgeted with the edge of her sleeve. She'd been stupid to go out by herself. But then to drop the shotgun, to render herself completely vulnerable the way she had… Stupid didn't even come close to covering it. She clenched her jaw, willing the shivers to stop. "He tried to warn me, but I wouldn't listen." It wasn't the first time she'd rushed headlong into danger. It wasn't even the first time she'd almost gotten herself killed doing it.

She needed to grow up and get her shit together.

"Well…" Adam steered them around an area filled with sastrugi, the wave-like drifts of snow reminding Letty more of serpentine desert sand than anything she'd expected to see in the Arctic. Adam navigated the snowcat back to smoother ground. "Maybe no more solo trips for now."

"For now?" She gave a nervous laugh. "More like forever." She'd be damned if she was going to get caught out on the ice alone again. Hell, going to the bathroom by herself sounded like too much independence. Even though, if history was any guide, it was just a matter of time before she did something idiotic again. The need to know — to find answers in the field — had always been stronger than her common sense. "I tried to call Charlie a bunch of times. And the facility. Never could reach anyone."

"I'm not surprised." Adam's face tightened into a grimace.

She frowned. What did that mean?

He flexed his hands around the steering wheel. "It might be better if you don't go anywhere on your own for a while… not just the ice, but in general."

Her frown deepened. She'd known there might be repercussions from her investigation. Most of Sallow Bay either worked in the oil and gas industry or provided services to those that did. But she had never thought the backlash would get to the point where she'd need an escort to get to the grocery store and back. "What's Odele been telling everyone?"

"Odele?" He glanced over at her, his eyebrows raised.

Letty sighed. "She confronted me right before I left Charlie's shop this morning. Said I'm a 'clueless liberal out to ruin good people's lives. Blah, blah, blah.' Seemed pretty pissed about it, too. I'm not surprised she went and stirred things up." Although Letty had to give the woman props for speed. It had only been a few hours since they'd argued. For Letty to already be persona non grata town-wide, Odele must have been running her mouth nonstop. Letty managed to open the coffee and take a sip. Even if Odele had made the rounds talking shit, that didn't explain why no one but Adam had picked up the phone when she called.

"I haven't talked to her or heard anything—" They ran over a thick patch of ice, and the snowcat rocked them side to side in their seats. Adam waited until they'd gotten through the worst of it to continue. "Makes sense that Odele feels that way, though. She had a little too much to drink the last time I was here on assignment. I overheard her telling one of guys at the bar that she was the only one in her entire family who didn't work for an oil company."

"Oh." That explained a lot. "What'd you mean then, about not going out alone?"

He shifted in his seat. "A family in town died this morning."

Letty's teeth finally stopped clattering. Whatever she'd thought he might say, that wasn't it. She leaned forward, the thermos edge pressing into her sternum. "What?"

"A local fisherman shot his wife and kids, then himself." Adam's throat bobbed. "Half the village has been gathered outside the house since their bodies were discovered. The wife's sister came over after her shift at the mini-mart. Found them all sprawled on the living room floor, surrounded by the kids' toys. Blood everywhere." Another throat bob. "It's a small town, everyone knows everyone. It's horrible." He paused, as if collecting himself. "I'd bet that's where Charlie and the others were when you tried to call them. Probably gathered at the family's house or down at the church where everyone else is."

Letty let her head fall back against the headrest, trying like hell not to let the image Adam had painted spring into her mind in full, gruesome color. "That's terrible."

"I guess the whole family had been sick for a few weeks. And the man had been acting kind of off. Not just sick but... different." Adam's gaze flicked to her then back out the windshield. "From what I hear, he wasn't violent, though. No one had any idea he might hurt anybody. I guess he went out on his boat early this morning, brought in the family's catch, like he always did. Then..." He shrugged and went quiet.

Then he'd massacred his entire family.

"Jesus." How could someone do something like that? To his own family.

To his children.

Letty fought a burning behind her eyes. She'd passed a ragtag group of kids playing soccer in the road on her way in from the airport. They'd seemed so young, so joyful, so full of life. Had the children who'd died been there? The toothy boy at that awkward preteen, still-growing-into-his-body stage who'd dabbed a celebration dance when he'd scored a goal. Or the girl in the bright pink snowsuit who was too small to really keep up with the others, whooping as she ran behind the pack. Letty blinked fast, willing tears away.

She took a deep breath. Even if she had seen them outside playing, she didn't know those children. She didn't know the family or the friends who must now be grieving their loss. But between the waning adrenaline of the day and the exhaustion that seemed to have taken up permanent residence under her skin, the tragedy of such a brutal, senseless loss of life hit her hard. Both she and Adam fell silent, the rumble of the snowcat's engine filling the lull as town came closer. The blocky, uniform structures like houses on a Monopoly board but drained of color. Lifeless and bleak.

Adam finally spoke again, his voice rough. "That's why I was saying I think we should only go out in pairs... I don't want to sound crazy, but what if whatever's wrong with the animals is affecting people, too?" He glanced at her. "What if it's making them dangerous?"

Letty shook her head. She wanted to dismiss the possibility outright. To deny that there could be any connection between a murder/suicide and the local animals' unusual behavior. To call today a one-off tragedy, just another domestic disturbance. Another senseless shooting. After all — as horrific as it was — it wasn't like that kind of violence was new. Fathers killing their children, husbands killing their wives. People had been killing each other as long as there'd been people. More lately, it seemed. The news was full of it.

It would be so much easier to tell herself it was too far-fetched. Too big of a logical leap to make. Especially after what had happened in Chattanooga, when she'd come to a similar conclusion. And been wrong. But that didn't mean Adam was wrong now.

Something was making the animals of Sallow Bay sick.

And humans were no less animal than the others.

■   ■   ■

Under any other circumstance, Letty would have retreated under her covers with a bottle of wine and a laundry list of worries and self-recriminations. But that wasn't an option today. She paced outside the lab's glass doors. A Tribe Called Quest thumped loud enough through their overhead sound system to make ripples in a cup of milky tea left abandoned on the side table by the couch.

Musa and Hilde worked at either end of the long metal table running down the lab's center, both still sending her the occasional worried glance. They had both apologized profusely for not being there when she'd called. They'd only left the lab for an hour, drawn into town by the tragedy, just like everyone else. It was down to bad luck that them leaving had been right when she needed them. And the whole thing was her fault anyway, she had been the one to put herself in that position. She made a point to try and look reassuring anytime their gazes met.

Musa did stable isotope testing at a mass spectrometer — which would give them data on the animals' diets and any pollution in their environment — while Hilde prepared specimens for transit to an outside lab for hydrocarbon testing. That would tell them if there were petroleum byproducts in the animals' systems, which kind, and in what concentration. It was the first and most direct route to knowing whether Stafford Oil's, or any other oil and gas company's, operations had anything to do with the animals' behavior.

Everything they could do in the lab they had there was getting done, which left her at loose ends. She sighed and kept pacing. She had put a rush on the samples they'd be sending to the outside lab. Every minute that passed made it more likely the connection between Sallow Bay and the Katmai attack would become public. For Mark's sake—

No.

She shook her head, dislodging the thought. That wasn't it. For the foundation's sake, they needed answers before the press descended.

But there were limits on how fast these things could go. Even setting aside the time it would take to perform the tests, they had the transit time to consider. Sallow Bay was at the literal end of the Earth. Once securely packed, her samples would spend the night in the lab's refrigerator, then ship out on tomorrow's flight south. The only way out of Sallow Bay today was already long gone.

She sighed out her impatience. It didn't help anything for her to pace herself silly.

Not that she'd been able to stop wearing a hole in the carpet since her conversation with Adam. She made another circuit around the couch and back past the lab.

He was right. Something was off in Sallow Bay. And the answer to what it was could be sitting in their lab right now. She peeked back in the glass doors.

Hilde worked with the tip of her tongue pressed to the center of her top lip, a look of absolute concentration on her face. No one had said so, but after the events of the day and the unusual results they'd gotten from the first set of water samples, they were all a little on edge. No one was taking chances with sloppy lab work. Not that Letty thought Hilde or Musa ever would. She hadn't worked with them long, but she'd already grown to trust them. Both had the same no-nonsense, pragmatic grit as her team back at UGA.

She forced herself away from the doors and back to the kitchen, where her pan of ground beef and onions had finally begun to look the right shade of caramelized brown. Staring at her colleagues while they tried to work probably wasn't the best way to telegraph that vote of confidence. And if she couldn't be in the lab helping, she could at least feed everyone. She seasoned the meat, then dumped in a half-dozen assorted cans of beans, corn, and spicy tomatoes. The possibility that something out there could be making people sick, making them murderers, was almost too scary to consider. Too radical to be real. And for the roughly millionth time, she let herself dwell on the similarities between this situation and what had happened with the rabies cases in Chattanooga. She'd been wrong, and it had cost her her job. Almost gotten her killed.

In all likelihood, they'd find some other contamination in the samples. Some more pedestrian explanation for the animals' behavior. Something unconnected to the man who'd killed his family and himself.

She stirred the soon-to-be chili. As much as she didn't want to find any evidence of petroleum byproducts in their samples, even that would be preferable to what Adam had suggested. She glanced up at the wall clock, which seemed stuck in the same place as the last time she looked. She sighed again and took a sample taste from the pot. It needed more… everything. She put her now dirty spoon in the sink and went for another round of seasoning, this time heavy on the cayenne pepper. Then added a dash of hot sauce. She would put more on her own bowl when it was all done, but she didn't want to assume everyone else liked to set actual fire to their digestive tract the way she did.

She shot a quick text to Adam. "Almost done?"

He had stayed next door with Charlie after they'd come back in from the ice, helping to stow all the gear and get things set for tomorrow. The GFA showed a perfect window for them to get back on the pack ice then. Which would allow her to collect the second set of water samples. And, after apologizing profusely for her own idiocy, thanking Charlie a dozen times for the lend of the snowcat, and promising dinner in return, she'd scurried back into the research facility with her tail between her legs and a prayer that the facility's cupboard would turn up something dinner-worthy. Chances were good. In a place as remote as Sallow Bay, a well-stocked pantry and freezer could literally mean the difference between life and death.

Her phone dinged a response. "Be there in a few." Dots, and another text. "Helping Charlie pack the gear for tomorrow. He says we can leave at ten."

Hell yeah.

Had today sucked? Yes. Had she learned her lesson?

She wanted to say yes. But…

On the whole, it'd been worth it. She had the samples she'd gone out on the fast ice to find. And she'd get the rest of the water samples she needed tomorrow. Things were looking up. She inhaled the steam coming off the chili, which smelled delicious.

She, on the other hand, did not. She still had on the same base layer she'd worn out on the ice that day, and her shirt smelled like panic sweat.

Yick.

She gave the chili another stir and turned down the heat, leaving it to simmer.

With any luck, she could rinse off and have fresh clothes on before Adam and Charlie made their way over for dinner. She stopped outside the lab again on her way by, peering inside. Hilde and Musa had swapped ends of the table. Hilde's head now bobbed to the still-thumping bass of 90s Hip Hop, but nothing else had changed. Both looked perfectly in their element.

Letty left them to work, ducking into the bunk room without bothering to flip on the light. A rectangle of light cast by the hallway's overhead fixture lit up the space plenty for her to pull what she needed from the suitcase. Leggings, a soft off-the-shoulder sweater, and her last pair of clean underwear — which had tangled themselves around her laptop power cord and a random shoelace somehow separated from its shoe. When had she stopped being a neat, orderly person who had folded clothes and laced shoes?

She unwound the shoelace/cord/underwear tangle. Somewhere between UGA and nearly dying in Chattanooga, she'd stopped caring so much about controlling the little things. She didn't need to micromanage the details of her life to feel like she was living it. She still missed Jessa, still felt her big sister's absence every day... but she'd also stopped trying to use everyday minutiae as a proxy for what she really wanted to control. There was no way to force her jagged feelings into neatly cornered boxes. And that was okay.

She was okay.

She finished untangling her underwear and turned for the bathroom. Sometimes she was messy, sometimes her feelings were messy, and maybe that was normal. Or, at least, normal for her.

A glint of something metallic flashed from her bunk.

What the hell?

She flipped on the light, staring at what waited on her pillow.

A single, shining bullet.

CHAPTER 19

Sallow Bay, Alaska
October, 24, 2018

The helicopter swept due south, through a sky crowded with low, pallid clouds. The ice beneath them held none of the brilliant sparkle of the day before. Snow swirled in gusty spirals, a haze suspended in the atmosphere. It blurred the edges of the craggy pressure ridges lining the ice below. Everything the same and yet constantly changing. Not even the ground beneath them could be counted on. Letty shivered, trying to shake off the thought.

Of course the ice felt menacing. How could it not after what had happened yesterday? She didn't feel safe anywhere anymore. Not here and certainly not at the facility.

She had barely slept. Even with Hilde snoring softly in the bunk beside hers, Musa in the room next door, and Adam sleeping on the facility's couch to try and make her more comfortable, she'd jumped at every noise. Her dry eyes begging for sleep but refusing to close. She hadn't been able to stop watching the doorway, waiting for someone to come in.

Locked doors were cold comfort. They hadn't stopped the asshole who'd left the bullet from getting in the first time.

According to Musa, they sent keys to every team coming to work on site and rarely got them back from the scientists when their work at the facility ended. They'd planned to change the locks but hadn't gotten around to it. And there was no telling how many sets of keys were floating around out there. She tightened her safety belt, the thump of the helicopter's rotors beating in time with an exhaustion headache forming behind her temples. There was another possibility.

Hadn't the door been open the day she'd arrived in Sallow Bay? Musa had said it was commonplace in town to leave doors unlocked. And even if they hadn't done it on purpose, with all the mayhem in town after the shooting, it was just as possible he or Hilde had left it open by accident.

That made more sense than someone breaking in. There'd been no sign of the door or windows being forced open. Not that how the person had gotten in was the biggest question. What mattered was who had gotten in. Someone who wanted her investigation over. Someone with something to hide.

Someone who wanted her gone, wasn't giving up, and knew exactly where to find her.

Worse, when she had finally given up on sleep and climbed from bed, it had only been to find a series of texts from Gemma. A couple camping in Denali had gone missing overnight, their campsite found bloody, littered with broken gear and polar bear tracks. More than one set.

Which was confirmation of something part of her had already known. Given the number of sightings Gemma and Ranger Brenner had been reporting to her via email and text over the last couple of days, they weren't just dealing with two displaced bears that had migrated south. There were multiple polar bears moving from the pack ice into more populated areas, sick and hungry.

The helicopter banked to the right, and Letty slid against the door, her hands tightening into fists in her lap. Whatever borrowed time she had been living on had run out, and those Denali campers had paid the price. She wanted to think maybe they would be found alive but, what were the chances of that? And the longer it took her to figure out what was going on, the more people were in danger. The more people would die. She knew it wasn't her fault, not really, but it sure felt that way. Her fingernails cut into her palms, and she winced, loosening her grip.

It wouldn't help for her to focus on the things she couldn't control. Plenty of qualified people would already be out looking for the missing campers. And right now, she had a job to do. One she was damn sure going to finish.

If whoever had left that bullet thought she'd scare off that easily, they had another thing coming. She was onto something now. They would have test results back in within days. Answers were finally within reach. She wasn't going to let some loser with more ammunition than brains keep her from finding them.

Not when every minute that passed without them knowing why the bears were migrating south into populated areas meant another person in danger. And not when she was finally getting traction. She had taken three sets of water samples from the western quadrants of the bears 'territory today, and there were still enough hours of daylight left for her to finish sampling the next quadrant before Charlie took them back to Sallow Bay. She only wished Adam would have had the same luck.

He sat in the seat beside her, his camera again resting against his thigh. His face stoic. He hadn't taken a single picture from the air. And every time he'd come back from scouting the areas around where they'd gone so she could take samples, he'd gotten more quiet. She had tried to engage him the first couple of times, but his one word answers made it pretty obvious he didn't want to talk. She was trying not to take it personally. The cost for Nat Geo to fund his expedition must have been expensive, and so far as she could tell, he was coming up empty-handed. That couldn't bode well for his career.

He had not said a word since they loaded back into the chopper this last time.

"See any water?" Letty held the mic close to her mouth, trying to be heard over the thud of the helicopter's rotors. Given how long they'd been in the air, they should be approaching the edge of the pack ice — the marginal ice zone. If Adam was going to spot anything worth photographing, it would be in the MIZ, where floes broke apart and the ice melt was at its most advanced. Fish, birds, marine mammals. All normally congregated there to forage.

Charlie pointed to a shadowy spot in the clouds.

Letty looked at Adam, who shrugged. Charlie must have misheard her question. Even with the mics, the noise inside the chopper was deafening.

"Water sky." Charlie steered the helicopter toward the dark smudge in the clouds. Letty and Adam exchanged another glance. Adam looked as puzzled as she was.

Charlie went on. "When it's overcast like this, you can sometimes find the water's reflection in the clouds. See? It's darker than the reflection of the ice."

Cool.

For everything that'd gone wrong on this case, having Charlie as her guide had been an absolute stroke of luck. He hadn't even rubbed it in her face that he'd been right to tell her not to go out onto the ice alone, that Adam had had to borrow his snowcat to come get her, or that she'd come back without his gun. Over a small rise, a craggy break in the ice appeared. Then another, and another. The transition from sea ice to open ocean crawled with fissures and cracks. But there was still no sign of animal life. She glanced at Adam, whose expression held all the softness of stone. Where had the warm, charismatic guy who'd charmed her at the bar, saved her from the bear yesterday, and then taken up guard duty on her couch gone?

Charlie flew them over the MIZ, then circled back, scanning the ice. No doubt looking for a safe place to set down. The helicopter weighed six thousand pounds, he'd explained, which meant they needed ice at least eighteen inches thick to hold its weight.

The first time they had landed, Letty'd thought her heart might burst out of her chest from panic. You couldn't test to see if the ice was thick enough to land safely... without landing. Crazy. The whole time, she couldn't stop imagining the helicopter crashing through into the seawater below. Charlie and Adam trapped inside, her tether dragging her under with it. All of them trapped and freezing to death under a mile of Arctic sea.

She tried to make herself relax, forcing open the now white-knuckled fists in her lap. Charlie would keep the bird running, she'd go out on a tether and drill down into the ice. If it was thick enough, they'd unload all their gear and get to work. If it wasn't, she'd hop back on board, and they'd go to another spot and try again. She watched the ice grow nearer out her window, her anxiety rising the closer it got. Her hands closed back into fists.

They'd done this same dance a half-dozen times already today, so she knew the procedure. But this was their first landing near the MIZ, where the ground was peppered with melt pond formations. Like windows in the frozen ground. And, thanks to climate change, multiyear ice had been replaced by thinner, first-year ice. Not a comforting thought when you were landing on untested ground.

She took a deep breath and let it out slowly. She trusted Charlie to know what he was doing. He seemed to have a sixth sense for where it would be safe to put down. Part of it was the ice's color. Thinner ice tended to be darker, thicker ice a pure white, but there was obviously more to it than that. He'd circle an area five or six times before selecting their spot. Each time, when he'd put them down, the ice had been more than thick enough.

So far.

Charlie settled the bird onto the ice. Letty checked to make sure her tether was properly connected, and she climbed out, ducking even though the rotors spun well above her. If the bird had seemed loud inside, it was absolutely thunderous now, pulsing in her ear drums. Air pressed down around her, plastering her hood against her head, whipping loose strands of hair into her face. She blinked against the onslaught of wind.

Adam handed out a two-inch Kovacs auger attached to a cordless drill. She had it preassembled with a three-foot bit and immediately set to boring a test hole, keeping her face turned away from the helicopter's buffeting draft. It would be easier to work without the rotors running. But having them going helped to minimize the chopper's weight until they knew it was safe. It was a sacrifice she was happy to make. The bit punched through the ice, and she pulled it free.

Twenty-four inches.

More than enough. Letty let out a sigh of relief, her stomach unclenching. She leaned the bit against her leg and shot Charlie a thumbs-up.

He cut the engine, and Adam climbed out to help. "Want me to stow that?" He reached toward the auger.

"Thanks." She smiled at him, glad to hear his voice again, even if it was for something so simple as that. She passed the auger to him and reached down to unclip her tether. The wind finally quieting as the blades slowed above her head.

Red streaked her snow pants where the bit had rested. "What the hell?" She looked up to Adam to see if he'd noticed.

He stood, half out of the helicopter, staring down at a trail of crimson spots marking the ice, where the bit had dripped as Letty passed it to him.

He looked up at her, his eyes wide. "Is that... blood?"

They peered down into the narrow hole at her feet. But it was too deep, too confined for them to see anything but shadow.

No way for them to know what might wait beneath.

■   ■   ■

Letty stepped into the warmth of the facility, sweating in her jacket as she balanced the heavy sample case against one hip. Chris Stapleton crooned from somewhere inside, a clear sign that Musa had control of the sound system. Hilde's taste leaned exclusively toward Hip Hop. The louder, the better. Letty wobbled through the living area, her biceps straining against the case's weight.

She balanced it on the wall, catching her breath before she knocked on the open lab door. "You ready for me?"

Musa swiveled the lab stool to face her. When he worked, he wore thick red-framed glasses that made his eyes look comically large. He owl-blinked at her behind his lenses. "Let's see what you've got."

Letty tried to gently lower the case. It thunked to the floor. "Crap." At least everything inside was well packed and insulated. "One second." She stripped out of her gloves and heavy jacket, leaving a shower of icy flakes on the lab floor. She did her best to wipe them up with her hat as she pulled a sample from the case. "Here."

Musa took it with raised eyebrows. "This is… not what I expected." He swirled the sample, and crimson liquid painted the sides of the container. "When you said on the phone that you'd pulled a red water sample, I assumed it was Mesodinium rubrum." Another swirl. "It's caused red tides in the Arctic before."

She lifted her hair from the back of her neck, fanning her sweat-damp skin. "But now you don't think that's it?" Once she'd gotten over the initial shock of the water's color, she had come to the same conclusion. Harmful algal blooms had caused red tides everywhere from Japan to Florida. And, in the Arctic, HABs tended to be found right where she'd pulled this sample. The blurry edge of the pack ice allowed enough light through the ice to stratify the water column, keeping phytoplankton at the surface and allowing them to bloom.

"Nope." Musa swirled the vial again. "Mesodinium rubrum is a red ciliate that preys on cryptophytes and partially retains the cryptophytes organelles, including the plastid, which allows it to—" He looked up at her no-doubt vacant expression and owl-blinked again. "Sorry. What I mean to say, is that a red tide caused by Mesodinium rubrum would be pinkish, not a true red like this. This is too pigmented." He turned back to the table, preparing the sample to view under the microscope. "Something different."

Well, crap.

Letty started stowing the rest of her samples while Musa set up. Even if what she'd found wasn't Mesodinium rubrum, chances were good it was some kind of HAB. And if this was a toxic HAB, it could explain the lack of animals on the pack ice. She hummed along to the catchy tune playing overhead. If a neurotoxin-producing species was filtered from the water as food by fish or shellfish, it could accumulate in the larger species that consumed them. And then in those animals' predators. With this biomagnification continuing throughout the food web, it could, ultimately, cause mass mortality in fish, shellfish, birds, marine mammals and beyond. Potentially leading to the absence of wildlife on the ice.

Letty reached for another sample, her hand hovering over the vial. It could also explain why her bears had migrated down to Katmai. If their food source had become untenably scarce, they'd have little choice but to look elsewhere for sustenance. She sat back on her heels. The only thing it wouldn't explain was the animals' strange behavior. She stopped humming.

Or could it? Toxic algal blooms could cause respiratory illness to anyone close enough to inhale the aerosolized toxins. And they could cause serious illness or even death to those who consumed contaminated shellfish. Why couldn't a neurotoxin have caused the animal behavior they'd been seeing in Sallow Bay? She had a vague recollection that Alfred Hitchcock's movie The Birds was based on an actual seabird attack caused by the birds' ingestion of toxic algae.

Just like the birds who'd attacked that plane at the King Salmon marina.

She'd sent samples of the blood and tissue she'd found on the plane back to the JDF before she'd climbed on her plane to Sallow Bay. But she hadn't heard if there'd been any results yet or any conclusions drawn from them. She made a mental note to follow up, even though those particular birds had been no where near the affected water. Still, once she knew what they were dealing with here, she'd want to test for it.

She kept loading today's samples. As much as she wanted the answer to be that easy, the likelihood of a neurotoxin causing so many species to react in the exact same way — with violence — seemed as unlikely as it was terrifying. She wasn't jumping to that conclusion again. Not until she had real hard evidence to support it. It was far more probable, the animals' behavior was part of the greater global crisis they were dealing with. Some unrelated phenomenon they had yet to get to the bottom of.

And the only way they were going to find those answers was if Congress gave the JDF the authority to manage a global response. She forced her mind back to the task at hand. Getting answers here was the best way she could help make that happen. She put the last of her samples in the lab's refrigerator and closed the door.

"Let's take a better look at what we've got, shall we?" Musa scooted his stool closer to the work table and went quiet. He adjusted the microscope's focus and stared into its lens for what felt like forever. He raised up, opened his mouth as if to speak, then pressed his eye back to the lens again.

"What is it?" Letty got back to her feet. "What do you see?"

"Take a look." He stood up with a strange look on his face and gestured for her to sit. "It's a dinoflagellate. I want to say Alexandrium catenella, but…"

Letty frowned as she took his seat, spinning back toward the microscope. A dinoflagellate made sense. The algae often caused red tides, but— "Isn't it too cold for Alexandrium all the way up here?"

"It should be, yes." Musa said, his implication clear. For several decades, the Arctic had been warming at roughly twice the rate of the rest of the world. It was just a matter of time before the ecosystem changed with it.

She looked into the eyepiece. Under the microscope, the water showed a thriving mass of algae. "Wow, there are so many of them." The sample teemed with tiny creatures, their movements jerky and unpredictable. The plankton were unicellular with two swirling ribbon-like feelers they used to swim, called flagella. Each had a transverse groove running around its center. Definitely dinoflagellates.

But, unlike the ones she'd seen before, these had no variety in form. "Why are they all the same? That's odd isn't it? I remember when we studied them in undergrad, there were like two thousand different species and, other than the basics of a common structure, none looked alike."

Musa hummed his assent. "What else do you see?"

Letty looked again and gasped. "They have two apical horns." She looked up at him. Dinoflagellates had a single horn-like protrusion from the tops of what she thought of as their heads. Not that they had any actual morphology similar to a human's. Instead of one unicorn-style horn, these creatures each had two, like a devil's. "I don't think I've ever seen that before." It was a dinoflagellate, but it wasn't. Or at least, it wasn't like any she knew of.

Musa shifted his glasses to his head. "Me neither."

"What are you guys looking at?" Hilde said from the doorway, her hair still wet from the shower. She looked up at one of the speakers in the ceiling, crinkling her nose at the country music still playing overhead. Now Toby Keith's cheerful ode to a Solo cup.

"The water sample I pulled from the MIZ today." Letty got up from the stool so Hilde could sit. "See what you think."

Hilde plopped down, a waft of strawberry scented shampoo drifting after her. "Holy crap." She adjusted the focus. "What the hell am I looking at? I'd say Alexandrium, except for the horns." She made another adjustment to the microscope, then looked up, flicking her gaze to Musa. Her words came out fast and bright. "Have you sent an image to Dr. Fulton or Dr. Diliplaine?"

"Not yet." Musa shook his head. "We've only just now seen it ourselves."

She gave a quick nod. "I think we should get samples out to them, too. ASAP. It's a dinoflagellate, but not one I've seen before. This is something new." Hilde's eyes glittered with excitement.

Letty knew the look well. Every scientist dreamed of discovering something novel. Of solving some previously unanswered question. Letty smiled, just as Hilde's face fell. Like some realization had burst the happy bubble of the discovery.

"What?" Letty asked, her own smile faltering. "What's wrong?"

"Could be totally unrelated, but..." Hilde reached for the sound system's remote, cutting Toby Keith off mid-verse. The room fell into heavy silence.

"You're worried about the cyst fields." Musa leaned back against the work table, his expression pinched.

"What cyst fields?" Letty asked.

Hilde swiveled the stool to face her. "An expedition earlier this year found a massive Alexandrium cyst field in the Chukchi Sea. Covering something like 400 miles of seafloor."

Musa nodded, his face still tight. "With roughly 17,000 cysts per square centimeter."

"Jesus." It was hard to imagine the magnitude of it. When conditions grew too cold, Alexandrium could enter a dormant resting stage, where it formed into a cyst, fell to rest on the ocean floor, and waited until the water grew warm enough for it to germinate. Letty's mind spun with the implications of a cyst field that size suddenly coming to life. "If that many cysts were to revive, the resulting bloom would be... massive."

Musa grimaced. "To put it mildly, yes."

Letty crossed her arms, tapping her fingers against her elbows. Even if that were what was happening, it wouldn't explain the tension on Musa and Hilde's faces. Huge algal blooms weren't unheard of. In the summer of 2010, one had covered more than seven hundred and seventy thousand square miles of ocean between Hawaii and Taiwan. Then disappeared, as if nothing had ever happened.

Except that bloom hadn't been a dinoflagellate.

And it hadn't been whatever this new, potentially toxic variety might be.

"Yikes." Letty closed the sample case and sat on the lid. A toxic bloom of that size, especially if currents carried it south toward more populated areas, could be catastrophic to the ecosystem. And to anyone who came in contact with it. Respiratory illness, nausea, vomiting, even death in cases where the exposure or reaction was serious enough. But— "we don't know if this has anything to do with the cyst fields or even what this algae is, right? It isn't like any form of Alexandrium we've seen before."

Hilde tilted her head back and forth, as if weighing her words. "Alexandrium could be evolving. Reacting to some change in environment or some contaminant in the water." She twisted her still-wet hair into a knot on the top of her head. "Could also be something else entirely. A novel dinoflagellate that's been dormant on the seafloor so long no one's seen it before."

Letty nodded. Data science on harmful algal blooms only went back about thirty years. It was entirely possible other previously undiscovered algae waited in cyst form under the Arctic ice. Especially given that both north and south poles had once been warm enough for them to be lush and green. There was no telling what might be hiding there, just waiting for the water to warm enough so that it could spring back to life.

Musa took off his glasses and rubbed at his eyes. "I'll check all the other samples you pulled today, but given the concentration of algae in this sample, I'd bet we find a lot more of it under the ice." He set his glasses on the table, the worry in his eyes no less pronounced without their magnification. "And I'd be lying if I said the complete lack of any other life forms in this sample doesn't concern me."

There were lots of reasons why there might not be other plankton in the sample, but Musa was right. Their absence combined with the sheer volume of the two-horned dinoflagellate in the sample she'd drawn didn't look good. It looked like this new algae might be unusually toxic, even to other plankton.

Letty pulled her phone from her back pocket. It was long past time she reported what they'd found to Mark. Her stomach clenched with the same mix of anticipation and nerves she always had where Mark was concerned these days, but there was no more avoiding him. "Let me go make a quick call to the foundation, then we can talk about what to do next."

She took a deep breath and stepped out of the lab, pulling the door closed behind her. If they were going to handle this the right way, she and Mark needed to be able to work together. No more hiding from the memories he brought back. Or ignoring the queasy sense of shame she carried around. As if pretending she hadn't fallen in love with her sister's fiancé and then basically put Jessa on the boat where she'd lost her life made it any less true. She tapped the cell phone against her palm, working up her nerve. The only way the JDF was going to succeed was for her to suck it up, put history behind her, and do what needed doing.

CHAPTER 20

San Diego

Dishes clattered from the restaurant's kitchen, paper lanterns swayed in the breeze of a wobbling ceiling fan overhead, and outside the front window, a line of people waiting for a table curved around the block. Even before five o'clock on a weekday, Yamato Sushi drew a solid crowd. Mark loaded wasabi onto his spider roll and dipped it in a ramekin of soy sauce. He usually got his sushi fix from a takeout container at his desk. If he did go out to eat, it was for business or just before closing, on nights when his apartment seemed too quiet to go back to. Too empty.

It felt that way a lot lately. And normally, he would enjoy being out with Aunt Kath. Would embrace the novelty of a break in the sometimes soul-crushing monotony of his workload. But that was hard to do when the break wasn't one of his own choosing. He wasn't on vacation.

He'd been fired from his family's company. Or, okay, not fired but "temporarily relieved of his position." Whatever that meant.

He lowered the chopsticks back to his plate. This place was his favorite. He'd been known to order so much it wouldn't fit on his table, and he could swear he'd seen the sushi chef wipe his brow and put on a game face when Mark had come in the front door.

But tonight, the poor man was either going to be sorely disappointed, or relieved. No matter how delicious Mark knew the food would be, he had no appetite for it. Or anything else.

"You need to eat, Mark." Aunt Kath took a sip of her wine, the chilled white almost the exact same shade of blonde as her hair. "I know you're stressed about the investigation, but I promise I have it under control. I would tell you if I'd seen anything you needed to worry about." She pulled the paper from her chopsticks and circled them at him. "Honestly, it looks like much ado about nothing so far." She cracked the sticks apart and skewered a piece of sashimi. "Reid is going to have so much egg on his face by the time this is over." She hummed her approval of the bite, then scooped up her wasabi and deposited it on Mark's plate.

Despite the worry tightening his gut, Mark smiled at her. She'd been passing spicy food from her plate onto his as long as he could remember. He made himself eat a bite of his sushi. It had the same magical burst of flavor and texture as usual, the soft-shell crab's crunch a perfect counterpoint to the buttery richness of avocado, but he barely tasted it.

He chewed and forced it down. "If anyone can manage Reid and his cronies, it's you."

Except, Kath didn't actually know everything she was dealing with. The allegations of self-dealing were one thing. He hadn't actually done that, which meant those issues should be resolvable. But he'd definitely breached a fiduciary duty. And, unlike an internal investigation, an outside investigator like Owen Lockwood would leave no stone unturned.

How long until the board's investigator uncovered the paper trail for the deals he'd quietly torpedoed because they put profitability over sustainability? Or the environmentally friendly ones he'd signed off on, burying the projections that clearly showed a net loss. The numbers he'd falsified to keep it all hidden. He might not have stolen from the company, but as far as the board was concerned, acting against the company's financial interest, hiding it from them… it would be just as bad.

He could tell Kath, and all of this would be so much easier. If he did, she'd still be on his side. He had no doubt about that. Aunt Kath had been there for him his entire life. But, she would also cover for him — like she had for his father — and Kath would be just as culpable as he was.

That was something he couldn't live with.

She looked down at the sushi roll on his plate then back up at him, waiting until he picked up another piece before she went back to her own meal. "Reid wouldn't be such an issue if your godfather would just put his foot down. Jimmy could sway the rest of the board however he wanted if he wasn't such a goody-two-shoes." She sipped her wine. "I get that he needs to appear neutral, but that doesn't mean he couldn't apply some quiet, well-placed pressure to Reid and the others. They can't actually think you've been stealing from the company."

Mark wouldn't put it past Jimmy to muscle the board in Mark's favor, but only if he felt confident Mark was in the right. And it was becoming pretty obvious now: Jimmy didn't. Mark hadn't heard from him since the last board meeting. He pushed his food around his plate.

His phone lit from where he'd left it on the table. A call coming in. He'd taken the picture that flashed on his phone's screen two years before. It showed a beautiful brunette windblown on Ocean Beach pier, a grin splitting her face, a sardine-sized perch hanging from the fishing pole he'd let her borrow. The fish too small to eat, barely bigger than the bait they'd used to catch it.

Letty.

Shit.

He flipped the phone over and glanced up, hoping Aunt Kath hadn't noticed.

"Need to get that?" She held her wine glass by the stem, slowly spinning it between two fingers.

"Nope, all good." He picked up the piece of sushi he'd abandoned, shoving it into his mouth to avoid having to give any more of an answer. He'd promised Kath he would deal with what she'd said was Letty's apparent distraction from the Katmai investigation. Some fixation she'd developed about Crawford's disappearance.

But, of course, he hadn't.

Every time he thought of talking to Letty, he found himself tongue-tied. As Jimmy would say: useless as tits on a boar hog. Mark braced himself, swallowed his food, and glanced up, hoping Kath might've moved on. But, of course, that was as likely as her getting a neck tat or voting a straight Democratic ticket.

She glanced down at his phone, then at him with pursed lips, the wine glass still turning in her hand. "Mark, I know that you have history with—" The glass stopped so abruptly, wine sloshed over the rim. She stared at something over his shoulder, her face tight, a muscle ticking her jaw.

"What is it?" He turned, following her line of sight to a breaking news graphic scrolling across the TV behind the bar: "Authorities say Katmai bear attack may be tied to Stafford Oil's controversial operations in Sallow Bay." Then in closed captioning: "One of the first offshore rigs permitted in the Beaufort Sea, protests over the Stafford Oil's drilling in the area are credited with sparking several rounds of subsequent environmental legislation."

"Oh shit." Mark turned all the way around in the booth so he could see better. He didn't need to keep reading to know the history of his company's off-shore drilling legacy. And that wasn't what mattered anyway. What mattered was what came next.

The image on television shifted to a familiar hallway. Burgundy wallpaper, sedate artwork, clustered groups of interchangeable bureaucrats. The Capitol.

The few pieces of sushi he'd managed to eat went sour in his stomach.

Senator Hilliard marched down the same gauntlet Mark had braved a week before. The senator held up a hand to block the cameras, a persistent "no comment" on his lips. He reached a turn in the hall and stopped, his face a study in conflict and contemplation. The expression too perfect to be sincere.

Here it comes.

Hilliard waited for the press's clamor to subside, the camera zooming in to catch every nuance. His words flicked across the screen in the blocky letters of closed captioning. "I can assure you, the committee and I are hard at work getting to the bottom of the troubling allegations against Stafford Oil that have recently come to light. These are early days, but I can tell you this… if Stafford Oil does bear responsibility…" He looked around, making eye contact with each of the gathered press. "I can't imagine how Mr. Stafford's foundation could be trusted with any aspect of investigating or managing the government's response to the alleged increase in animal violence or disease." He glowered at the cameras and turned to go, talking over his shoulder. "You'll all know more as soon as I do."

Mark pushed his plate away, not able to meet Kath's gaze. Everything he'd worked for was slipping out of his grasp. The company. The foundation. The chance to help people, to do something important in Jessa's memory. The chance to figure out why she'd died. To keep others from losing their lives for no reason, the way she had. His stomach churned again.

All of it, as good as gone.

CHAPTER 21

Sallow Bay
October 25, 2018

Letty waited for Charlie in his office, which still smelled like sock-flavored coffee. For the sake of her sanity, she needed to put a game plan in place for them to get back on the pack ice. She had passed Charlie on the way in. He had been helping Odele retrofit an outboard motor onto a traditional skin boat: a nine-foot whalebone frame stretched with seal skin and oiled until it was waterproof. It was the first of the traditional Inuit boats she'd seen since she arrived, and she had desperately wanted to stop and take a closer look. If it had been anyone but Odele with Charlie, she would have. But she was in no mood to deal with Odele's bullshit, and, thankfully, Charlie had waved her inside to wait until he was done.

Letty rubbed her hands over her face and peered out of the room's one tiny window. At half past ten, the sun hadn't yet hefted itself over the horizon, and the sea crashed a relentless cadence against the shore. In the moonlight, it looked like a black and white photo, with all of life's color drained away. She'd spent most of the night before looking at this same view through the facility's window next door. Listening in on conference calls or pacing while Hilde and Musa debated possible explanations for what she'd found under the pack ice. Throughout it all, snow fell, suffocating and thick.

Which was crazy.

According to what she'd read online, Sallow Bay usually got less than two inches of precipitation this time of year, and, this morning, there had to be at least two feet of fresh powder on the ground.

Even weirder, if the forecast were to be believed, this snowfall was just the start. A massive storm front had gathered somewhere out over the Beaufort Sea and now howled west at an unprecedented clip. This morning's GFA showed it hitting Sallow Bay late tomorrow afternoon. Which was, by no means, a certainty. The GFA was only reliable for about a four-hour window, as Charlie was fond of reminding her. But all the weather websites she'd checked showed the same thing: the storm was coming. It was huge, unpredictable, and — given what she'd found under the ice — had piss-poor timing.

Mother Nature could be a real bitch. If what they needed was on the fast ice, she could go today. Load up the snowmobiles, this time with an escort, and get what they needed. But, of course, it couldn't be that easy. The data she needed was on the pack ice. And that meant waiting until the weather would let them fly.

If they didn't get there and collect samples before the next storm hit, there was no telling how it could change things. She chewed the inside of her cheek. Chances were, the shifting wind and currents would scatter the specimens she needed to collect — just like what had happened to the incident site in Katmai. Without the rest of their data, they'd have no way to know for sure whether the algae bore responsibility for the Sallow Bay animals' unusual behavior. No way to know if the bloom might somehow be responsible for the polar bear attack that had brought her to Alaska to begin with, or the apparent migration of all the other animals off the pack ice. The sample size so far was simply too small for concrete answers. She couldn't tell how far it had spread, the size of the bloom, whether the concentration was consistent, or how it impacted the areas it left behind. She held her only lead between the edges of her fingertips, and it was a hair's breadth from slipping away.

"Fuck." She refocused out the window, where the snow seemed to have slowed. Or even stopped? She stared out at the darkened sky. It was entirely possible the flakes she saw drifting through the air were just those blown up from the ground, recirculating like Arctic tumbleweeds skittering over the ghost-town landscape. There was a solid chance the weather forecast could be wrong. That she could get out on the ice, get what she needed, and prove by this time tomorrow that the whole thing was down to some innocent, solvable cause. Something completely unrelated to Stafford Oil. She stared out at the snow, knowing how improbable that was even as she—

Something was out there. A mark along the ice, too uniform to be natural.

Letty shifted Charlie's desk chair out of the way and moved so close to the window, she could feel the chill coming through the glass. What had she seen?

She wiped condensation from the pane. A single line of bootprints cut across the snow.

Someone had circled behind the facility, recently enough for the tracks not to be obscured by snow. Which, now that she was closer, she could tell was still falling. She bit at a rough spot on one of her cuticles, then moved to the next. She'd been on edge since finding the bullet, and the idea of someone sneaking around outside the facility didn't help. If she hadn't already been losing sleep, she would be now. She forced herself to stop chewing her nail.

She had no reason to think the tracks had been made by anyone who didn't belong there. Charlie or Odele had probably been outside working this morning while Letty had been in the shower or trying to caffeinate herself into consciousness with Hilde's secret supply of Columbian dark roast. She looked back outside. Could the bootprints be explained by something so simple? Or were their edges still too sharp for them to have been left that long ago? Not enough snow filling them in.

"Sorry that took so long." Charlie stepped into the office. "We were supposed to deliver that boat over to the marina yesterday, and we're running behind."

"No problem." She pasted on a smile and shifted away from the window, suddenly aware she'd been standing behind his desk. In what Charlie probably thought of as his private space. She moved back to the far side of the counter. "You think we could get out onto the pack ice and back again tomorrow morning if we leave at first light? Make one more trip before the storm hits?" Normally she'd wait out the weather, but they didn't have that option.

"Maybe yes, maybe no." Charlie wiped his hands on an already filthy rag. "Not sure it's a good idea to try it. And the bird you were originally supposed to have is still grounded in Barrow. Did you talk to Adam?"

"Not yet." Which was shitty of her. It was his flight she'd be hijacking, his employer who'd be paying the cost for her to do it. His hide on the line if they spent the money to get out on the pack ice, only to be turned back by weather. Weather that would make it much harder for him to get any of shots he actually needed.

She should've gone to him first, but she hadn't really wanted to. No matter how attractive Adam might be, the hot and cold game he'd been playing over the last couple of days was a turn-off. Helping her then ignoring her. She'd called twice, sent a text. And gotten nothing back. Which could be because the only bear they'd seen so far had been on the fast ice, where he could go with a snowmobile. Or maybe he had just gotten tired of her. Either way, his sudden silence made her realize how little she actually knew about him.

Like with Pete.

Letty suppressed a cringe.

"Hmmm." Charlie tossed the rag onto his desk, a frown line creasing the center of his forehead. "I think we should start there."

She nodded. If she'd given more than a half-second's thought to it, she would have known she couldn't avoid keeping Adam in the loop. For all intents and purposes, he was Charlie's client, not her. "I'll give him a call."

"Good." Charlie pulled the desk chair over and sat, wiggling an ancient mouse to wake his desktop. From her angle, she could just make out the morning's GFA open on the screen. "We'll see what he says, but, I'm not liking the look of this weather." He clicked over to a satellite image, showing an angry purple-red blotch churning its way over miles of sea. "From what I can tell, storm's gonna roll in here around three o'clock tomorrow. That wouldn't give us much daylight to get out and back… sounds like asking for trouble."

Odele's voice floated in from the garage. "Some people are nothing but."

Letty pretended not to hear her, even as irritation prickled under her skin. "I'll talk to Adam. Assuming he's on board, why don't we see what the weather looks like in the morning and make a final decision then?" There was a chance the storm would dissipate overnight or blow in somewhere else. Sallow Bay never saw severe weather so early in the season. She dug out her phone. "I can call him now and—"

The phone rang in her hand, the foundation's number flashing on the display.

Mark.

A hum of anticipation made her fumble with the phone. "Sorry. I've got to take this." She hadn't been able to reach Mark last night, which in a way had been a blessing. She knew way more now — after hours of collaboration via phone and Skype with other scientists and researchers from universities all over the world. She could give him concrete answers or at least an educated start toward some.

Letty stepped into the garage bay, where Odele glowered at her from behind the boat's new engine, and hurried the rest of the way outside before she connected the call. "Hello."

"Dr. Duquesne? It's Kathryn Stafford."

"Oh." By now, she should be used to Kathryn calling on the foundation's line. Letty coughed and cleared her throat, hoping her reaction didn't sound like disappointment. Not that she was upset to avoid Mark. If anything, she was relieved. This would be easier, simpler. "Hello, Ms. Stafford." Letty managed a more even tone, despite the fact that she still hadn't sent the updates Kathryn had asked for. An oversight she was sure hadn't gone unnoticed. "Thanks for the call. It's been a busy few days here."

"I'd say so."

Letty frowned. What did that mean? She shrugged as she zipped her coat and pulled her hat over her ears. Gemma must've given Kathryn the broad strokes of what had been going on. Letty launched into an update on everything that'd happened since they last spoke: the red tide, the bear who'd attacked her on the fast ice, the bullet, and finally, what she'd found under the pack ice. She stared off toward town as she ran through the details, explaining why they were in a holding pattern for the day.

Sallow Bay seemed to be enjoying an unusually busy day. With the sun finally coming up, twice as many people as usual emerged from their houses to walk the streets. Several clustered in groups; a few walked with purpose toward the hotel. In the distance, the tail of today's turn-around flight in and out of Sallow Bay slid over ragged rooftops. It taxied the runway in the still-tepid morning light, carrying her samples of the bloom to other scientists who could help confirm what they'd found. Letty finally wound down her update, trying to think if there was anything she'd forgotten to cover. So much had happened, hitting all the highlights might not even be possible. But finally, half-convinced she'd said the same thing twice or maybe left out something vital, she stopped for breath.

"And who else have you spoken to about all of this?" Kathryn asked.

Letty blinked. Why would that matter? Except, of course, it did. The foundation would want to make sure the conclusions she'd reached had been properly vetted. "Dr. Becker and Dr. Adeyemi have been working closely with me here on the ground. We've looped in their colleagues at the University of Alaska Fairbanks and shared data with several scientists from the WHOI, NOAA, and several other research institutions who specialize in harmful algal blooms. Everything so far confirms that this is a new HAB. It's a form of the dinoflagellate, Alexandrium. We've named it Alexandrium diabli. A little dramatic sounding, I know, but that's what they look like under magnification. They've got two apical horns. And this new strain is particularly toxic.

"It would make sense that, if the bloom has tainted or destroyed their food supply, animals might migrate to other areas." Letty cleared her throat and continued. "And, given that polar bears' usual migration patterns can take them more than a thousand miles, it also makes sense that they'd be among the displaced animals we'd find furthest South." Which seemed confirmed by the reports she'd been getting via email and text from Gemma and Ranger Brenner. More sightings piled up every day, most unconfirmed, but still. "From what we—"

"I'm assuming you've seen today's news?"

"I—"

What?

Letty wrinkled her brow, waiting for Kathryn to start making sense. Something else was going on, Letty just couldn't tell what. The plane she'd been watching took off into an empty sky, like an escape pod launched into the vacuum of space. "No." She'd barely taken the time to brush her hair, much less turned on the television. "Why?"

"Someone spoke to a reporter at the New York Post, alleging a connection between Stafford Oil's Sallow Bay operations and the Katmai attack."

Letty wilted back against the nearest building. It was just a matter of time before word got out. There were too many people in Katmai who had known the bears came from Sallow Bay for it to stay quiet, although the Post seemed like a strange choice for them to reach out to. It was the least credible of the New York papers and, why New York? Why not a local paper or, at least, one on the west coast. Her mind flew to Adam. But that made no sense. It wouldn't benefit him to give the story to another journalist.

"They have documentation showing both the connection… and the foundation's awareness of it." Kathryn paused. "JDF documents."

Letty straightened, prickles of apprehension finding their way down her spine. "How would they—"

Oh.

She clenched her hands into fists to stop them from shaking. "You think I told them." Which was ridiculous. A gust of wind whipped around the side of the garage, tossing her hair into her eyes. She batted it away. She would have no reason to leak anything to the press. Especially not to a paper that had all-but-endorsed a climate change denier's run for the White House. There was no way they would be sympathetic to anything the JDF was trying to do. She glanced behind her. Odele stood arms-crossed in front of the skin boat, not even pretending she wasn't listening.

"That's ridiculous." The words jumped from Letty's mouth before she could stop them. She took several steps further away and lowered her voice, fighting to keep her anger out of it. "Let me assure you, I didn't have anything to do with a press leak. I have no idea how JDF documents got into their hands, but they didn't come from me." Her voice rose despite her best efforts, and she made herself take a steadying breath before she continued. "I'd have no reason to bring the press down on us. I'm here doing everything I

can to prove Stafford Oil's operations have nothing to do with it."
Saying the words out loud twisted something in her gut. She didn't
want to think of herself as a biased researcher, as someone coming
into an experiment with an agenda. She wouldn't have tipped the
scales in Stafford Oil's favor, no matter what she'd found. But that
didn't stop her from praying Mark's company came out unscathed.

"Are you?" Kathryn huffed out a half-laugh. "Because I have it
on good authority you've been conducting some sort of
unauthorized investigation into Cody Crawford's disappearance
instead."

Letty's mouth gaped open. Her mind struggled to catch up, even
as Kathryn continued, "And you've been using JDF resources to do
it."

"What?"

Oh crap.

Letty closed her eyes. The only resources she'd used had been
her time… and Gemma's.

If she had gotten Gemma in trouble, put her job in jeopardy,
she'd never forgive herself.

"While I appreciate that the loss of a colleague is an emotional
thing… you've essentially interjected yourself into what is a police
matter. This not only reflects badly on you but on the JDF as well."
Kathryn took a deep breath. "We'll get to the bottom of the leak. I
can assure you of that. What concerns me now is how the JDF
handles things from here."

Kathryn's next words came out wrapped in steel. "Too much is
at stake for me to stand by while this investigation runs off the rails.
Mark is like a son to me… I know he trusts you." She sniffed.
"Though, honestly, I can't see why… I was there after his fiancé
died. Did you know that?"

Letty couldn't answer. Her throat had closed entirely.

Kathryn continued. "When I got to the hospital, he was alone
and in pain. I understand what you were going through, how hard
it must've been to lose your sister like that." She didn't sound like

she understood anything. Except that Letty was a complete and total piece of shit. "But you owed Mark better then. And you owe him better now."

Letty tried again to respond, but she couldn't get any words past the pain. All the anger she'd felt at Kathryn's false accusation faded away, replaced by the thick, familiar poison of shame. It coated her throat, spreading down into her body, wrapped its sticky tendrils around her lungs and squeezed.

Kathryn wasn't wrong. Jessa had died swimming off the Nápali coast, attacked by box jellyfish, and Mark had almost died trying to save her. Neither of them would have been there if Letty hadn't cancelled their plans for that week. Begged off of the wedding planning they had intended to do together because she had been choking on feelings for Mark she couldn't control. The trip to Hawaii had been a last minute stand-in, entirely Letty's fault. And what did she do after? She'd disappeared. Left Mark alone with his pain and his grief. What kind of person did that?

Not a good one.

She had spent every day since trying to make up for it. She still was. "I wouldn't do anything to hurt the JDF, or Mark. Going to the press is the last thing—"

"I know what happened in Chattanooga." Kathryn cut in.

This time, there were no words to force out. Letty's mind had gone entirely blank. Kathryn had delivered a perfect one-two, knock out punch.

"That won't happen here." Kathryn paused, and then her voice finally softened. "I don't mean to sound harsh, Dr. Duquesne. This is nothing personal. My priority is Mark's well-being, and right now, that means ensuring the JDF's well-being."

"Nothing personal."

Right.

Kathryn hadn't just gotten personal; she'd gone for Letty's fucking throat.

Kathryn went on. "I'll make sure someone qualified is assigned to handle the Sallow Bay investigation going forward. Until they can get there, you say nothing more to the press. If you're put on the spot, it's 'no comment' or nothing. Do you understand?"

Someone qualified?

"Got it." Letty choked out the words.

A yell came from somewhere behind the facility, then another. But she couldn't make out what had been said. And right then, she didn't care. Her face burned, and saliva pooled in the back of her mouth while Kathryn's accusations swirled toxic in her gut. If she didn't hang up soon, she was going to vomit. She hadn't had anything to do with the press, but she wasn't blameless. The rest of what Kathryn had accused her of was absolutely true. No matter how much Kathryn judged her for it, she judged herself even more.

Charlie ducked out of the hangar, with Odele on his heels. "Did you hear that?"

Letty nodded as another yell sounded. For help? This time, the voice was a woman's, but the words were still too garbled for Letty to understand.

"Something's happening. I've got to go." She hung up before Kathryn could respond. It wasn't like the woman could think any less of her.

Letty followed Charlie around the side of the hanger toward a growing hum of voices. A smattering of people stood near the water. Some she recognized from town, others she didn't. Several of the newcomers, probably fresh from today's turn-around flight, were woefully underdressed for the weather. Likely press. They all stared out at the water.

The tide had come in a bright, blood red.

CHAPTER 22

Mark shoved his sketchpad into his desk drawer. Given that trying to work had been an exercise in futility since he'd arrived at the foundation's offices that morning, he'd been hoping to lose himself in the soft scratch of his pencil against paper. To find distraction in the absolute focus of creating something from nothing. The way he had since Aunt Kath gave him his first art set when he was a boy. But his brain wouldn't quiet down. He glanced up at the TV, where CNN replayed the same cycle of headlines he'd already seen twice. They still hadn't mentioned the JDF's press release.

Which was exactly what he'd hoped for. He had kept the foundation's statement as standard corporate-speak as possible, trying to bore the press — and the public — into losing interest. "The Jessa Duquesne Foundation is dedicated to the thorough and compassionate investigation of all unusual instances of zoonotic disease transmission and animal on human attacks, including the recent unfortunate attack in Katmai National Park... blah blah blah." Nothing he hadn't said about the JDF's mission countless times before in interviews, podcasts, or from behind a podium.

So far, the gambit seemed to have worked.

The press's emails and calls had dwindled to an almost manageable rate. Or, at least, they'd slowed enough to where they became background noise to the JDF's usual buzz of activity. No matter what peril the foundation's future was in, the work they did wouldn't wait. Scientists came in from the field, others prepared to leave on assignment. Gemma buzzed back and forth between her office and theirs. Everyone engaged in what they should be doing.

Except for him.

For the second time in a week, he had spent the morning holed up alone in his office. He'd scoured the news and tried not to panic over the JDF's future, even as his thoughts spun in an endless cycle of what-if's: What if the foundation lost the public's confidence it had only now started to gain? Without it, local authorities might stop seeking their help. Congress could decide not to let them manage a global response. They could lose the chance to gather reliable data worldwide. He leaned forward, rubbing the heels of his palms into his eye sockets. And now, of course, he had the added joy of obsessing over how a reporter had gotten an internal JDF document.

The obvious explanation was that it had been leaked by an employee. Someone who had been convinced Mark's relationship with Stafford Oil would color the outcome of the investigation. He dropped his hands, blinking his eyes clear. He hated to think anyone would be afraid to raise the fear with him directly. But even he could see how naive that was. If they thought he would skew the results of an investigation for his own personal gain, there's no way they would come to him with the concern.

Still, he couldn't for the life of him imagine anyone within the foundation doing such a thing. Either he or Kath had hand-picked every one of them, choosing who to hire not only based on their exceptional professional qualifications but because he had felt a connection with them in their interviews. A common purpose, a dedication to what the JDF was trying to accomplish. People with a single-minded focus on righting whatever had gone wrong in nature.

He grimaced. Exactly the same kind of people who would whistle-blow if they thought the JDF was no longer serving that purpose.

He rearranged the stacks of files on his desk. Even if that was true, half of his staff hadn't known the Katmai investigation was ongoing. Most of them were in the field. And beyond that, it was just him, Gemma, the janitorial staff, and a few temps here and there.

Could that be it? The hiring process for temps was nothing like what he'd done for the rest of the staff — with the obvious exception of Letty. Was it paranoia to think Senator Hilliard could have planted a spy? Or, for that matter, Reid or one of his cronies?

Mark stared out his office window, where heat shimmered off the freeway in transparent waves. Traffic sat at a standstill, while commuters baked in the sun. It was usually warm in San Diego in October, but this was ridiculous. It had to be ninety outside.

He leaned back in his chair.

What if the culprit hadn't been someone in the foundation? He didn't know enough about cybersecurity to say how hard breaking into their email system would be. He pulled out a notepad and pen, jotting down a quick to-do list. First, he'd ask Gemma to see if the system's security had been compromised. He glanced back at the TV, where Nancy Grace was busy schooling a younger reporter on cold case files. Mark tapped the pencil against his pad. He didn't know much about computers, but he was pretty sure the history of any electronic document could be traced. Maybe the same was true for an email.

A knock came from his door.

"Come in." He called out, and Gemma stepped inside. She looked tired. Her eyes red, her hair a mess of tangles barely contained by a leopard print scrunchie.

He stood and circled the desk. "Are you okay?" He pulled up a chair and gestured for her to sit.

She obviously wasn't. She hunched as she sat, her hands clasped tight in her lap. "I'm all right." Her nails had been chewed to the quick and half her polish was peeled off, leaving splotches of black behind.

She looked like she needed a hug, but he didn't know her well enough for that. He sat in the chair next to hers instead. "What's going on?"

"I need to apologize." She kept her gaze on her lap.

Mark's skin went cold. Of all the people in the office that could've leaked the email, he would never have suspected Gemma.

"I know digging into what happened to Cody Crawford wasn't something I was supposed to do." She looked up, her bloodshot eyes meeting his.

His brow creased with confusion. "You did what?"

She coughed out a laugh, looked away and back at him. "I guess I've outed myself then." She gave a small, tired smile. "I thought Kathryn would have told you. Letty and I have been looking into Crawford's disappearance. Mainly just poking around online, trying to figure out why he might've disappeared, where he might've gone." Her face tightened. "Although I did go through his employee file, too." Her gaze met his again. "I know that was probably inappropriate, but at the time, it seemed in the service of a greater good. And I didn't do any of it on company time. I promise you that."

He relaxed back into the chair. He didn't fault Gemma or Letty for wanting to know what had happened to Crawford. He did, too. If he'd had the time and the bandwidth, he would have done the same thing. Which was probably why Kath hadn't told him Gemma had been involved. She would have expected that to be his response.

Gemma spoke again before he could say so, her voice thick. "This job is really important to me. I wouldn't do anything to jeopardize it." Her throat worked. "I don't know if you realize what you did for me when you offered me this position."

He shook his head. "If anyone got the benefit of the deal, it was us." He might have taken a chance when he'd hired her — she'd had gaps in her resume and no formal education beyond the secondary school she'd attended in London — but she had more than proven her worth since. Gemma was an office manager, human resources manager, and IT support all wrapped into one. She didn't just do her job, she treated it like a vocation.

"You don't understand. And I think, if you're going to, you need to know everything." She shifted in her seat. "Noah's dad is trying to take him from me."

"He's what?" Mark blinked, not sure what to make of the non sequitur.

"It'll help if I start from the beginning." She took a deep breath, and Mark nodded. Whatever Gemma needed to get off her chest, he wanted her to feel comfortable sharing it.

"I met Donny in a pub when I was eighteen. He was on a study abroad. And I was young and a fool. I'd never had a real relationship before…" Gemma shrugged. "I got swept up in him, in his life, in the drugs he always seemed to have lying around the flat." She gnawed at a cuticle. "We got married a week before the term ended, and I followed him back to the states. He got clean, but I didn't. I took classes in computer science, but never graduated. I couldn't hold down a job. Couldn't get my shit together in general. Not until Noah. He changed everything."

She looked out the window, where the sun glared off the windshields of passing cars. "For me, and for Donny. After Noah was born, Donny couldn't handle that not everything was about him anymore." She gave a sharp smile. "And I was harder to control once I was sober."

"I'm sorry." Mark said, keeping his voice as gentle as he could. He couldn't imagine Gemma letting anyone control her, especially not someone who sounded like such a narcissistic asshole. "Why are you telling me all of this?"

"Because the only way I can afford to fight Donny in court, is to keep this job. And Kathryn seemed so upset about my having over-stepped, I—"

"You have nothing to worry about." Mark straightened in his chair. "This place would fall apart without you."

She nodded but didn't look at him as she pulled a shirtsleeve down over her palm and used it to swipe her eyes. He gave her a moment to collect herself, but he wasn't going to let her leave his office until she understood she'd always have a place at the JDF.

As long as there is a JDF.

He fought a wince at the thought, and the vortex of worries that had been plaguing him all day rose back up again. This time with a fresh, guilt-inducing nuance. If the foundation failed, everyone he'd hired would lose their jobs. People who had moved across the world because they'd believed in what he was doing, who believed they could make a difference. And for Gemma, it was so much worse. If they failed, she could lose her son.

He hunched; his worry for the foundation had been like heavy chains weighing him down since he'd first realized the Stafford Oil investigation could put the foundation's future in jeopardy. Those chains had now grown rusted and barbed, cutting into him even as he bent under the weight. He forced himself to refocus on Gemma. "You'll always have a place here. And don't worry about the Crawford thing. I would've done the same in your shoes."

"Thank you, Mark." She sniffled into her sleeve. "You don't know how much that means. I'd do anything for Noah. Anything."

Anything.

Like selling a private email to a reporter? He hated the thought as soon as he'd had it. But he also couldn't quite let it go. Gemma obviously needed the money. She was desperate to keep her son. He didn't want to believe it could be true, but…

He looked away, and his gaze fell on the television. It showed a satellite image of an enormous red mass just off the Alaskan coastline. "Holy crap."

Gemma turned, following his gaze with red-rimmed eyes. "What is that?"

The ticker on the bottom of the television read: "The next Azola?"

He reached across his desk for the remote control, turning up the volume.

The image on screen flipped to an aerial shot of a blood red tide lapping against an icy shore. An anchor's voice cut in. "Early reports indicate the giant organic mass discovered off the northeastern coast of Alaska is an algal bloom, massive in its scale. Early concerns have been raised by the scientific community that a bloom this size could trigger a catastrophic change in Earth's climate. Some have likened it to the Azola event, where an Arctic bloom of the fern Azola changed Earth from a greenhouse climate — hot enough for palm trees to grow at the north and south poles — to our current climate. More on this as…"

"Jesus." Gemma said, under her breath. The aerial photo shifted south, over a small cluster of blocky buildings with an airstrip slashing along one edge of town.

Sallow Bay.

CHAPTER 23

Letty checked her watch. It wasn't even 6:30, and outside the town hall's cracked, dingy windows, night had already fallen. Every day here got shorter, daylight dwindling until each hour seemed precious. They'd barely had seven hours today.

Snowflakes blurred in the glare of the parking lot light outside. A silent, unending reminder of the storm heading their way. Now a full Arctic cyclone. It promised twenty-foot waves, a massive influx of warm southern water... and the complete destruction of the data she needed to understand what was lapping at Sallow Bay's shore.

On one hand, the tide making landfall in Sallow Bay gave them more data, which was never a bad thing. She, Hilde, and Musa had spent most of the day taking samples from it. But having that information did nothing to alleviate her need for more data from the pack ice. They needed to establish a baseline for how the tide impacted the areas where it had already been. What exactly did it do to the environment?

So far, tests showed nothing living in the tide's wake, other than Alexandrium diabli. And there should have been something else alive in that water. She didn't want to jump to conclusions, but if they had to go solely on the samples they had so far...

Alexandrium diabli was an ecosystem annihilator.

And the coming storm was going to blow it God-knew-where.

Like déjà vu, all over again. Only now, her inability to get the data she needed wasn't just because of the weather. Letty's replacement would be on the next flight into Sallow Bay.

The idea of being replaced. Of what Mark must think of her... Letty swallowed what felt like barbed wire. The shame of what she'd done long ago, and of what she hadn't done. Knowing that Jessa would never have been in danger if it wasn't for her, that Mark had almost died, too, because of her... it pulled and tore all the way down. Like it had every time she'd let herself digest what Kathryn had said.

You owed Mark better...

The words had been rattling around in Letty's head all day, knocking things loose she'd worked so hard not to feel. She pressed her palm into her forehead, as if she could push all her thoughts back into place. Keep everything where it belonged. She had too much to do in the few hours she had before the storm hit to let herself get lost in a would-have, should-have spiral.

The town hall smelled of cheap carpet, decades of hot dish potlucks, and people quickly growing too warm in their coats. Except for the spot she'd saved for Musa, every seat had been filled. Letty unwound the scarf from around her neck, and her shoulder knocked into Charlie, who'd been deep in conversation with the man to his other side since she'd arrived.

He turned her way. "Glad you made it."

"Me, too," she said, as a text dinged from her phone.

Brenner: "Reports say the bears are hunting in packs. Getting closer to populated areas."

Two other unopened messages waited above that one, both from Gemma. "Results came back from the dead bear you found on the fast ice, positive for Alexandrium diabli." And, "Testing on the samples from the bird strike is inconclusive, so far. Following up now." Letty sent a quick thank you text to Gemma and Brenner, then forced herself to look away from the phone. She'd need to process what that all meant later. She looked back at Charlie. "Seems like the whole city's here."

He gave a short nod, his weathered face tight and unreadable. "People want to know what's happening."

She looked out over the crowd. Some, she recognized. Odele. Two of the roughnecks from the bar. A few others she could identify as reporters. They wore credentials or stood with cameras in the back of the room, their rapid click click click a steady punctuation in the growing noise around them. None of them looked good. Hands rubbing at temples, bodies braced against the walls.

Letty unzipped her coat, needing some air in the claustrophobic, too-crowded room. "I just wish we'd had another chance to go out and get better answers." She lowered her voice. "Especially with the press here."

Charlie didn't look at her when he spoke. "Heard anything from Adam?"

"No." She blew out a slow breath. Charlie had already made his position clear. They weren't going anywhere in his chopper without Adam's buy-in. Only, Adam still hadn't responded to any of her texts or voicemails. She scanned the crowd. No shiny black hair, no broad flannel-clad shoulders. He wasn't there.

Letty's gaze landed on Hilde, who stood at the front of the room behind a podium with a complicated scaffolding of microphones attached to the top. She fiddled with wires attached to the back of a laptop, no doubt a PowerPoint failing to cooperate — as they always did in the moments before a big presentation. The meeting had been scheduled for half an hour ago, and the room thrummed with restlessness. Voices raising, people shifting in their seats.

Poor Hilde.

There were bound to be questions she couldn't come close to answering. None of them could with what little information they had. Letty looked back out the window.

A man stood smoking at the far edge of the parking lot. For some reason choosing to stand in the snow rather than under the protection of the building's eaves. He had his hood up, and it cast his face in absolute shadow. The man lifted the cigarette to his mouth. Its tip flared a sharp, shock of flame in the dark frozen night. He could've been looking at anything, or nothing in particular, but she could swear she felt the press of his stare on her.

She shivered. Seated so close to the window, in the bright overhead lights, she might as well have been spotlighted on a stage. The man raised the cigarette to his mouth again, the lazy arc the same motion she remembered from the man outside Crawford's hotel in King Salmon.

Another shiver ran through her, and she shifted in her seat, looking quickly away.

Don't be stupid!

The motion of raising a cigarette wasn't unique to anyone. Smoking was smoking.

An echoing thud, thud, thud came from the front of the room. Then Hilde's voice, loud but muffled by the microphone. "Sorry for the technical difficulties, everyone. We should be able to get started here in just a moment."

"This is a fine mess." The man to Charlie's other side leaned forward. He had a beard, mustache, and eyebrows so overgrown, Letty couldn't make out the contours of his face beyond the wiry mix of red and gray hair. He crossed beefy arms over his chest, meeting her gaze, then Charlie's. "People are starting to lose it."

"Half of town's talking about some government conspiracy, saying they're trying to scare us off our land to take the oil underneath." Charlie leaned closer to the man, keeping his voice pitched low. "The other half's saying not to drink water from the tap, even though everybody knows the reservoir is freshwater and a good half mile inland." He shook his head, making as clear a bless-their-hearts expression as she'd ever seen.

"Like I said, crazy." The bearded man gave a dark chuckle and shrugged. "Still, something doesn't feel right. Everyone's…. off."

Letty paid closer attention to the people around them. A wiry woman in the row in front of them rubbed at her temples with cigarette stained fingers, as if trying to massage a headache away. The man sitting beside the woman pulled at the neck of his shirt. All around her, people's faces were flushed, their expressions pained. Every one of them looked worried, on edge.

"Watch yourself." A man's voice barked out, and Letty snapped her gaze to the other end of their row of chairs. A big man in a trucker hat and overalls glared at Musa as her friend tried to edge his way down the aisle.

"My apologies." Musa eased past the man's thick knees, negotiated another half-dozen human obstacles, and let out a held breath as he got to his seat. "Thanks for saving me a spot."

"Glad you made it." Letty said, as she tucked the tote bag she'd used to commandeer his seat under her chair. He'd been retesting samples all day. She didn't hold out much hope for new information but… "Anything new?"

He shook his head, his face lined with disappointment as he sat down beside her. "Sorry I'm late. There was trouble in town."

"Surprised anyone was still there to make trouble." She glanced around the packed room.

He pulled his cell from his pocket and tilted it to show a picture of a police cruiser parked crossways on the main road. Yellow police tape had been strung between phone poles behind it. Beyond that, barely in frame, an ambulance. "Some kind of fight at the market. The police have the road closed off, so I had to go around the long way."

In a town the size of Sallow Bay, two violent incidents in as many days seemed highly unusual. And the fact that the ambulance's lights hadn't been flashing in the photo didn't bode well for whoever had been in the fight.

Something flickered in the back of her mind. A thought she'd had days before but hadn't had the time, or maybe the guts, to look at too closely. The animals' odd behavior, the red tide, the uptick in violence… "I was thinking about what happened with the man who shot his family." She kept her voice low enough she hoped only Musa could hear. "He was a fisherman, right?"

"Not professionally, that's not legal here." Musa was slow to answer, probably adjusting to her abrupt change of topic. "But subsistence, yes."

That made sense. Commercial fishing might have been outlawed, but the locals had been fishing to feed their families as long as people had inhabited this part of Alaska. And as much as she hated to think it… "What if the fish or shellfish he caught were contaminated with Alexandrium diabli? If the sea creatures ingested the algae, and then he and his family ingested the tainted seafood…"

"They could get sick." He nodded his head, as if what she was saying was obvious. "Just like shellfish poisoning."

She tried again. "What if the same thing that's making the animals violent is what happened to the fisherman?" She glanced back at Musa, watching his face for reaction. Imagining the public's panic if they believed that were possible. Imagining Kathryn's reaction if Letty were to cause a panic and turned out to be wrong. Not for the first or even thousandth time, what happened in Chattanooga invaded her thoughts: she'd convinced herself the facts that didn't add up meant she'd stumbled on some novel pathology.

And almost died because of it.

Still. "What if eating the tainted seafood is what made him do what he did?"

Musa didn't answer right away. "That's quite the logical leap, but… it's possible." He finally said and nodded, slowly. "I don't want to say it is, but I can't dispute that it might be."

Letty looked around the room again. At all the red, clammy faces. The people squinting as if fighting a headache. The men leaning against the walls for support.

Inside her coat, despite the overheated room, Letty's entire body went cold. She hoped she was wrong again, but there was no way they could take that chance.

One way or another, they had to find the truth.

CHAPTER 24

Letty sucked in air so cold it burned in her lungs. For once, she welcomed Sallow Bay's relentlessly frigid climate. The town hall had gone from uncomfortably warm to stifling over the course of the meeting, the temperature rising with the angry voices that still boomed through the closed door behind her. What a colossal waste of time. She looked off toward the path Hilde and Musa had taken back to the facility, their bootprints lost in the myriad marking the snow. Her friends had scurried out as soon as Hilde finished her presentation, letting the mayor take over his part of the Q&A.

If it hadn't been for the chance someone there had information she didn't, Letty would've left with them. She wished now she had, given how pointless it'd been. The clamor inside the town hall made it hard to think — even before the mayor had lost control of the crowd — and once she had let herself admit aloud that the HAB could be sparking violence, she'd had trouble focusing on anything else.

The possibility of an algal bloom turning animals, or people, into killers made what little she'd eaten that day churn uncomfortably in her gut.

God, what a horrible thought.

At least now she could go back to the facility where she could think in peace. Where she could puzzle everything through and, hopefully, come up with some less terrifying explanation.

She stepped out from under the short overhang of the town hall's eave. Snow pelted her face, each icy shard stinging as it struck. Letty pulled up her hood and followed the trail of footsteps leading toward the facility.

She couldn't think of anything much scarier than the idea of Alexandrium diabli as not just an ecosystem annihilator, but one that drove those affected mad — made them violent, even homicidal. She shivered inside her coat as she hustled down a block filled with darkened houses. Sallow Bay, it seemed, really had emptied itself into town hall.

Even knowing why the village looked so empty, it was creepy as fuck. Snow dampened every sound but the crunch of her own boots over ice. Blocky houses loomed around her in the dark. Like a ghost town. Apparitions silent and waiting.

She sped up, keeping to the road, where the snow had been packed down by tires. It meant a greater chance of slipping on ice, but it was a hell of a lot easier than walking through the deepening snow drifts to either side. She rounded a block. Was she crazy to even consider that the HAB and the violence they'd seen were related? She tilted her head up toward the sky, and snowflakes drifted into her eyes, making her vision blur.

She turned her head down again, taking care where she stepped. Was she jumping to the worst case scenario too quickly? Like in Chattanooga. Might there be some other explanation she was missing?

Not that the explanation behind what had happened in Chattanooga had been anything she could've predicted.

Pete had been a special kind of evil.

She fought the urge to spit the taste of his name out of her mouth, even if she hadn't spoken it aloud.

There had to be some reasonable explanation she'd missed. And it was her job to find it. Which was what she'd do first thing tomorrow. Tonight, the best she could do was to get her head screwed on straight, her gear ready, and then a good night's sleep so she could wake early and rested enough to tackle this whole shit circus fresh tomorrow. She pulled out her phone and dialed Adam again. Maybe she hadn't been clear enough in her last message.

They had to know what they were dealing with before the weather dispersed the bloom into more populated areas. Before Alexandrium diabli did to other people whatever it was she feared it might've done to the people of Sallow Bay. And in the end, going benefited Adam, too. His assignment in Sallow Bay had to have changed since the red tide came in. Photographs of the bloom from the air, a real time documentation of their fight to stop its spread. Nat Geo would have to be crazy to turn that down. That's what she should have led with. He should want to go as badly as she did.

The phone made three loud tones in her ear. Call failed.

Shit.

She was out of range for Wi-Fi. And there was no cell service here otherwise.

A soft thud came from behind her. Then another. Footsteps.

Letty stopped and turned, listening. Searching the shadows for what she'd heard.

She knew better than to be out alone right now, with animals having shown their willingness to stalk and terrorize anyone who was.

With the people of Sallow Bay the way they were.

Her nausea solidified to a stone in her gut. Hadn't she just promised herself after what happened out on the fast ice that she wouldn't put herself in this position… again?

Fuck.

When would she ever learn? Another thud fell in the snow behind her, and she squinted, trying to find the source. Every muscle in her body tensed.

Movement flickered in the darkness.

An animal?

She held her breath.

The shadows shifted again. This time, coalescing into the shape of a person. Whoever it was waited under a lean-to that'd been tacked onto a building about a half a block behind her. Not moving. An image of the man smoking outside town hall flashed in her mind. But that was crazy, wasn't it?

It could be someone leaving the town hall or headed elsewhere… but if it was, why had they stopped when she did?

Whoever waited in the dark was following her. She knew it in her bones. And she wasn't sticking around to find out why.

Letty broke into a run. A cold sweat slicked her skin as she glanced back again. The shadow was closer now. Definitely a man. Too big to be a woman.

She peered into each house she passed. But except for the weak glow of a porch bulb here or there, the lights in all of them were off. Were people asleep? Or still at the town hall? Musa had said most everyone left their doors open, but if she slowed to stop and check, the man would catch up.

At least she knew where she was, knew where to go. Two more blocks down, a right turn, and she'd be at the facility. She'd be safe. She looked back again, hating the precious seconds the move cost her but not able to keep herself from doing it. He was so close now, she could see breath huffing out from beneath his hood.

The snow fell even faster. More blizzard than storm. It came down so hard, it muted what few lights broke the darkness. The single bulb outside a gas station, shuttered for the night. The glow of the airport terminal too far in the distance for her to get to.

No sign of the police presence she'd seen in Musa's pictures.

A flash of light appeared through the gaps between houses.

Adam's hotel.

Her steps faltered. Could she get there before the man caught up?

The hotel sat on the next street over, the lights inside warm and bright.

Adam hadn't answered his phone in days. Maybe he'd left town altogether. But someone would be there. Someone who could help her.

There had to be.

She cut between houses, remembering too late how thick the snow would be where it hadn't been tamped down or cleared.

Shit.

The snow grabbed at her boots, holding her back. Like an insect caught in flypaper. The man was close enough now, she couldn't distinguish the thunk of her feet in the snow from his.

She forced herself to keep going. To push. To move. Her legs cramped, but she didn't slow. Her heart pounded too loud for her to hear how close he was behind her now. But she felt him there, coming nearer even as she stumbled the last few feet from the alley to the packed snow of the hotel's driveway.

Thank God.

Now if she could just get inside.

She raced the last few feet, stumbling up the hotel's front steps.

Please be unlocked.

She yanked open the door, her breath a painful heave in her throat. The relief of finding it unlocked a quick flash in a sea of panic. "Help," she called out, her voice too rough to carry far enough to matter.

The front desk stood empty.

.   .   .

Wind rattled the lobby door in its frame, as if it'd gotten caught in the hungry exhale of some giant creature waiting beyond the glass. But in the rectangle of light sneaking out from the lobby, the front steps stood empty and accusing. Only Letty's bootprints marked the stairs' thick coating of fresh snow.

Where the hell did he go?

Letty pressed a hand to her chest, trying to keep her hammering heart from breaking through her ribcage. "I'm sorry…" She sawed a harsh breath into burning lungs. "…if I scared you." She turned to the pretty Iñupiaq woman who had hurried out of a back office when Letty stumbled inside, yelling for help.

"Is there someone I can call for you, ma'am?" Behind the polite, professional veneer, the clerk's dark eyes flashed with distrust. She glanced out at the still-empty front steps. "Seems like maybe we should ring the police."

Letty shook her head, still trying to find her breath. The last thing she wanted was to draw the authorities' attention. Not only would whatever clown show followed keep her too tied up to get out on the ice in what little time she had left, her report of what had happened would be a matter of public record.

More fodder for the press, and worse, Kathryn would find out.

That couldn't happen. Letty forced in a gulp of musty damp-carpet scented air, then another. Mark's aunt already thought Letty had forced her way into the limelight in Chattanooga and again here by leaking documents to the media. If she reported an attacker that had literally vanished into thin air... Letty would lose whatever little credibility she had left.

Lose whatever chance she had to convince Mark she was still the right person for this assignment. There were dozens, maybe hundreds, of scientists with experience more germane to harmful algal blooms than her own — but, right now, she was the only person in the right place to get the data they needed before it was lost for good. Her team there in Sallow Bay right now were the only ones who could get out on the pack ice before the storm hit. The only ones who could find out what the red tide might actually mean for those affected.

"No." Letty cleared her throat. "No need to call the police. I must've just gotten spooked." She straightened from behind a dusty, plastic ficus where she'd taken shelter. Because clearly that made sense. "With the animals behaving strangely, and the red tide and all. I'm a little on edge." Letty leaned against the scratched veneer of the front desk with what she hoped — and probably failed — to pull off as casual embarrassment.

"It really is best to only go out in pairs, especially at night." The clerk worried the end of her short black braid, adjusting and readjusting the band that held it in place as another gust of wind rattled the door. "Still, maybe it's best if I have someone come… take a look around?" She said the last words as if they were a euphemism for 'have you committed' and picked up the phone.

This wasn't going well.

Letty shifted on her feet. After everything she'd been through — the threatening note, the bullet, the man who'd attacked her in Katmai, and now the man who'd tried to chase her down tonight — a well-meaning receptionist couldn't be what stopped her from doing the job. She glanced down at the woman's name tag.

Letty read it out loud: "Anika Quinnayuak." It was a long shot, but… "You're not related to Charlie, are you?"

"My dad." Anika put down the phone. "You know him?"

"I'm working at the research facility. He's been my guide on the project, and he's been amazing." Letty's face must have shown the sincerity of her gratitude, because Anika blushed.

"Don't tell him that." She finally cracked a smile. "He's hard enough to live with as it is."

Letty let herself relax.

Saved by Charlie.

Again.

"I have a friend staying here at the hotel. Adam Wan." Letty shrugged out of her coat, realizing, only now that her terror had started to wear off, how warm the lobby was. "Would you mind calling his room for me?"

"Of course." Anika snatched the phone back up and punched in an extension.

Letty tried to keep her face neutral as she waited, watching the front steps from the corner of her eye. Anika's gaze flicked up to her, and Letty forced another smile, pointedly not looking toward the front door, which continued to rattle in each gust of wind.

Nothing to see here.

Letty gave an inner eye-roll.

Just your average sane person, yelling about invisible stalkers.

Anika shook her head. "No luck."

"Could I go up and knock?" Letty asked, hoping the miracle of Charlie's implied seal of approval might be enough to sway the clerk into bending the rules.

Anika hesitated, then pointed toward a half-flight of stairs to the right. The carpet tan at the edges and a dull brown down the middle from years of tracked in snow and ice. "Go up that way. Last door on the hall."

If Adam wasn't answering the phone, chances were good he wouldn't answer the door either, but she had to try. There was no way in hell she was going back outside alone. "Thank you, I'll do that." Letty hurried up a short flight of steps, down a long, dim hallway, past a clunking ice machine, to the final door. Room 213.

No noise came from inside.

What was she even going to say if he answered? Unlike Charlie's daughter, he knew, or at least suspected, how dangerous their situation was. The red tide might be on the news, but their fears over what seemed to be happening to people who'd been exposed were hardly public. Add in the fact Adam knew about the bullet on her pillow… and chances were good he'd insist she call the police. But what choice did she have? She took a deep breath and knocked. "Adam?"

Nothing.

Her stomach sunk. Now that she could get on to the hotel's Wi-Fi, she could call Hilde or Musa, but she didn't want to ask them to come get her any more than she wanted to go back outside. Not with the man who'd chased her still out there somewhere.

Letty knocked again, this time harder. "Adam, it's Letty. Are you there?"

More clunks came from the ice machine. But, otherwise, the hallway stayed silent.

She closed her eyes, then patted her pockets, searching for her phone. Maybe Hilde could borrow Charlie's truck and—

A shuffling sound came from behind Adam's door.

She knocked again. "Adam?"

After another long, silent minute, the door swung open.

Adam looked more disheveled than she'd ever seen him. He wore low-slung PJ pants and a gray t-shirt that had been washed so many times the cloth had grown thin. The planes of his chest showed through, hard and defined. He had on oversized noise-canceling headphones, and an open laptop hung from one hand. "Letty?" He pulled off the headphones and stepped back, in a silent gesture for her to come in. "What're you doing here?"

A fair question, after he'd ignored her all day. Under other circumstances, she'd be embarrassed. But she didn't have time to worry about looking clingy or desperate, after calling and texting so many times. She needed Adam's help, no matter what he thought of her.

Letty stepped inside, the door closing slowly behind her with a soft click. As many times as they'd been together, this felt different. Alone, in a hotel room. Blackout curtains covered the only window. They were really and truly alone. A week ago, she would've begged for this situation. But now? No one would know what happened behind that closed door, and she couldn't decide if the flutter in her belly was the good kind… or nerves.

Get a grip, Duquesne.

She shifted her jacket from one arm to the other, trying not to look as awkward as she felt. "I was on my way back to the facility, and…" She hesitated, still not sure how much she should tell him. He was the press. Or, at least, press adjacent.

But now that she was finally somewhere safe, her adrenaline had nowhere to go. The words refused to stay put. "Someone came after me, when I left town hall just now. He chased me through town, I didn't know where to go, and—" The fear she'd forced down in the lobby rose again in her throat, like she was back outside again. Like the shadow man was back. Her entire body trembled, and she couldn't make it stop.

"What? Holy crap." Adam stepped closer, taking her jacket. "Come, sit." He led her further into the room and stopped, as if realizing only then there was nowhere for him to take her. His room was a wreck.

Clothes and photography gear covered every surface. Cameras, lenses, and ink-covered notepads lay scattered across the bed. A coat had been draped over an ancient, boxy television. And an entire North Face catalog worth of fleece and outerwear buried what she assumed was a small desk and chair underneath. Adam rubbed the back of his neck. "Sorry about the mess." He shifted a tray with the remains of what'd probably been his dinner — an empty beer bottle, an orange peel, and the crust of a sandwich — from the foot of the bed to the floor, making room for her to sit.

"I'm not usually such a slob." His face reddened in a way that told her he definitely was. He put her coat on top of his. "Now, start at the beginning, and tell me what happened."

She perched on the edge of his mattress. "I heard someone behind me after I left the meeting. When I realized he was following me, I tried to run, but he was so fast—" She rubbed her hands up and down her arms, for comfort more than warmth. "I wasn't even sure you'd be here. I tried to reach you a bunch of times…"

He blinked at her, his eyes red and bleary. "You did?"

She frowned. He had to know she'd called. She hadn't been subtle. She'd left messages, sent texts, she'd even tried email.

He sifted through the papers on his bed, unearthing an iPhone. "Oh crap." He looked up at her. "I'm so sorry I didn't answer. I've had it on silent and all the notifications shut off on my computer."

Was that even possible? He looked sincere, but—

"I'm on a deadline. With everything that's been happening here with the press making the connection to the Katmai attacks and now the red tide, Nat Geo wants to run something sooner. They insisted I have sample shots in by tomorrow morning, and I've hardly got anything to submit. I need to make sure what I do send them is perfect. I've been hunkered down, editing for..." He glanced at his watch. "God, I'm not even sure how long. All day, I guess." He rubbed a hand through his hair, which looked deliciously rumpled.

She had the irrational urge to stroke her hands through it.

She forced her gaze back to his.

"God, Letty. You must've been scared out of your mind. I'm so sorry I didn't call you back earlier." He retrieved a bottle of vodka, a Russian brand she didn't know, from the scarred table holding the TV. "It's warm, but..." He unwrapped the plastic from two paper cups marked with the hotel's logo, and glugged a healthy pour into each. "Sounds like you could use it." He handed her the cup then leaned back against the wall and glanced down at his phone. "Did something else happen before that? It looks like you've been calling me all day." He had the decency to look bashful.

She had no idea where to start. Letty drank the vodka, wincing at the sting. She took a deep breath and dove in, telling him everything that had happened since she saw him last — the storm, the tide, her fears about whether and how it might be impacting the human population. She even told him what had happened with Kathryn, about her replacement coming in. It might not paint her in the best light, but she needed Adam to understand the situation they were in. She needed him to appreciate how important it was that they get back on the ice ASAP. That they get the data she needed before it was gone for good. That it might actually help him to get it. Whatever pictures he caught out on the ice tomorrow would be worth their weight in gold.

When she finally fell quiet, he pushed off the wall, retrieved the vodka, and refilled both their cups. "I'm in, even without the pictures. That's insane."

Relief fell over her like a sunbaked blanket, warm from the clothesline. She was going to get back out on the pack ice. Going to get what they needed. She nodded. "It kind of is." She threw back the vodka. It burned the whole way down, but less than the first time around. And it left a pleasant hum in its wake.

"Tell me more about the guy following you. Did you get a good look at him?" Adam watched her over the rim of his cup. "Any idea who it might be?"

She shook her head. Even with the after-effects of knowing she'd be able to do what she needed to and the alcohol loosening her tongue, she wasn't willing to say what she really feared. That the man who'd chased her might be the same one who'd attacked her in King Salmon. That the same one who'd smashed her windshield hundreds of miles away had followed her here to leave a bullet in her bed. If she was trying to look sane, that theory wouldn't help.

Even if it was starting to seem more and more like the truth.

Whoever wanted her gone had lost patience in waiting for her to go quietly. "I didn't get a good look at him. He just came out of the shadows and then, when I got to the hotel, he disappeared into them again. Like a freaking ghost." Her words went tight. "I have no idea what he wanted. What he would've done if he'd caught me."

"I can walk you back to the facility, if you want." Adam sat his cup next to the vodka bottle, took her empty cup, and sat it beside his. "But I don't think you should go back tonight." He turned back toward her, his gaze unguarded as it swept over her. If there'd been any ambiguity about his intentions before, there wasn't now.

The last thing she wanted to do was go back out into the storm. And damned if she didn't want to take him up on whatever hot, sweaty distraction he was offering. But staying here with Adam seemed like one more in a long line of questionable choices. She got to her feet, intending to make her excuses. To gather her coat and let him walk her back to the facility.

She stepped toward him instead, his gaze holding hers. Their bodies so close now, her chest nearly touched his with each breath. Nothing about this was safe.

He leaned in slow. Gave her every chance to stop him.

She didn't move. He smelled like pine needles and spice, and just slightly of the sharp medicinal scent of vodka. Letty bit her bottom lip. She should stop before this got any further out of control.

But she didn't want to.

She lifted her hands to Adam's chest, and his breath caught. His body stilled, even as his pulse jumped so hard, she could see the flutter under his skin.

He waited until she twined her hands behind his neck before he lowered his head to kiss her. Soft at first, then as she opened her mouth to his, more urgently. His tongue stroked hers, and she melted into his touch. Into the comfort. Into the feel of someone's hands on her. Of his body pressed hard against hers. She'd almost forgotten how good this could feel. She wanted more of it, all of it. Even as she knew she shouldn't do this. They shouldn't. As much as she wanted Adam, she already knew what they had didn't go beyond the physical. She didn't trust him, didn't know him really…

She faltered. She'd made this mistake before.

He pulled back, a question in his eyes she didn't want to answer.

This might be a mistake, but it was one she damn well wanted to make.

She fisted her hands in his shirt and pulled them back together. All the soft parts of her body lining up with the hard parts of his. He deepened the kiss, his hand slid behind her head, his fingers tangling in her hair as he tilted her head so that their mouths could seal together.

She let out a sigh against his lips. "Okay."

His hands moved down her body, drifting from her back to her ass and back up again, as if he couldn't stop himself from exploring every curve of her. She leaned into his touch.

"You'll stay?" His thumbs brushed soft against the undersides of her breasts. Lighting her nerves on fire. "Are you sure?"

No.

"Yes."

CHAPTER 25

Sallow Bay
October 26, 2018
The harsh trill of Letty's phone ripped her out of a much-needed deep sleep. She blinked into the absolute darkness only blackout shades could create, flailing her hand in the general direction of the side table, trying to grope her way to where she'd left her phone dangling from Adam's spare charger.

Her hand smacked the base of a lamp, and the hotel room burst into focus. It looked like a bomb had gone off, even worse than it had when she'd gotten there. Clothes and gear scattered everywhere. Adam lay next to her, him on top of the covers, her under. Both of them, more or less, still dressed. The details of last night came back to her all at once, and Letty blushed. Not that she had any real reason to. She hadn't done anything.

Because I'm an idiot.

Adam shifted a pillow to cover his head, and a garbled mumble came from underneath. The words, still muffled and thick with sleep, finally took shape. "Think that's yours."

The phone rang again.

"Sorry." She forced her sleep-addled body into action and yanked her phone from the cord. Gemma's face filled the screen. She'd taken the picture the day before Letty left San Diego, showing off the bright salmon pink she'd just dyed her hair. It was a color only Gemma could pull off.

Letty sent the call to voicemail. She could call Gem back when she wasn't in bed with someone she conspicuously hadn't slept with the night before. God, she was a mess. Who turned down sex with someone who looked like he did? Her gaze darted up to the time on the phone's display.

9:15.

"Shit, Adam. We overslept." Charlie had been perfectly clear. Even if she did convince Adam to take the chopper out again, if they weren't on the ice before ten, he wasn't going to risk taking them out with the storm coming in.

They needed to go. Now.

She leapt out of bed, stumbling over a half-zipped duffel bag before catching herself against the wall.

"What?" Adam sat up, rubbing at his face. "I swear I set an alarm."

She cast around, looking for her fleece, coat, and boots — all of which were buried somewhere under the mess of clothes and equipment they'd cleared off Adam's bed so they'd have a place to sleep.

He picked up an old-fashioned clock radio from his bedside table and groaned. He fell more than climbed out of bed, one leg bound up in the throw he'd used as a blanket. "I hit PM instead of AM." He dropped the clock back onto the table and hurried toward the bathroom, stopping only long enough to scoop a set of clothes up from the pile on his desk. "So sorry. I'm such a dumbass. I'll be ready in five."

She fumbled her foot into a boot. "Let's just get there as fast as we can."

Her phone rang again, and she puffed out an irritated breath. She glanced at it long enough to see it was Gemma again but didn't answer. Where the hell was her other shoe? She pulled on her fleece, found her hat and gloves under one of Adam's lens cases, and ignored the ringing. She didn't have time to do anything but hustle her ass to Charlie's shop. She yanked on her hat and stopped. "Shit."

Gemma wouldn't be psycho-calling her without a reason.

Letty snagged the phone, trying to keep the anxiety out of her voice. "Hi, Gem." She still didn't see her other boot. "Everything okay?"

"Owen Lockwood is here."

Letty dropped down on her hands and knees, searching the floor. "Who?" She swept back an unnaturally stiff bedskirt, not wanting to think about what could've gotten on the fabric to cause it to be that way. Her missing boot lay on its side, hiding behind the rigid cloth. She'd need to bleach her hand, but at least she wouldn't be flying out onto the pack ice in one shoe.

"The investigator. The one looking into the allegations against Mark."

"Oh." Letty shoved on the boot, trying to focus on what Gemma was saying. She'd known the board's investigation was ongoing but wasn't sure she'd ever heard the man's name before. "Why's he at the foundation?" The JDF might be funded by Mark's company, but they were two separate entities. Lockwood had no business being there.

"Kathryn set up a conference room for him here with all the documents he requested. His team's been in all morning. I guess that's why she and Mark cleared out of the office. You know, to avoid them. But they've been a right pain in the ass. 'What's the wi-fi, again?'" she mimicked, with a particularly western twang. "And you'd think none of them ever learnt how to make a coffee themselves and—"

"Sorry, girl." Letty pulled on her coat as the sound of Adam's electric toothbrush came through the bathroom door. "I need to call you later." She ran her tongue over her teeth, which felt like they had fur. She swigged from the half-empty water bottle she'd left on the side table the night before and chased that with a lonely, and only slightly dusty, mint she found at the bottom of her coat pocket. It was the best she could do until she got back to the facility and her toothbrush. "We're on our way back out the ice this morning, and that storm we talked about is coming in fast, I need to get moving."

Letty yanked open the blackout curtain. Outside, the morning was gray but clear. The proverbial calm before the storm. The fact that yesterday's GFA had been accurate, that this morning did, in fact, give them a flight window, seemed like a gift.

One she wasn't going to let pass her by.

A burst of optimism shot through her, like a double-shot of espresso. It was about fucking time she had a stroke of luck. "Let's talk when I get back, okay? Should be mid-day, early afternoon at the latest." If they weren't back by then, they were going to be in a world of hurt. Not even Charlie could fly in the kind of storm that was headed their way.

"I—" Gemma sighed. "Okay, but look. One of Lockwood's people asked me for help with the printer, and I found a document jammed inside. I know I shouldn't have looked at it, but..." Another sigh. "I mean, how could I not? It's some kind of chronology, and I did some digging and... I'm worried. I don't know who else to talk to about it. I'm going to text it to you. Just take a look, okay? See what you think."

"Of course." Letty said, but her mind was somewhere else. She turned to find Adam waiting by the door. He had his feet shoved into unlaced boots and two camera bags criss-crossed over his chest. She tilted her head in a 'let's go' gesture and followed him out of the room. "I'll look as soon as I can, Gemma. I promise. But I'm sure it's nothing. Mark is always on the up and up." She glanced over at Adam as she exchanged goodbyes with Gemma, but if he'd heard a word of her conversation, he didn't show it. As ever, he looked ruggedly handsome as he walked down the hall beside her. He now had his own phone pressed to his ear and seemed entirely focused on whoever was on the other end of the line.

"Sounds good." He glanced over at Letty and gave her a thumbs up. "We're on our way now."

"Charlie?" She mouthed the question.

He nodded then followed as she hurried down the half-flight of stairs into the lobby. They had an immense amount of work to do and barely any time to do it, but with Charlie on board, they at least had a shot.

Adam spoke from behind her. "He says he'll have the chopper ready when we get there. Musa got your text from last night, and the gear's already packed, so we can be in the air as soon as we arrive."

A burst of gratitude bloomed in her chest. She turned back, catching his sleeve as he finished zipping his phone into the pocket of a camera bag. "Thank you." She smiled up at him. "For everything. I know it's been more than you signed up for when you offered to share your helicopter." But she couldn't have done any of it without him. And she'd definitely underestimated him. He'd been amazing last night, backing off as soon as he'd realized she wasn't sure she was ready. He'd been so chill about the whole thing, it hadn't even been awkward. Which was saying something; she could make anything weird. She went up on tiptoe and gave him a soft, thank-you kiss. "You're a good guy, Adam Wan."

A throat cleared behind her.

Adam looked up and stiffened.

Letty turned, her hand still gripping Adam's sleeve.

Mark stood in the lobby doorway, a rolling bag behind him.

And a look of absolute fury on his face.

■　■　■

Of all the things Mark had been prepared to face when he landed in Sallow Bay — the looming storm, the potentially devastating threat of the red tide, the media hounding them every step of the way — he'd never expected whatever it was he just walked into.

"Mark?" Letty finally let go of the Henry Golding look-alike who was standing way too close behind her. The man she'd just kissed. Who, by the look of the cameras hanging from his neck, was press.

What the actual fuck?

"What are you doing here?" She lifted a hand to her mouth, as if realizing what he'd seen, and moved toward him.

Mark took a step back. He hadn't wanted to believe the things Aunt Kath said about Letty, but maybe he hadn't been seeing her clearly.

She stopped short, a flicker of hurt on her face.

He ignored it. She didn't have any right to be hurt. He'd dropped everything to come help. To make sure the foundation had what it needed to deal with the threat of the tide. All while she'd been busy shacking up with some random guy she met on assignment. Some guy who probably had a press pass. Mark forced himself to let go of the white-knuckle grip he had on his suitcase. "I brought reinforcements. We got on the plane as soon as we saw the news. I dropped everyone else at the research facility, came here to make sure we'd all have a room. I know it's pretty booked up with all the press in town…" He steeled himself and turned to the man who still stood silent behind Letty. "I don't think we've met. I'm Mark Stafford. I run the JDF."

"Adam Wan. Nice to meet you. I'm here during some work for Nat Geo." The man stepped forward, waiting for a group of rough looking guys in coveralls to pass them on their way from the opposite wing of rooms through the lobby before he extended his hand. "Letty and I have been sharing a helicopter to get out on the ice."

Among other things.

Mark stifled a grimace. The words were the last ones he wanted to say right then, but… "Thank you for that. I hope you'll be willing to let our team join you again today." Mark accepted the handshake, squeezing a little harder than was absolutely necessary before he let go. "I understand with the storm coming in, we have a limited window to get data."

"Of course." Adam's gaze darted between Mark and Letty, as if trying to get a better read on the situation. Whatever he saw had him draping an arm over Letty's shoulder. "It may not be the images they sent me here to capture, but I'm sure my boss will be even happier with photo-documentation of the tide."

Letty smiled up at Adam in a way that made Mark want to punch something. Preferably Adam. Which was not a thought he wanted to look to closely at, or even acknowledge. What was wrong with him?

She checked her watch, then looked back at Mark. "We should get going. Our guide, Charlie, has the helicopter ready. If we hurry, we should be able to get out on the ice, get what we need, and—"

"That won't be necessary." Mark cut her off. "Ines and our new marine scientist, Dr. Keegan, are at the facility now. They can take it from here." He hadn't intended to cut her out of the investigation. The team would only benefit from the continuity provided by her involvement, but in that moment, he couldn't imagine working with her. He'd barely slept in his rush to get there, and she was here doing... this? He pointedly avoided looking at Adam.

Letty's face flushed red.

Adam looked between the two. "Why don't I let you two sort this out? I'll go find Charlie. Make sure everything's ready to go." He squeezed Letty's shoulder and, with one worried glance back, disappeared through the hotel's front doors.

Letty turned to Mark. "I know Kathryn had planned to have reinforcements," she said the word like it meant something else, "come in this morning, but I'd really like to stay on and work with Ines and Dr. Keegan. Do whatever I can to help before I head back. I have a whole lab team here in place. We have samples in process. I know exactly where we need to go to take the remaining data."

Mark raised a hand. "The guide will know where to take us, and I'm sure your work is well-documented. Between Ines and Dr.

Keegan, they've got thirty years of experience with harmful algal blooms. They're already at the facility now, getting up to speed." He'd planned to have them all work together. But Letty hadn't been at the facility when they'd arrived.

She'd been here.

She opened and closed her mouth again without forming a word. The clamor of the roughnecks' complaining to the desk clerk about their rooms' lack of a mini-bar grew suddenly loud in the open space.

Mark pushed down a swell of guilt. It wasn't that he didn't want Letty on the job. "Given the size of the tide, the danger it could pose, and the public interest — not just in it, but in the JDF's handling of the investigation — we need to put the most qualified people we have on it."

She held a hand to her throat, her brows pinched. "What?"

He tried again. "That came out wrong. I'm not saying you're unqualified. Just that there are others more qualified to investigate this particular case. Your field experience isn't in the Arctic, and it isn't with plankton or polar bears." He took a deep breath and spit out the rest. "The public interest in this tide is overwhelming. Everything we do will be picked apart by the press. The oversight will be oppressive. Given where things stand with Congress and with what happened in Chattanooga…"

She closed her eyes, shaking her head. "You don't understand."

He clenched his jaw. He hadn't wanted to say anything. Hadn't wanted to add more pressure to an already volatile situation, but… Letty was the one who wasn't getting it. And they didn't have time for him to be gentle. "The fisherman who survived the Katmai attack died this morning."

"Paul Reardon?" Her question came out as barely more than a croak. "But they said he was expected to make a full recovery."

"Complications during surgery to repair some of the damage to his face. He died while I was on the last leg of my flight here." While she was busy getting laid. "And the bear who did it is still out there, along with God knows how many others."

The words had come out like an accusation, and he fought to clear his throat. That hadn't been what he'd meant. Not really. It had been a step too far, and even he knew it.

Her face paled.

Shit.

He was making a mess of this. He needed to stop and regroup. He wheeled his suitcase to the front desk and left it with the desk clerk, buying himself a minute to pull his head out of his ass.

He came back to where Letty waited. Her face still looked pained, but now she had her arms crossed over her chest. That couldn't mean anything good. The look on Letty's face was the same one Jessa always had when Mark had done something spectacularly stupid. It usually preceded a full, Duquesne-style meltdown.

"Listen." Mark tried to make his voice as even and soothing as he could manage, but the longer she stayed silent, the faster his words came out. "We should have had someone else step in after what happened to you in King Salmon. It's entirely my fault for not taking action earlier. Call Gemma and get her to put you on the next flight home. We can regroup once—"

"You know what, Mark?" She stared him down, the fire now bright in her eyes. "I'm done with this shit. All of it." She walked past him and yanked open the lobby door without looking back. "I quit."

CHAPTER 26

The bar's generator choked and rattled, like an old gas-powered lawnmower on its last legs, but it kept the lights on, the beer cold, and the drinkers warm. Letty pointed at her empty glass. The bartender — who was a heavy pourer, handsome in a rough-around-the-edges kind of way, and, most importantly, not Odele — nodded and grabbed the pint glass for a refill. Letty turned to check the door while he worked, but Adam still hadn't shown. She'd texted him after the brutal scene in the hotel lobby with Mark to let him know she wasn't coming, and he had promised to meet her at the bar after he got back to let her know what happened and help her drown her sorrows. But she had heard nothing from him or anyone else, and the view outside the bar's front window wasn't helping her anxiety. It was long past dark and near perfect white out conditions.

The storm hadn't just hit Sallow Bay. Since making landfall a little before four that afternoon, it had pummeled the village with wind, snow, and ice.

She tapped her phone, making sure she was still connected to Wi-Fi and had service. She was, but still had no missed calls, no texts. And it was now well after six. Hours since Adam, Charlie, and the others should have been back from the pack ice. For two beers now, she'd been bouncing between worry about what could have gone wrong and the fact that this wasn't the first time Adam ghosted her.

The bartender dropped off her beer. "Wanna close it out?"

Letty shook her head. Alcohol might be her only company. "Thanks, though."

She sipped the IPA. As much as her fragile ego leaned into the idea she had been ditched again, this didn't really feel like that. She'd shared something with Adam last night. Nothing romantic, not really, more like they had understood each other. He knew what the stakes were. He would know she'd be waiting on pins and needles to find out what had happened on the ice. She couldn't reconcile the guy who'd been so amazing yesterday with him standing her up today.

What if there was a reason he hadn't texted?

God, please let them be okay.

The lights flickered, the generator choking out a wheeze before it roared back to life. There had to be some innocent explanation… But even if Adam had stayed to help unpack the chopper, stowed all of Charlie's gear, checked in with Nat Geo, and dropped his equipment off at the hotel, he should still be here by now. They had a hard stop to be back off the ice by 3:00 p.m., at the latest. She'd already texted him once. She tapped the phone against her leg. She could just go back to the facility and see what was happening. All her stuff was still there, and she had no where else to sleep tonight; it wasn't like she could stay away forever.

But what if Mark was there?

That's a no.

She'd just have to wait him out. He would have to go back to his hotel, eventually. Then, she could go the facility, pack her stuff, and book herself on the next flight home. God, she really hoped it was that simple.

She typed in a message to Hilde: "Did everyone make it back?"

Letty stopped before hitting send. It felt weird to just shoot off a text after what had happened this morning. Hilde and Musa had been her team, along with Charlie, and even Adam. And she'd walked away from all of them in the middle of something important. Something dangerous. It was a seriously shitty thing to have done, no matter that she'd felt she hadn't had any real choice in it. She'd technically quit, yes. But in that moment, it had felt more like she'd been removed from the project. Her intentions called into question. Her capability called into question. Normally, she would've fought to stay and prove him wrong, but…

The bear who did it is still out there.

She winced, just like she had every other time she remembered what Mark said. Even worse, the look on his face when he'd said it. There'd been no missing the accusation in his eyes, the insinuation that in failing to find and contain the second bear, she'd put more people at risk.

Voices raised from the other end of the bar. Two of the guys in Northrup Grumman caps glaring at each other over a dilapidated pool table. The bartender hurried toward them. "You two know the rules. You want to stay where the booze is flowing, you gotta play nice."

Letty turned back to her beer. She couldn't work where people didn't respect her, and both Kathryn and Mark had made it clear they didn't. She rubbed at an ache in her chest. It hurt to know that Mark, of all people, could see her as someone who couldn't be trusted to see things through, to do the right thing.

She took a long swig. Maybe the fact that she kept losing her job was a sign she wasn't meant to be doing this kind of work at all. She'd always loved science. Loved working in the field, being outside, in nature, exploring the world, answering what had been thought to be unanswerable questions. But maybe loving it wasn't enough. Maybe she was on the wrong path. Chasing the wrong things.

The thought settled heavy in her chest. What had she thought was going to happen? Working with Mark had been a completely ridiculous idea from the start. Not when she still felt the way she did about him. She rubbed at a spot where the chest pain had gone tight. They had too much history. What she needed now was a new plan. One that would get her as far away from Mark as possible. She sniffed a laugh. Because that was going to be so easy…

Right.

She'd left academia behind to join the foundation. Then quit that job less than two months after she'd started. Add that to what had happened at UGA last spring, and her resume had more red flags than it had bullet points. Even if she could somehow find a university willing to take her, she'd probably end up right back where she started. Forced out of the field into a teaching position, fighting the same publish or perish race she'd watched so many friends struggle through.

The only place where she'd get to do what she truly wanted to do was at the JDF. This was where she could do right by Jessa, where she could make a real difference. And, instead, she'd shit that bed in spectacular fashion. She finished her beer and sent the message to Hilde.

It wasn't like she could hide from her mistakes forever. She owed her team an explanation. And an apology. She could have stuck it out, despite Mark basically ordering her to fly back to California. She should have at least stayed on to explain everything to her team, no matter how hard it was. No matter how much it hurt to know Mark didn't want her there. Her phone dinged in her hand. "Finally."

A message from Gemma. "I heard what happened. Are you OK?"

Crap.

She tried to think of any response that wasn't either a lie or something that would result in an immediate talk-her-down-off-the-ledge phone call she had no interest in having, but came up empty.

Lies it was. She sent off an "I'm okay" message and stared down at her phone, waiting for it to ring. There was roughly a zero percent chance Gemma would let her off that easy. Above Gemma's check-in text, the document she had sent Letty that morning still waited in their thread, unopened. She'd been so busy, so caught up in her own drama, she had completely forgotten about it.

It shouldn't matter anymore. Not to her, anyway. Mark wouldn't want her help.

But Gemma had sounded really worried that morning, and it wasn't like Letty had anything else to do. She opened the document. Irregular lines creased the page, where it had obviously been crumpled up and flattened again. It looked exactly like what Gemma had said, a chronology of some sort. A list of dates beginning in early 2015 and ending in December of 2017 ran down the left side, each correlated with information that seemed to have been pulled from a flight log. Three of the flights had been highlighted. All of those departed from either Houston or San Diego and landed in Gulfport, Mississippi. She'd bet money the chronology reflected flights made by Stafford Oil's private jet. A third column listed people's names she didn't know and, on some, stated either "500 barrels" or "750 barrels."

It would make sense for Lockwood to be tracking Mark's use of the jet, to make sure he hadn't diverted that resource for personal use. But this looked like something else. Proving Mark's use for business wouldn't require the specific details of each deal. And one of the names in the left-hand column had been circled every time it appeared: Randy Freer. The name didn't ring any bells. Letty enlarged the screen so she could read the notes scrawled across the margin in Gemma's messy handwriting. "Sun Herald article dated 11/5/17 reports Freer facing five years for unauthorized dumping of petroleum byproducts." And, after that: "Sun Herald 12/18/17, 'Pediatric Cancer Cluster Linked to Unlawful Dumping.'"

Letty dropped her cell to her lap. This document made it look like Mark had used the company jet to meet with Randy Freer on the dates listed. That each time, they'd agreed on some off-the-books deal with Freer to dispose of Stafford Oil's petroleum byproducts. Worse, when taken with the articles Gemma found, it looked like what he'd done had made people sick. Made kids sick. Which was crazy. Mark would never do anything like that. Cutting that kind of corner might save a little money, but it was short-sighted and unbelievably dangerous. Mark would know they couldn't get away with it forever. It ran directly contrary to the entire purpose of the foundation he'd given his heart and soul to. And, most importantly, he would never put profits over people's lives.

She couldn't let Lockwood paint Mark as a cold, profit-hungry consequences-be-damned CEO. Mark might hate her, he might think she was unfit for her job, but he was none of those things.

She started back at the top of the document and went through it again, line by line. Gemma had obviously already had a go at looking up the names listed online if she'd found Freer's arrest record. And, knowing Gemma, she had dug up everything there was to find. But Letty couldn't stop herself from trying for something more that would help.

She got to the bottom of the page and started over a third time. None of the other entries seemed relevant. She ran a finger down the dates… and stopped. "Holy shit."

Letty yanked on her coat, threw money on the bar, and hurried to the front door. If Adam had been planning to meet her, he certainly would've been there by now. And what she'd found couldn't wait.

She stepped out into a freezing gust determined to push her back inside. She leaned into it, forcing her way forward until she finally made it over the threshold. The wind whipped the door from her hand and slammed it behind her.

This felt closer to a hurricane than a storm, only the wind was thick with snow and tiny biting shards of ice. She hunched over, pulling her coat tight, and keeping her face turned down. Out here, the generator was even louder, more jet engine than lawn mower. She turned the corner of the building and choked on a cloud of thick exhaust the wind whipped into her face, but it was gone in an instant. Replaced by another gust that pushed her back two steps before she could keep moving forward again.

She needed to get to the facility ASAP. Without the weather, it was a ten or fifteen minute walk, now… God help her.

Letty rounded the back of the bar, sighing at the reprieve it offered from the wind. As long as she stayed behind a building, the gale coming in off the water would be buffered enough she could make decent progress. Even without that resistance, the going was slow. The snow fell thick and wet, tugging at her boots with each step. Maybe if she stuck to the paved streets, she could at least keep herself from getting mired down? She lifted her head enough to look around, wincing at the sharp sting of ice against her cheeks.

She couldn't see any sign of where the streets might be. Snow blanketed everything, and the houses around her were too uniform for her to tell apart most days, even without the weather. It was worse tonight, because none had lights on inside. So much for that plan. The only benefit of the storm was that she was likely the only person dumb enough to go out in it. No shadow man to worry about.

She hoped.

Letty came to a gap in buildings, and, after a deep, bracing breath, she stepped out into the wind. Snow whipped around her again, so thick it hid the world behind it. She leaned into the draft, her body tilted forward at a hard slant so she could keep moving.

Her gaze caught on a flash of orange in the snow. Something big in a snow berm beyond the darkened buildings. "Hello?" She called out, but the wind captured her words, taking them away as soon as she'd uttered them. Letty slowed, closing in cautiously as the orange blob became a jacket, the dark spot beneath, a pair of legs. A body. She gasped in air so cold it stung. She knew that jacket.

Adam.

He lay face down in the snow. She let out a strangled scream and raced to his side, struggling to turn him over. Snow caked his face and stuck in his eyelashes. Blood stained the snow beneath him and ran in rivulets from his scalp and down his cheek. His eyes were open but unseeing. Still, she dug through the layers of his coat and scarf, pushing down his fleece to press her fingers to his neck.

No pulse.

His skin was unnaturally cold under her touch. He was already gone. Tears left warm trails down her cheeks. He'd been on his way to meet her when this happened.

He wouldn't have been out here if it wasn't for her.

"I'm so sorry." She brushed the snow from his face. Had he slipped on the ice? Hit his head in the fall? She got slowly to her feet, taking in the bloody scene. Something about it didn't add up. She'd found him face down. With an injury to the back of his head. Her heart dropped.

Oh my—

Something cracked against the back of her skull. Pain exploding out from the point of impact.

Her vision dimmed at the edges. She stumbled forward, falling over Adam's legs, flailing as she landed hard in the snow. Her breath whooshed out, no air left in her lungs for her to scream.

The shadow man.

A spike of pure terror crackled through her veins. She had to get out of there. Had to get away. She jerked up to her hands and knees, scrabbling forward, clawing for purchase. The ice jabbed into her palms, hard and sharp, even through her gloves. It didn't matter. Nothing did except putting distance between her and him.

Move Letty, move.

Snow crunched behind her.

"No!" She shrieked as another blow crashed into the back of her head, sending her sprawling face forward into the snow. Her head ringing, the world spinning around her, she sucked in a breath. But she couldn't make her body move. She tasted snow on her tongue. Smelled the musty tang of stale cigarettes. Felt the cold press of ice against her cheek.

And then, nothing.

CHAPTER 27

Old school Hip Hop thumped inside the research facility's onsite lab, so loud it reverberated in Mark's chest. The facility had been a hive of activity all day. People in and out of the lab. His team from the JDF, the facility's scientists, Charlie — everyone firing on all cylinders, knowing how important the work was and how little time they had to do it. Mark paced the facility's main living room, walking a circuit between the couch and the huge window looking out toward the sea.

First, there'd been the frenzied push to get his team out onto the ice. Then a whirlwind of managing the press that had been camped on the facility's doorstep when he got back from the debacle at his hotel, and, after that, straight into monitoring the weather to make sure his people stayed safe while they were out on the ice. A feat he couldn't have managed if Kath hadn't stepped in to handle the worst of the press, and the Sallow Bay mayor's office. Add to that, a particularly ill-timed call from Lockwood, demanding a date for his interview — which he'd understood, in no uncertain terms, was really an interrogation — and the day had been one of the longest of his life. Mark made another circuit and rubbed at his eyes. It did nothing to ease their grittiness or relieve the dull ache building behind them.

He'd agreed to Lockwood's preferred date without sparing more than half a minute of worry about where it would lead. Aunt Kath would have his head about agreeing to something so easily or so soon, but he had more pressing worries. He paused his pacing in front of the window and glanced back into the lab, where the two scientists who'd been working with Letty before he'd arrived were hard at work processing today's water samples.

Dr. Musa Adeyemi seemed to feel Mark's gaze. He looked up, the thick lenses of his glasses magnifying the distrustful squint he gave in return before refocusing on his work. Dismissing Mark the way he and his colleague, Dr. Becker, had been doing for most of the day. They'd been polite when Mark's team first arrived, open and professional... until they realized Letty's absence was more than a coincidence. Mark cringed.

And now that his team had gone back to their hotel, Letty's people had made themselves pointedly scarce. They might not know exactly what had gone down with Letty, but it was obvious they blamed Mark for the fact she wasn't there with them.

Which was fair.

He blamed himself. His pacing picked up tempo, a knot of regret pulling tight in the pit of his stomach. What had he done? Wind lashed at the window, ice ticking so hard against the glass it would probably be etched by tomorrow. The weather blocked any view he might have had of the surf battering the shore outside. But the storm's roar left no question it was there. Not even the pounding music coming from inside the lab could drown out what sounded like a freight train headed their way.

Except this storm was no longer coming. It had arrived. And Letty still hadn't come back to the facility.

Should he call her? He made another lap around the common room and down the hall, striding past the shared bathroom and a wall of tacked-up photographs showing only unfamiliar faces. No, that wasn't going to work... as mad as she'd been when he last saw her, she wouldn't answer anyway. Plus, this conversation seemed like one they really needed to have in person. He had spent too much time avoiding the weirdness between them since she'd come to work at the JDF. And that cowardice was half of what had gotten them in this position to begin with. They needed to clear the air and get back to a place where they could just be Mark and Letty, where they could be as comfortable as they had been before Jessa died. That had been his hope when he asked her to come on board. He had imagined them working together. Doing good together. He turned back at the end of the hall.

But then he'd gone and messed it all up somehow. Let things get awkward between them, then acted like an ass when he had come all this way, just to find Letty shacked up in some photographer's motel. He pinched the bridge of his nose, willing the headache to subside.

He glanced at his watch. Almost seven. He'd expected her to come back to the facility hours ago. Mark stopped by the open door to the women's bunk. All of Letty's things were still there. Her suitcase spilling over in the bunk room, her bed unmade. A soft depression in the pillow where she'd lain her head. He had the irrational urge to go in and touch it.

What's wrong with me?

He went back to the common room, picking up the same well-tread path he'd been pacing before between the couch and the window. He'd thought, after she cooled down, she would come back, even if just to pack up her things. It wasn't like there were that many other places for her to go in Sallow Bay. And that would have given him a chance to talk things through with her. To make her understand that he hadn't been blaming her for what had happened or questioning her abilities. No matter how bad what he'd said had sounded, that wasn't what he'd meant.

Ice ticked hard against the plate-glass beside him.

He scrubbed a hand though his hair. He'd let his personal feelings color his reaction. He knew she was a grown woman, a brilliant scientist, and really an all-around badass. But she was also Jessa's sister. And he couldn't stop thinking of her as someone he needed to protect. Never mind the fact that she and Jessa had been taking care of themselves long before they'd been adults; their parents were hardly worthy of the title. Never explicitly cruel or abusive, but they had only been there for their daughters when it fit into their lifestyle. When they weren't off on some half-cocked retreat or pilgrimage of "self-discovery." They were the perfect picture of loving neglect.

And with Jessa gone, he'd felt like the only person left who could take care of Letty. Like she was his little sister, rather than Jessa's.

He grimaced. Letty wasn't his goddamn little sister. That wasn't what he felt for her, and he knew it. But he couldn't go there. It had only been a year and a half since Jessa died, which didn't seem long enough for him to have feelings toward anyone else.

And, shit, was there ever a time when it was okay to have feelings for your fiancé's sister? He let his hand rest on the rings under his shirt.

No. There wasn't.

And yet, somehow, despite knowing that in his bones, he'd made an ass of himself. Seeing Letty with that handsy photographer had pushed him past the point of reason. Made him say things he didn't mean.

He'd had no right to draw conclusions or pass judgment on whatever she chose to do. Or whoever she chose to do it with. The ache behind his eyes grew into a persistent throb. What mattered was that he'd done something stupid, and he needed to fix it.

But she hadn't come back.

Maybe she wasn't coming back.

He couldn't text her, could he? That would be too much. Too… inappropriate. He was her boss, and that was all he was going to let himself be. Another angry gust of wind smacked against the window. Letty was probably with the photographer again anyway. Adam had left the facility as soon as they'd returned from the ice. He hadn't said where he was going, but Mark could guess. The two of them were probably back in Adam's hotel room now. His hands curled into fists. "Fuck."

Mark slumped onto the couch. A small shipping box resting on the center cushion tipped toward him. It had the foundation's address scrawled on top, but it hadn't been sealed closed. He lifted one of the flaps, peering in at what looked like a case file. He skimmed the top page. A preliminary incident report filed by one of the responding officers at the Katmai attack. Nothing he hadn't seen before. He shuffled absently through a few more pages of similar, official-looking documents. Crawford's file.

Letty must have finally been packing it up to send to the JDF when the tide had diverted her attention.

Or something else had.

He bristled but pushed the thought of what exactly that "something else" might be away, thumbing through the file without really seeing anything. There wasn't much to see. The details set out in the file were gruesome, yes. But he knew most of them already, and the documents' most striking feature was the lack of any annotation. Every page remained clean. They held none of the notes he was used to seeing in the margins of the JDF case files he reviewed.

"Weird." He sifted to the bottom of the box, his interest piqued. The last document was of a different size and style than the others, the paper thinner and worn around the edges. Not a copy of some official report or site map. A note. He squinted down at it.

He knew that hand-writing.

Knew the signature at the bottom.

The hair rose on the back of his neck as he read the message again, his fingers tracing over the familiar crabbed scrawl: "I can't be the man you need… Know that I will love you both always."

There was only one reason for Crawford to have it.

Mark dropped the paper, his throat going tight.

Oh my God.

CHAPTER 28

An icy, unwelcome breath tickled loose strands of Letty's hair across the nape of her neck. She shifted, her limbs heavy and her eyelids heavier. She wanted to stay asleep, to rest, to be somewhere the throbbing pain in the back of her skull couldn't find her.

The breath came again. Freezing cold and, this time, wet. She swatted at it, her eyes fluttering open to find nothing but a haze of impenetrable white-gray. Snow as far as she could see, covering every surface, thick as fog in the air. She lay half-covered in it, her arms and legs stiff from cold, painful as she rolled to her back and eased up into a sitting position. What the hell had happened? She explored her scalp with her fingertips, wincing when she found the source of the hurt. She had a knot, and a small gash, but nothing that felt like it'd need stitches. Still, when she pulled her hand away, blood wet the fingers of her glove.

She stared at it, black-red in the dim glow of the moonlight, remembering. She'd been looking for Mark, found Adam in the snow, and then… and then…

Letty burst to her feet, the world canting under her. She stumbled, the pounding in her head doubling as she turned in a circle — searching for Adam, searching for signs of the shadow man. But there was nothing. Or, at least, nothing she could see beyond the snow swirling around her, so thick it obliterated the rest of the world. Its claustrophobic sameness pressed in on her from all sides. Making it hard for her to breathe, to think. She turned again, but her head seemed two steps behind, a jarring, woozy mess, and she fell again, landing hard on her butt in an icy patch of snow. Another stab of pain flared across the back of her head, and her vision blurred, but, this time, with tears.

What if the man was there, waiting, watching, just far enough away that she couldn't see him? Her heart pounded in her chest as her mind raced.

Or what if she hadn't been attacked at all? What if she'd fallen and hit her head? Or suffered some form of neurologic damage from exposure to the algae? She blinked back the tears, her mouth going bone dry.

Could she have imagined Adam's body?

No way.

She knew what she'd seen, what she'd felt. The orange flash of Adam's jacket in the snowdrift. The unnatural chill of his skin beneath her fingertips. The agonizing crack of something hard against the back of her head. But if she'd seen what she had, why wasn't Adam there? Could he have come to while she'd been out and gone to find help? Or had he woken hurt and confused, like she had, and wandered out alone into the storm?

That seemed so much more likely. She couldn't imagine him leaving her there, any more than she would've left him. "Adam?" She called out, but the storm muted her words. Everything muffled by the snow around her. She turned in another slow circle, this time careful not to go so fast she made herself dizzy again. But she couldn't see anything beyond the puff of her own breath, and no one answered.

She needed to get help. Now.

She patted her pants and jacket, searching for the hard outline of her phone.

Her wallet and keys were right where she'd left them, but her cell definitely wasn't. She yanked down her coat's zipper, bracing at the sudden rush of cold that swirled in underneath as she dug through every pocket of the oversized JDF parka.

Like freaking cargo pants. So many damn pockets.

But still no phone.

"Fuck." Could she have dropped it when she got knocked out? Maybe it had skittered away somewhere, probably covered by the steady fall of snow while she'd been unconscious. She couldn't have been out long, or she would've frozen to death. But at the rate the snow was coming down, it wouldn't take long for something so small to get buried.

She scanned the ground by her feet, kicking at the accumulated drifts. But it was like searching the beach for a lost stone. The phone could be anywhere, and there was only so much time she could waste looking for it. She worked what turned out to be a chunk of ice free with the toe of her boot. "Shit." She stopped with a shiver.

What if the shadow man had taken her cell with him?

Either way, it didn't matter now. If she couldn't call for help, she'd have to go find some. Letty zipped her jacket and huffed hot air into her hands. The real question was where to find someone. The few lights she could make out were nothing but a dull glow in the distance. The storm had left the landscape so uniform, she couldn't tell north from south, which would be less of a problem if she'd thought to stuff her compass into her pocket. Only the bootprints scattering the ground around her gave her any sense of direction at all.

The relentless fall of snow had softened even the deepest of the prints, but she had no doubt they weren't all hers. She took a slow breath in and scanned the ground as far out as she could see. Two, or maybe three, sets of prints extended off into the distance to her right. One set trailed off to the left. One must be hers, one Adam's. The other, her attacker's. But all were too indistinct now for her to tell if the person who'd made them was coming or going. And given their poor quality, she couldn't even say for certain each set was only made by one person. It would've been easy for her attacker to trace back over their bootprints as they left.

She turned again in a slow circle, searching the swirling abyss for anything that might tell her which way to go, but there were no landmarks to find. She couldn't even make out the moon. The snow both blocked out and amplified its glow, the night as bright as an overcast afternoon. Which made the few lights from town even harder to see. But they were there. A few scattered to either side of her.

Letty set off toward the brightest of the bunch, a series clustered together beyond the single set of prints. Her body ached with each step, stiff with the cold and bruised from her fall. She rubbed at the knot on the back of her head but made herself keep going. The road had long-since been lost to the snow. She couldn't tell if she was still on it, much less which one it might be. But where there were lights, there was power still on, and that meant people. That meant help. She looked back to where Adam had lain in the snow, with a wash of unease.

Her boot sunk into the snow with her next step, her back wrenching as she stepped into some sort of hidden depression in the ground. A ditch or a gulley? She had no way to know. Letty fought her way through it, her breath coming heavy. Adam had been coming to see her when he'd gotten hurt. All while she'd been warm and safe, sitting on a bar stool being pissed at him for not showing up. She scraped her teeth over her bottom lip, hard enough to tear the skin. And now he was out here somewhere, alone, hurt, and probably confused. Her foot slid out from under her, a hidden patch of ice yanking her off balance. She jerked out her arms, finding her footing. Barely avoiding another fall and tasting blood in her mouth.

She made herself focus on her feet. One in front of the other, she watched where she stepped, careful not to trip over any half-concealed debris. She matched her steps to the tempo of the pounding in her head. The further she went, the more the wind picked up. Both a blessing and a curse. It pressed against her but also made it easier to see, sweeping the snow from the air. And the lights were definitely getting brighter, closer. She stumbled forward, and the marina came into view. The wind blew even stronger here, enough to clear her view entirely.

A man worked to pull a boat from the water. Something he should've done hours ago, before the storm had hit. The moron was going to get himself killed. Even if the storm hadn't been battering the coast, the water itself had become a danger.

She hurried her pace, putting her head down as she walked into the wind. She glanced up. The man wasn't pulling the boat out but putting it in. She slowed her steps. That made no sense. Why would anyone go out in a storm like this? Whatever his reason, he obviously didn't know about the algal bloom. In the dark, he probably couldn't see that the water was discolored.

He didn't know that even now, he waded ankle deep in something that could kill him.

She opened her mouth to call out but let the warning die on her lips.

The man loaded a series of small, yellow packages into the boat's prow. Plastic wrapped tubes of… something. Drugs?

He bent down, hefted something heavy from the ground, and tossed what turned out to be a fat duffel bag over the gunnel. He shifted to adjust his cargo, moving just enough for her to see the body in the bright orange jacket laying on the ground behind him.

Letty's hands flew to her mouth, barely stopping her gasp. Adam lay sprawled in the snow. And if she'd had any delusion he was still alive, she didn't now. Something about the way he lay there left no question in her mind: Adam was gone.

Panic fluttered up through her chest and fizzed across her skin.

This was no fisherman. This was the shadow man. She backed up, slowly. Not wanting to draw the man's attention. He'd killed Adam, tried to kill her and was now preparing to do what? Dispose of his body?

He must've carried Adam here, planned to come back for her.

If she hadn't woken up when she did…

Her body flashed hot, then cold. Every muscle spring-tight. Her breath sawing in and out, so loud she couldn't hear herself think beyond the overwhelming need to get away. Letty scrambled back, her boots sliding in the snow. She was only three or four blocks from the police station. If she could just—

The man turned toward her.

The marina's emergency lights shone down onto his face. The sickly yellow glow lighting up features she knew.

Crawford.

CHAPTER 29

Letty gaped as the man rounded the back of what she now recognized as the skin boat she'd seen at Charlie's shop. The bow bobbed in a foamy surf that crashed and receded from shore, as if it was shrinking away from him. She did a double-take, her mind at first refusing to accept what she was seeing. But she would know Crawford anywhere. She had spent hours looking up everything she could find about him online. Staring at his photo on the JDF website, worrying about what had become of him.

And here he was. Not dead, not missing. Stalking toward her in long strides that seemed to eat the distance between them. Almost nine hundred miles from where he'd last been seen in Katmai.

With Adam's body at his feet.

The wind whipped over the water and landed an icy slap to her face, breaking through the jumbled buzz in her head. She jerked backward, scrambling to put space between her and Crawford. As much as she didn't understand what was going on, the animosity coming off of him was unquestionable.

"Dr. Duquesne." He stopped a few yards away. Even with his voice raised to be heard over the wind, he said her name like he was savoring the taste of the words. "Nice of you to save me the trip back."

The words hit her like another slap. Confirmation of what she already feared — if she hadn't woken when she did, he'd have come back and finished the job. Not that she'd helped herself much. She'd gotten free of the web only to offer herself up to the spider.

He reached under his jacket and pulled something from the waistband of his snow pants.

A gun.

Letty stifled a gasp, and her fear became a living, breathing thing. Too big for her to control. The frantic thump of her heart, like an animal trying to claw its way out of her chest. "What do you want?"

Crawford's face gave nothing away as he came even closer, pointing the weapon at her.

She fought the urge to run. She wouldn't get far. Not with the gun trained on her and his finger already on the trigger. "Why are you doing this?"

"You didn't give me a choice." His face hardened. "You just keep ruining things for everyone else. Like my brother."

"Your... brother?" Letty's hand drifted to the knot on the back of her head. She'd been off since he'd hit her, her head woozy. But even under the best of circumstances, she was damn sure none of this would make sense. Hadn't Gemma said Crawford was an only child? And what the hell did his brother have to do with anything?

"Always peacocking around." He muttered under his breath, and she almost didn't catch what he'd said over the roar of the wind and sea. He flicked the gun toward the water. "Let's go."

She looked out at the empty, roiling waves, then back at him. "Go?" There was nowhere to go. The closest towns were Barrow or Prudhoe Bay, and both were miles beyond where one tank of gas in an outboard motor could take them. Especially with the storm slowing them down.

Crawford gestured the gun toward the boat again. His mouth made a thin, grim line.

She made herself start moving toward what could only be a death sentence. She'd skipped right over "don't let them take you to a secondary location" and signed herself up for a boat ride to nowhere, in a blizzard, with a gun-toting murderer. Letty swallowed hard. "You don't have to do this."

He laughed, the sound as cold as the ice beneath her feet. "It wasn't like I didn't warn you. Didn't tell you over and over again to just go home. But you wouldn't, would you?"

She grimaced. He wasn't wrong. She hadn't listened to the threat on her windshield or the bullet on her pillow. Hadn't been scared off when he'd attacked her or chased her through town. She was only here because she had refused to give up and go away. And she'd make the same choice if she had to do it all again. The day she stopped fighting was the day her life was no longer worth living.

"Should have just left me alone," he said with a grunt.

Left him alone? This was all because she had tried to figure out what had happened to him? That made no sense at all. She stopped by the boat's stern, turning to ask for more of an explanation. But Crawford still had the gun trained on her, and the look on his face told her not to bother.

"What now?" She finally asked.

Crawford glanced behind her and pursed his lips, his eyes narrowed in thought. "The jacket. Take it off him." He nodded in Adam's direction as he stripped out of his own coat. He traded the gun from one hand to the other as he pulled off each sleeve, keeping the weapon pointed at the center of her chest. Then threw his jacket into the boat. "Now."

This fucker was straight crazy. But what else could she do?

Nothing.

She turned to Adam, a sticky film of panic sweat breaking across her skin. The idea of touching him when he was like this, taking something from him, felt impossibly wrong. Crawford must have sensed her hesitation, because he advanced on her. His boots crunched sharp in the snow, a promise of violence that finally forced her into action. Tears welled back in her eyes, and she pushed down a whimper as she unzipped Adam's coat and eased it off him, the thickness of her gloves making everything harder.

I'm so sorry, Adam.

Sorry for everything.

Once she had finally worked the jacket free, she tossed it toward Crawford.

He put it on, using the same awkward process he'd done before, shifting the gun hand to hand as he dressed, never taking it off her. He looked down at himself and pulled up the hood. "That'll do it." He was several inches shorter than Adam, but from a distance, there would be no way to tell them apart.

What the hell is he up to?

Crawford zipped the jacket. It barely closed. He might be shorter than Adam, but he was heavily muscled. Strong enough he'd been able to haul Adam to the marina. Strong enough Letty would have no chance against him if he attacked her. Which was beginning to look less like an if and more like a when.

Crawford gestured with the gun. "Now get him into the boat."

"You want me to— " How the hell was she supposed to do that? Adam had to outweigh her by sixty pounds or more. "What?"

"I'd offer to help, but... my hands are full." He waggled the gun at her and smiled, the expression slippery and awful.

It took Letty five or six tries and, by the time she had Adam in the boat, she was sweating inside her jacket, the pounding in her head had doubled, and one of her shoulders radiated an excruciating ache from where she had overextended it. She rubbed at the joint.

"Get in." He commanded.

She hated doing as he said but couldn't see any other option. Letty climbed inside, sitting as far from Adam's body as she could get. He lay crumpled toward the back of the boat, his legs splayed over the middle seat. She didn't want to see him like this. Didn't want to think of how his body had looked and felt as she'd hefted it on board, his skin tinged blue, his limbs now rigid with cold. Or maybe rigor mortis. She had no way to know how long she'd been knocked out or how long he'd been dead. Letty shuddered.

She couldn't think of Adam now. If she let Crawford take her out to sea, she wasn't coming back. Which meant she needed to do something now to get control of the situation.

The boat wobbled as Crawford pushed them one-handed from shore and climbed in behind her, dividing his attention between her and trying to start the motor. If she was going to have a chance to get the upper hand, this was it.

But how? She didn't have anything she could use as a weapon. Especially with the gun's eye still staring right at her. She scanned the inside of the boat, trying not to let her gaze rest too long on Adam. Crawford's duffel was too far for her to reach, and even if she could get into it, there was no way for her to know if she'd find anything useful inside.

She eyed the plastic wrapped bricks she had seen Crawford load into the prow. Now that she was closer, they looked less like bricks and more like tubes of some sort. Wrapped in a yellow oiled paper, the writing so small she had to lean closer to make it out: "Trinitrotoluene." What the hell was that? She squinted down at the fine print. "Explosive. Danger. Explosif."

Holy shit.

Crawford wasn't transporting drugs. The packages lining the front of the boat were TNT. The blood drained from her face, as the engine kicked on, and, after a brief lull, the boat powered out into the water. Letty held on tight, her grip slipping with the ocean spray coating everything. Her lips, her face, her hair. Everything slick with whatever poison now lived in the surf.

Even if she escaped whatever Crawford had planned, she was covered in the stuff. It could kill her, or maybe just drive her mad. And she wasn't sure which of those possibilities was more terrifying. The boat smacked against the water, jarring her bones, clacking her teeth together. She clamped her mouth closed to keep from biting her tongue as Crawford steered them out to sea, one hand on the tiller, the other holding firm to the gun. Realization prickled across her skin.

She knew exactly where they were going.

Stafford Oil's drilling rig was just off-shore, hidden behind the fog of snow. And they were heading right for it.

With a boat full of explosives.

She gripped the gunnel tighter, even inside her gloves, her fingers had gone so cold they were numb. Her mind flew through everything she knew, trying to make it make sense. The boat slammed down over another wave, and a memory flickered to the surface of her consciousness. Avalanche-control. Gemma had said Crawford worked on a ski resort, managing the risk of avalanches, which would mean explosives. Which explained how Crawford might've gotten them. And, more importantly, meant he'd know how to use them.

Shit.

That realization sucked the last of her breath from her body. He was going to blow it up. Going to kill all the people who were living and working on the rig. How many would that be? Fifty, maybe sixty souls doing nothing but their jobs, with no idea of what was coming for them?

She couldn't let that happen. Even if it meant she never made it back to shore.

"What... fuck!" A voice carried out over the sea, muted by the roar of the motor and the pounding of the hull against the waves.

Letty whipped around in her seat.

Odele stood on the shore, scissoring her arms over her head. "Get back...!" The rest of her words got lost to the wind and pounding surf.

"He's going to blow up the rig." Letty yelled at the top of her lungs, pointing toward where she thought the rig was hidden behind the snow. She tented her hands around her mouth, praying her words could reach shore. "You've got to warn—" The boat lurched forward as Crawford gave it full power, tossing Letty backward. She landed hard, her head cracking against the gunnel, her shoulder bouncing painfully off the middle seat. A wave of nauseating pain rolled out from the shoulder, she clutched at the joint, moaning as she rolled off of it. Only to find herself inches from Adam's cold, unseeing eyes.

She yelped, trying to push herself up. But her left arm wouldn't move. Something cold and hard pushed into the top of her head, forcing her onto her stomach. Crawford held the gun to her scalp, point blank. She twisted to look at him.

He sneered back. "Stay down."

.   ∎   ∎

The drilling rig's substructure loomed above the boat, casting the water below a deep fathomless black. Letty leaned over the side, trying not to lose sight of Adam's body as it slipped beneath the inky waves. As if keeping her eyes on him would make him any less gone. No matter how hard she stared, the faint outline of Adam's outstretched arms faded away, like a ghost in the darkness. Even knowing how pointless it would be, she fought the urge to dive in after him, her heart echoing a hollow beat of loss and blame.

"Why are you doing this?" She asked Crawford again, turning to him with her bad arm cradled against her chest. Her words came out thick, as much from the fact that she'd helped put Adam in the water as from the throbbing pain radiating out from her shoulder. She didn't expect Crawford to answer. He'd hardly spoken to her since they'd seen Odele, who was probably back at the bar telling anyone who would listen that Letty and Adam had stolen the skin boat.

The frustration of not understanding what was going on, why she was here, what Crawford wanted… it made her want to scream. But she'd already tried that once, calling for help when they'd first motored close enough she thought someone might see or hear them. And all she'd gotten was a backhand for her trouble. Anyone manning the rig was probably too far above them to hear anything happening below, especially over the noise of the storm.

She rubbed the bruise on her cheek. That scream had landed her back on the boat's bottom, where Crawford held her at gunpoint while he had done whatever he'd come to do with the explosives. He'd only ordered her to get back up when he had needed help getting Adam over the side — not that she was much of that with her dislocated arm useless and screaming in pain. All she could tell then was that the explosives no longer lined the front of the boat. She stared up into the dark recesses of the substructure. Where the hell were they? It only made sense he'd planted them somewhere. But she couldn't see any sign of them.

"Couldn't be helped." Crawford's voice startled her attention back to him. "It was hard enough losing my mother before I found out who killed her." His breathing got heavier, his words spilling out all at once. "Something like that can't go unanswered. Things need to be made right... he took away the one person I ever loved who loved me back. It's only fair I do the same to him. Even if he's not here to see it."

"I don't—" Letty shook her head. Hadn't his mother died from cancer? "I don't understand. I'm so sorry you lost your mom, but what does any of that have to do with me or with Adam?"

His face turned an ugly red. "I didn't lose her. She was taken from me." He blew out a breath as if to calm himself. "I won't let a photo tip my hand before I can burn the whole thing down." He turned back toward the motor, and it roared to life.

A photo? She hunched against the wind as Crawford steered them back out to sea. What the hell was he talking about? Clearly his mother's death had caused him to have some sort of mental breakdown. The boat slammed into a brutal wave, and the impact sent her flying. Her jaw smacked together, her tongue catching between her teeth. She tasted the tang of blood but ignored it as she gripped the rough edges of her seat, holding on for dear life. Only one possibility really made sense. Adam had captured something on film he hadn't been meant to. Which wasn't surprising given that he was always taking photos, snapping candids wherever they were — in town, on the ice, even in the hotel last night. He wouldn't have missed the chance to document the storm coming in.

He had probably gotten a shot of Crawford doing something in Sallow Bay without even knowing what he'd captured on film. And chances were, no one would have ever noticed or cared. If Crawford himself hadn't.

She gripped the seat even harder, her knuckles turning white. That accident had meant the end of Adam's life. She looked up at the night sky, trying to blink away tears. Maybe the end of hers, too. She had no idea why she was even still alive. Whatever Crawford had planned would surely be easier with her dead, too. She shivered from the thought as much as the damp, leeching cold. Every slap of the boat sent up an icy spray. Clouds shifted to cover the moon, like the lid of a coffin sliding closed. She shut her eyes against the wind, listening as the waves beat a relentless tempo against the keel. She kept her feet braced, her hands clenched, every muscle in her body focused on one task: Don't let go.

Because if she did, if she got thrown out into the freezing Arctic water, the madness that followed wouldn't matter. She'd freeze to death in minutes. Her mind conjured the image of Adam disappearing under the waves, lost to the sea. Like Jessa. She forced the image that sprang to mind away. Her sister sinking through the waves. That wouldn't be her; it couldn't be.

"Here we are then." Crawford cut the motor, the boat coasting to a stop, leaving them in a sudden silence but for the howl of the wind and the slap of water against the boat's sides.

She looked around. They were nowhere. At least a hundred yards from the rig and too far from shore for her to see any sign of it. Her teeth chattered in the cold. "What?"

He flicked the gun toward the water. "In you go."

"What?" She asked again, louder this time, panic clawing its way up her throat.

"All you have to do is swim to the rig and wait for help to arrive." He said it like it was nothing. Like he'd offered the perfect solution, and she was just too dim to see it.

"We both know there's no way I'd make it." Not with her arm dislocated and the water thirty degrees, at best. She'd either drown or die from hypothermia. And that was before she took the explosives into account. "If you'd planned to kill me all along, why didn't you just toss me overboard with Adam?"

He hesitated, and she wasn't sure he would bother giving her answer. But, finally, he gave a deep, exasperated sigh. "You weren't exactly going to go quietly, were you? It's unlikely anyone on the rig would hear, but why take that chance? Especially if you needed... motivation." He wagged the gun again and shrugged. "This spot is far away the sound won't travel, and it works just as well."

Shit, he was right. A gunshot would be loud. And something told her he didn't really want to use the gun either way. If he did, he would have already. Bullets left evidence behind. Ballistics and — if he'd been dumb enough not to wear gloves when he'd loaded the gun — DNA. And, maybe even more than that, a gunshot wound wouldn't fit the narrative he was trying to create. He'd put on Adam's coat to make sure anyone who saw them would think Adam had been driving her out toward the rig. He had dropped Adam's body there to be found amongst the wreckage. And now, it seemed he planned to leave hers nearby. As if the two of them had set the explosives, either intending to die in the blast or mistiming it so that they'd missed their chance to escape.

"Okay, all right." She got to her feet. She had no doubt he'd shoot her if he had to, but, if he had other plans...

He might hesitate to pull the trigger.

She pretended to stumble, her good arm jutting out for balance as she staggered closer to his end of the boat. A few more steps, and she'd be within reach of the gun. "Whoa..." She took another big step forward, bridging one foot over the boat's middle seat. "Hard to get a good footing."

He narrowed his eyes at her, tilting his head toward the water. "That's far enough, I—"

A siren yelped out over the water, and Letty whipped around, this time stumbling for real, her knee knocking against the center seat. The boat rocked under her as red and blue lights flashed in the distance. A garbled voice floated out over the water, its edges made rough and staticky by a bullhorn. "Stay where you are… police."

Letty wilted into herself, the relief so palpable she could taste it. But she wasn't free yet. Her only hope was to throw herself at him. To try and get control of the gun. Her chances were better in the boat, even with a gunshot wound. At least the police could find her there. She braced herself and turned to Crawford, ready to do whatever she needed to.

But he hadn't moved.

He had his eyes pressed closed and one hand tucked inside his now open jacket. His lips moved in some silent prayer or mantra.

The realization of what he was doing spider-crawled its way up her spine. "No—"

A blast of noise and fire and heat rolled across the water, knocking her off-kilter. And over the edge. She had an instant to process what was happening, a split second as she flew through the air when she knew what was coming, but she had no way to stop it.

She crashed into the icy waves. Plunged beneath the surface. The underwater world silent, black, and freezing. She gasped in the sudden cold, and the water rushed in with her breath.

She kicked hard, pushing to the surface, where she coughed and spat out the salty, nasty water. Trying not to think about what toxins she might be ingesting as she fought against the ocean's pull, trying to tread with just her feet and her good arm.

She forced her head above water. The surface looked like hell on Earth. Nothing but flame and destruction. One side of the rig creaked, metal shrieking against metal in an ear-splitting scream as the massive structure collapsed in on itself. There were people inside that structure, and she was likely watching as they died. But she couldn't focus on any of it. Not then.

Not when she had to save herself.

The snowsuit and boots that had helped keep her safe from the cold were absolutely deadly in the water. Sodden and heavy, they pulled her down as effectively as if she'd been wrapped in weighted chains. She had to get it all off. Her left arm blared with pain as she fought the jacket while trying to keep herself afloat and failed. Maybe if she had two working arms, she could unzip herself and peel out of her layers. But there was no chance of that now. She could barely keep her head above water.

She bobbed under. Once, twice. She could do this. She would do this. She kicked her feet harder. But every effort met more resistance than the last. Her body tiring, her muscles already fatiguing in the freezing water. Still, she forced herself up and gasped for air, searching for the boat. For the police. For Crawford.

The outboard motor roared to life behind her.

She spun toward the sound. Crawford must have held on to the boat somehow, despite the explosion. Knowing it was coming maybe giving him time to prepare. She tread in the wake, her arm screaming in pain as he raced away, disappearing into a growing plume of smoke. The police would surely follow the boat, and it would be too late by the time they realized she wasn't on it. Her only chance for survival, gone.

"Fuck!" She sobbed and sucked in a mouthful of water, forcing herself to keep kicking her legs, to keep afloat. Her shoulder screamed, her good arm ached from doing the work of two, and she shivered so hard it hurt.

Still, she forced her good arm through the water, again and again. Even though her body was becoming painfully heavy, so heavy half of her couldn't tell if her legs were moving anymore or if she was just imagining they were. Shit. She didn't even know what she was swimming toward. What was left of the rig was in flames, the boat gone, the police nowhere to be seen. The snow picked up again, ice pelting her face every time she managed to rise above the waves. Scouring her skin. She was freezing in a ball of fire. Or so it seemed. Flames shot into the sky, the inferno popping and roaring.

The fire reflected across the ocean's surface as if the whole thing was ablaze. But it was too far away to give her any actual warmth. Another series of pops in the distance, a roar of what she prayed was a boat engine but was probably just the rig consuming itself. Her head went under again, and everything went silent.

She kicked back up, and this time it took every bit of effort she had to clear the surface. To draw in one more breath. Just one more.

At least, it didn't hurt as much anymore. Not really. The shivering had finally abated. She'd gone numb. Even the pain in her arm seemed to recede, which made everything easier. She bobbed under again and didn't fight as hard to come back up as she had before. She was so tired. Everything was so hard. Too hard to keep fighting, when it wasn't a battle she could win.

She'd be gone soon. Lost at sea.

She and Jessa finally together again, in a way. Almost like something that was meant to be. Letty's head dipped under the waves, and this time, she didn't kick back up.

She let herself sink. The surface a glitter of fiery red, just out of reach.

CHAPTER 30

October 27, 2018
Sallow Bay, Alaska
Something growled.

Letty tensed, listening. The low rumble was like a warning she couldn't heed. Not when she wasn't there. Not really. She'd retreated somewhere far away from the ache of her body, in a floating dull nothingness where she was safe and at peace.

Generator.

The word came to her unbidden. An echo of some other time and place. The bar. She grimaced, pushing away the memory. She wanted desperately to go away again. To escape the headache pounding behind her eyes, the ache in her throat, the throb in her shoulder. But it was too late. The pain caught her and anchored her there, where each inhale came short and dry, and her lungs burned.

She tried to force in a deeper breath, but a sharp pang flared between her ribs, stopping her mid-inhale. Like someone had stabbed her with a pin knife.

She went to press a hand to the ache.

Her arm wouldn't move.

She cracked an eye and blinked the world into focus. Darkness shrouded everything outside the cast of a single light above her head. It was both too bright for her sensitive eyes and too weak to illuminate much of anything. A sling held her left arm to her chest. She lay in a bed with rails, and she had an IV attached to her good arm. She must be in a hospital or a clinic?

How the hell had she gotten here?

She closed her eyes again, trying to remember things that, now, only came back in shards. Adam face down in the snow. The rig consumed with flames. The boat disappearing into the smoke, leaving her to die. Her heart pounded, and she gasped. Or tried to. Pain flared again across her chest, and Letty curled into herself, the IV tugging against her arm.

Something shuffled in the darkness beyond the light's glow.

Her eyes flew open wide, her heart galloping in her chest. "Who's there?" She sat up, ignoring how much it hurt as she gripped the sheet to her chest. She searched the edges of the darkness.

"Just me." Kathryn shifted into the light. She pulled a battered chair to the side of Letty's bed and sat. "I'm so glad to see you're awake."

"What? Where am I?" Letty blinked the sleep from her eyes. "How are you here?"

"In a clinic, still in Sallow Bay. I came up with Mark. We left as soon as we saw the news about the tide. Even with the jet, it took all night, but we made it."

Letty let herself sink back onto the bed, the unclenching of her muscles hurting almost as much as sitting up had. No matter how badly their last conversation had gone, Letty couldn't be sorry Kathryn was there. She needed answers. And anything was better than being alone.

Kathryn poured a cup of water from a pitcher on the bedside table and handed it to Letty, canting the bendy straw toward Letty's mouth. "The doctor says breathing will hurt for a while. After nearly drowning, your lungs will be sore."

Nearly drowning.

Letty's skin went cold as the rest of what had happened came back, all at once. The explosion, the icy-shock as she'd crashed into the water. The suffocating, claustrophobic quiet as it had closed in around her. Her hands shook so hard, she sloshed water out of the cup, splattering the sleeve of her hospital gown. "How did I—?"

Kathryn steadied the cup, holding it so Letty could take another drink. "Your friend raised the alarm."

Letty blinked in confusion, closed one eye, and looked at Kathryn through the other. "My friend?"

"I believe her name was Odele."

Letty definitely had a concussion.

Kathryn shrugged. "She called the police as soon as she saw you by the marina, but it took time to get the boats out. Given the weather. You were lucky they got there when they did. If one of the police officers hadn't seen you go in, there's no way they would've gotten to you in time."

Lucky.

She didn't feel lucky. She had almost died. She'd been submerged in toxic water. Ingested it. And there was no way to know how it might affect her. Would an acute exposure like hers have the same effect as the long-term exposure had on the fisherman? Would she lose her mind and kill the people she loved? Tears burned behind her eyes. And that wasn't even the worst of it. "How many people died in the explosion?"

Kathryn's thin brows furrowed. "Thirteen, either confirmed dead or... missing." She grimaced as she said the word. If the missing hadn't been found yet, in those conditions, they were obviously dead. But Kathryn had the tact not to say it. She tucked an icy blonde strand of hair behind her ear, a diamond stud glinting in the overhead light. "It's tragic. But really, it could have been so much worse. We've already notified the insurance carrier. We're in the off-season, so the rig wasn't operational. There's no sign of any leaks or spills, and we only had a skeleton crew manning the rig. Most of the workers had already come onshore in advance of the storm."

Letty knew she should be able to feel grateful more lives hadn't been lost, for the fact that the explosion hadn't caused the environmental catastrophe it might have, but all she felt was rage. So many people dead, and for what? Letty made herself take another drink of the water. It hurt like hell going down. She handed the cup back to Kathryn, harder than she intended. "Thanks." She softened her voice. None of this was Kathryn's fault.

Even if she had been a bitch the last time they spoke.

Kathryn nodded as she put the cup on the bedside table, where Letty could reach it. Then turned back and hesitated before she asked, "What happened out there?"

Letty suddenly wished she had the cup of water back. Her mouth went bone dry. She still had more questions than answers, but she did her best to explain. She had to close her eyes to keep tears from falling as she went through the whole thing in as much detail as she could remember. Adam, the boat, the rig, the explosives. She had to be able to get through it. She'd have to make a statement to the police. This was good. A test run.

She steeled herself and kept going. "After I fell in, Crawford took off in the boat. I couldn't see which way he went, the smoke was too thick by then, and I could barely keep my head above water, and—"

"You're sure it was Crawford?" Kathryn's question cut in.

Letty had to clear the lump from her throat before she could answer. "Positive."

Kathryn rubbed a hand across her forehead, probably trying to figure out how Stafford Oil was going to handle that PR nightmare. "Did he say why he did it?"

"He didn't say much." Letty shrugged, and her shoulder twinged. But it didn't hurt nearly as much as it had before she'd passed out. Someone must've popped it into place while she'd been unconscious. "And what he did say made no sense. Something about his mother having been killed and him being on some quest to destroy what her killer loved. But I don't know what any of that has to do with blowing up the rig." A lump rose in her throat. "I think I know why he killed Adam, though. It sounded like he'd accidentally caught Crawford on film." A lump rose in her throat. "I don't think we'll know the whole story of what else Crawford was up to until the cops catch him."

Kathryn sat back in the chair. "He's dead."

"What?"

"I just overheard one of the officers talking about someone who shot at the police after the explosion. A man fleeing the scene in a small boat." Kathryn said. "They returned fire, and the shooter didn't make it."

Either she'd been wrong about his willingness to use the gun… or he'd seen no other option, in the end. How close had she gotten to getting herself killed? She rubbed a hand across the lump on the back of her head. Her scalp was still bruised and tender but didn't hurt nearly as much as the pounding inside her skull.

Kathryn leaned forward again, her hands clasped on her knees. "Did he say anything else?"

"Not really. Something about his brother? Nothing that made sense." She wished he had. Right now, none of what had happened fit any logical explanation she could come up with. Kathryn was probably thinking the same thing. She was going to have to face the press with no real answer for what had happened or why.

Kathryn gave Letty's good arm a reassuring pat. "The authorities will sort it all out once the storm's passed. You've been through so much. Try not to worry about the details now. I'm sure after everything, it's overwhelming. Confusing." Kathryn lifted the cup of water from the side table, and offered it to Letty again.

Letty shook her head no. She wasn't sure she could keep it down. The headache was now bad enough to be edged with a tinge of nausea.

"Your friends came by earlier to see you. Hilde, Musa, Charlie." Kathryn put the cup back down. "They wanted to make sure you knew they'd been here. Asked you to call them when you felt up to it."

She wouldn't be calling anyone until she got a new phone. Hers was either with Crawford or buried somewhere under the mountains of snow outside. Still, Letty nodded and tried for a smile. It wilted on her face. Everyone had come, except Mark. She cleared her throat, trying to force the smile. God knew it was hypocritical for her to expect him to be there for her. After all, she had abandoned him in the hospital after Jessa died. Which was so much worse. Mark and Jessa wouldn't have been out on that boat to begin it if it wasn't for her, and instead of going to say how sorry she was, she had run away. Her nausea threatened to make good on its promise.

"I'm sure Mark will come by, too, when he can." Kathryn said, as if she'd read Letty's mind. "He's with one of the workers who was pulled from the water. The poor guy's in bad shape, but they think he's going to make it."

Heat crawled up Letty's neck. Was she that transparent? Letty cleared her throat and instantly regretted it. It felt like she'd swallowed sandpaper coated in acid.

"Anyway." Kathryn got to her feet, grabbing an oversized Birkin bag from somewhere beyond the circle of light. "I should let you get some rest." Kathryn turned away, then stopped, stepping closer again. "I want to apologize for how abrupt I was when we spoke on the phone. Mark is like a son to me, and I'm afraid I can be a little overprotective. I'm sorry if what I said was hurtful."

Letty relaxed back into the bed's papery pillows. "It's okay. I get it." And she did. Mark and Kathryn were family. It would make sense for her to have his back. "I was actually on my way to find him, when I..." found Adam dead in the snow. She swallowed a lump rising in her throat. "When everything happened." She plucked up the water cup and made herself drink it, even if it did feel like swallowing fire.

"Really?" Kathryn glanced at the door, adjusting her purse against the crook of her elbow. "That's good. I'd hoped you two would reconcile at some point."

Awkward.

"No, I mean, I found something that might help him."

"That's nice." Kathryn now had the distinctly flat smile of someone humoring a friend who claimed alien abductions were real or that bubble gum ice cream was anything other than an abomination.

Letty made herself sit up again. One of the pillows behind her tumbled over the side of the bed and onto the floor. She was making a hash of this, and it was important that Kathryn understood exactly what she'd found. There was no way to know how long she would be stuck in the hospital, without a phone. Someone needed to know. "Mark didn't do what they think he did."

"I know." Kathryn nodded. "No one who actually knows him would think he would take money from the company. It's ridiculous."

"Right. You're right. But that's not what I mean." Letty rubbed at her face, trying to wipe away the last of the fog from whatever pain medication they'd given her. She needed what she had to say to make sense. "I'm talking about the illegal dumping. He wasn't there. He wasn't in Gulfport when they say he was."

"What?" Kathryn put the bag down by her feet.

Letty made herself slow down. She still wasn't making any sense.

She ran through all the details she could remember from the chronology, being careful not to say how it had come into her hands. The last thing she wanted to do was get Gemma in more trouble than she already had. "Mark couldn't have been in Gulfport on June 17th. Whoever met with Randy Freer, it wasn't him."

Kathryn stepped closer. "Tell me."

"That's my birthday. I was in San Diego for the summer break, but Jessa was off presenting a paper at a conference she couldn't get out of." And their parents had forgotten, as usual. "Mark and Jessa's best friend came over so I wouldn't have to spend it alone." A warmth lit in her chest at the memory of them showing up with

Letty's favorite donuts and his Netflix password. The three of them had binge-watched The Vampire Diaries for hours. Him arguing Elena should be with Stefan, the girls on team Damon. Obviously. "They were both there until at least midnight, which means he couldn't have been on a flight to Gulfport that day." Letty held her breath, waiting for Kathryn's response.

Kathryn's brows drew together in a look Letty couldn't read. Skepticism?

Letty tried again. "I know it doesn't disprove everything they're accusing him of. I don't know anything about the rest of whatever they're claiming he did, but it's a start, right?" After everything she'd been through, she needed it not to be in vain. It had to have all been for... something.

"It's more than a start. Thank you for telling me." Kathryn came around the side of the bed and picked up the pillow Letty'd knocked over the side. "I'll make sure the right people know and that Mark knows you came forward about it. But for now, you need your rest."

As she came closer, Kathryn's perfume invaded her space. A spicy, expensive scent that seemed cloying and out of place in a hospital. Letty's stomach clenched.

Don't barf, don't barf.

She turned away, breathing through her mouth as Kathryn leaned over her.

Something slammed over her head. The pillow, pressing down hard.

Panic flooded her system with adrenaline. She lashed out at her good arm but couldn't see what she hit, as she struggled to get free. Only the fact that she'd turned her head meant that she could breathe. That she could think.

She went still, holding her breath. Praying Kathryn took the bait.

The pressure on the pillow held, and Letty's already painful lungs caught fire.

Could Kathryn hear the pounding of Letty's heart? See the frantic flutter of her pulse in her wrist? Her lungs constricted, the need to breathe growing impatient, urgent.

Come on.

Don't breathe.

Was her pulse monitored by some device Kathryn could see? Letty couldn't feel leads on her chest, but would she? They could be there without her knowing. But she didn't hear any telltale beeps from nearby.

The urge to fill her lungs became overwhelming, irresistible.

Don't do it.

"I'm sorry it came to this." Kathryn said, her voice muffled by the pillow. She slowly released the pressure on Letty's face, her words becoming clearer. "He couldn't know."

Letty eased in a breath, hoping Kathryn wouldn't see. Trying not to cough, not to suck in giant gulps of air. One sip, then another. Until she was finally under control again. What the hell was happening? Why would Kathryn want her dead?

Whatever her reasons were, Letty wasn't going to let her finish the job.

She jerked up, and tried to yell out, but her throat was too raw and she couldn't push out enough air. She sucked in another breath to try again, but Kathryn rushed at her.

Letty couldn't get all the way out of the bed, not with the side-rails up. But she could damn sure get into a better defensive position than lying on her back. She scrambled to her knees and launched herself over the side, colliding with Kathryn.

She grabbed for Kathryn's throat and missed, her one good hand catching in the collar of Kathryn's shirt. They toppled backward, Kathryn's face going soft with surprise as she stumbled and fell.

Letty's leg caught on the rail, and the IV yanked free with a stinging pinch before she landed on top of Kathryn, hard. Her bad arm shrieked with pain, her head pounded, and the rest of her body joined in with a clatter of aches and bruises.

Kathryn shoved her off, nothing soft in her face now.

Letty scrambled away from Kathryn, her back smacking against the base of the bedside table before she struggled unsteady to her feet. "What the hell are you doing?"

Kathryn did the same, her eyes narrowing as she closed the distance between them. She grabbed for Letty's throat. "This has to end."

Letty pushed her hand away, and Kathryn's grip slid to Letty's bad arm. Letty cried out in pain, but Kathryn's grip only tightened. She wasn't letting go.

Letty widened her stance. If she couldn't run or yell loud enough to summon help, she didn't have any choice but to fight. She fisted her hands in Kathryn's shirt, shaking the woman hard back and forth. Something like a growl came from Kathryn's throat as she fought Letty's hold.

Letty dropped her head and yanked Kathryn forward, ramming the top of her skull into Kathryn's nose. The blow landed with a sickening crunch, and Kathryn collapsed to the floor.

A shaft of light cut into the room, and a startled voice asked, "What the hell?"

Letty looked from the body at her feet to a nurse standing in the doorway. Her eyes widened as she glanced between Letty and Kathryn, who lay crumbled and bloody on the floor. The nurse leaned back into the hall. "Security!"

CHAPTER 31

Mark strode down the clinic's central corridor, trying to figure out which one of the hallways branching off it led to Letty's room. It wasn't a big place, but every hall looked the same. Charlie had told him the room number, but he couldn't remember it. His brain felt like scrambled egg. First the bombing, and now his aunt attacking Letty? It was too much, all at once.

None of it made sense.

He passed another long hall. He could stop and ask someone, but chances were, he'd get kicked out if he did. It was well past visiting hours. He kept going, his mind still spinning. Kath had seemed happy to go check in on Letty when they had heard she'd been admitted. He had wanted to go himself, but the nurse he'd spoken to had assured him Letty was in stable condition, and there was no way for him to walk away from the families crowded into the waiting room. Half of them praying the wounded would recover and the other that someone missing would turn up alive.

Leaving them there, then, just didn't seem right. Not until he'd talked to every one, made sure they knew all their loved ones' medical bills would be paid. That Stafford Oil wouldn't stop looking until every soul who'd been on that rig had been found.

So Kath had jumped in to help, the way she always did. She'd given him a quick hug and hurried off with her usual calm efficiency, promising to update him as there was news.

And then she'd walked in and attacked Letty?

No, that couldn't be true.

There had to be some mistake. Something lost in translation. Like a kid's game of telephone. He spotted a hall marked "C" and slowed. Was that what Charlie had said? Mark turned the corner.

Aunt Kath sat on one of the puke green plastic chairs lined up against the left-hand side of the hall. She held an ice pack to her face and handcuffs shackled her wrists.

Her eyes went wide the minute she spotted him. "Mark, I—"

"What happened?" He stopped in front of her, glancing down at a policeman who was mid-conversation with one of the nursing staff a dozen yards away. The officer narrowed his eyes in Mark's direction.

Kath paled behind the ice pack.

Mark sat beside his aunt, who for the first time in his life looked absolutely undone. Her hair mussed, her shirt torn, her manicure chipped. He fought the urge to put his arm around her shoulder and make sure she was okay. First, he needed answers. "I don't know how much time we'll have. Better tell me fast."

She lowered the ice pack from her face. The bridge of her nose canted to the left and the stain of a bruise had already started spreading under both her eyes. "It's not exactly a short story."

He winced as he took in the state of her face. "Try," he said, but he kept his voice soft. He had known Kath his entire life and never seen her do anything violent. There had to be some explanation for what had happened.

"Cody Crawford was the bomber."

"What?" His question came out louder than he intended, and he flicked his gaze down to the police officer. The man had taken a step in Mark's direction and seemed to be wrapping up his conversation with the nurse. He had hardly had time since finding the note in Letty's things to process that he had a half-brother. Even less to think about the fact that this new brother was missing, that he might never get to know him. Now that brother was dead. And not just that, a murderer. A bomber responsible for the deaths of more than a dozen people. Grief warred with rage and guilt inside him. It was too much to process, especially when they could be interrupted at any moment. Mark turned back to his aunt. "Letty told you that?"

Kath nodded and blew out a long breath. "Your father was a complicated man. Conrad... made mistakes."

"My dad was an asshole." He didn't need Kath to waste time breaking the news about Crawford gently. Mark had known who Crawford was as soon as he had seen the note. His father had been unfaithful to his mother their entire marriage, even before she had disappeared into the comforting arms of booze, Valium, and God knew what else. The only surprise — at least before this conversation — was that his dad actually had feelings for one of his mistresses. That he hadn't insisted Crawford's mother "take care of it." If the note in Crawford's things was to be believed, his father had cared about someone other than himself.

Not enough to do the right thing by them, but still... it was side of Conrad Stafford Mark had never seen before.

Kath said nothing. Her lips pressed together in a thin line, and Mark immediately recognized his mistake. Sullying the Stafford name wasn't something Kath tolerated. It was the hill she would die on, and they didn't have time for that. He needed Kath to focus on whatever had happened with Letty, not their family's sordid history. "I know Crawford was my half-brother."

Kath cocked her head at him but didn't make any attempt to refute it.

Mark crossed his arms over his chest. "How long have you known?"

"His mother found me at Conrad's funeral. He had been paying Annemarie off for years to keep quiet about the affair. And, when he died, the tap shut off. She wanted me to turn it back on."

"So you did."

Kath nodded. "Crawford was an odd boy, not good with people. But once he channelled his energy into working with animals, he seemed to love what he did. I didn't mind paying for his schooling.

It felt right. And when the foundation started looking for people with his qualifications, it felt like it was meant to be. Then he wound up in Alaska, and I couldn't help but the see the opportunity it presented. The chance to help me help you."

A sour taste filled Mark's mouth, dread dropping through his stomach like a penny thrown into a well. If Kath was saying what he thought she was, if she had been involved in what Crawford had done, there would be no going back from that. Part of him wanted to get up and walk away before she could say any more. But he couldn't. "Go on."

"I knew Crawford would do whatever I asked. He owed me after everything I'd done for him." Kath let out a long sigh. "He was only supposed to disappear for a few days. I made arrangements for a boat to pick him up, for a cabin somewhere out of the way where he could lay low."

Mark leaned back, putting enough space between them that he actually felt like he could breathe. "You had him disappear from the Katmai job on purpose." Heat rose in his face, his anger winning the war for dominance inside him. "Right before I was supposed to appear before Congress, when you knew exactly how much I had on the line." His hands clenched into fists, and the penny hit bottom. The ripples of it, of what that meant — of what she'd been willing to do to him — rolled through him in angry, toxic waves. "You wanted the foundation to fail."

Kath reached over, grabbing one of his clenched hands in both of hers, the handcuffs clinking together. "No, never. The opposite. Crawford was just supposed to get 'lost' for a few days. Draw your attention back to the foundation where it belongs. I didn't realize his mother had passed right before he left or how it would affect him. I never intended for any of the rest of it to happen." She sucked in a breath, her words pouring out like a confession she could no longer hold in. "I really thought it would work. That you'd realize you couldn't run both the company and the JDF, not if you wanted to do both things well. It's too much for one person, and running

Stafford Oil never made you happy. It wasn't what you wanted. It was what Conrad wanted." She squeezed his hand. "I tried so hard to make you see that before, but you wouldn't listen. All you could see was your duty, even if it made you miserable."

"So you, what? Took the choice away from me?" His voice shook as he spoke. He wanted so badly to understand why she'd done what she'd done, for her to give him any reason to forgive it. But he had been down that road too many times. Felt the same way every time his father had disappointed him growing up. Each time had left his heart a little more brittle, and, if he wasn't careful, Kath was going to crack what was left of it in half.

"I tried everything. I tried talking to you, so many times. Do you remember? I could see how unhappy you were. But you just wouldn't listen—"

"So you sent the anonymous tip about me to the board." He knew he was right the moment he said it out loud. His fists so tight now, his knuckles ached. How could he have been so stupid? So naive? He had been so focused on all the money he'd lost in his early days as CEO, when he had been trying to refocus them on sustainability. The profitable deals he had left on the table when they didn't meet his standards. The deals he'd taken on, knowing they would generate a net loss. All the decisions that had put what was right above what was profitable — the ones he covered up and knew, even as he did it, the cover-up, more than anything else, would get him fired if anyone found out. That's all he had been able to think about when the investigation started. So much so, he had never blinked an eye when Kath had told him, over and over again, to just leave it all in her hands. It never occurred to him she had her own misdealing to cover up.

She grimaced. "I thought the board would see what I sent them and deal with it quietly. The worst of what your father did was too deeply buried for them to find. The documents I provided painted a clear enough picture, there was no need to go further. It wouldn't be in the company's interest to make any of it public, even if they did.

"And it would have worked, too. I could have gotten you out with no one but the board knowing why. You could have focused on the JDF, left me to manage the company the way it always should have been." She clenched her jaw, her eyes going flinty. "But then they appointed that damn investigator, and everything went sideways."

He put his hands over his face, as if by closing his eyes, he could actually block it all out. That's why the board was after him. Why Jimmy didn't trust him anymore. Based on the documents Kath had sent, maybe even created whole cloth, they thought Mark had continued his father's shady business practices or, at the very least, covered them up. When it was Kath who had been doing that his entire life. She still was now.

And it wasn't just out of some misguided fealty to the family name.

"You did it so you could run the company." He went completely still, the realization of what Kath had actually been up to ringing in his ears as he pulled his hands away and stared into her unflinching eyes. Now that the mask was off, he hardly recognized her. His stomach clenched, and if there'd been anything in it, he would have vomited it up. He had to force himself to stay in his chair. To ask the next question. "And Letty? What did she have to do with any of it?" It wasn't like there would be any question of Crawford's involvement once the police ID'd his body. There had to be something else, some other secret worth killing for.

"Okay, time to go." The police officer stopped in front of Kath's chair. "Doc's ready to set that nose." He took Kath by the elbow and helped her to her feet. Mark had been so preoccupied with his aunt's betrayal, he hadn't even heard the officer coming.

"One second, sir... please?" Kath's expression softened, her eyes wet with tears again as she turned to the officer. The look on her face made Mark sick. How many times had she turned her emotions on and off to get what she wanted? How many times had she done it to him?

The officer pursed his lips but eventually nodded.

"Keep it quick," he said, then stepped a few feet away to give them at least the appearance of privacy. Mark had no doubt he could still hear what they were saying. This end of the clinic was painfully quiet. All the doors closed, only the hum of the overhead fluorescent lights and the rumble of a generator somewhere outside. Under any other circumstance, he would have told Kath to keep quiet until she had a lawyer there. But it was too late for that. Too much damage had already been done in the course of protecting the Stafford name.

Done by her.

It was time the truth came out.

Kath turned back to Mark. "I didn't do it for power. I did it for you. Because I love you." Her voice cracked. "And I never meant to hurt Letty." Even with her face battered, Kath's grimace was clear. "I didn't know you'd sent her to King Salmon. She showed up at Crawford's cabin while he was inside gathering his things. I found out later he spent his time in hiding reading a bunch of his mother's papers he brought with him. Letty found one in the things he didn't manage to grab before she interrupted him."

"The note from dad."

"That's right." Kath nodded. "And once she found it, she wouldn't let Crawford's disappearance go. I told him to warn her off, but I didn't know how far he'd go. And it didn't work anyway."

Of course it hadn't. Letty wasn't the type to be intimidated. Anger twisted his gut, but he couldn't yell at Kath the way he wanted to. At least not yet. "So what did you do?"

"Nothing. Nothing, I swear. I didn't even know he'd followed her to Sallow Bay until he called me from there. And, when he did, everything was different. He was different. Angry. I guess he found a letter in Annemarie's papers. One she'd sent to Conrad that came back unopened, marked return to sender. In it, she told him she'd been diagnosed with HPV, wanted to tell him in case he didn't know he had it, to make sure he was okay." Another grimace, probably at Annemarie's naïveté. "That's what killed her, in the end. Not the STD he'd given her, but the cervical cancer it caused. And Crawford was livid. I guess he did the math, realized his mother was underage at the time. I tried to explain to him that Conrad had loved his mother as much as he was capable of loving anyone. Until he died, he had sent them money himself, every month like clockwork. He didn't do that for any of the others. I did. And that's when I made my biggest mistake…

"I told Crawford the truth, that Stafford Oil was Conrad's only true love." She winced. "I think that's why he leaked some of the documents I'd given him to the Post, and… why he bombed the rig. He couldn't lash out at his father, not with Conrad already dead. So he tried to destroy what his father had loved more than him. More than his mother. If he hadn't been killed in the process, I'm assuming he would've done more. Picked other company targets. Done worse, maybe."

What could be worse than what Crawford had already done? What Kath and Crawford had both done. Mark rubbed at his face, his head spinning. "None of that explains why you attacked Letty."

"No, I guess it doesn't." She gave a slow shake of her head. "The woman's relentless. She wouldn't stop digging. Not just into Crawford. But into the case against you. Against your father. Into the dumping and the corners he cut. I could've handled things, even with Lockwood. But not with Letty picking things apart. If the investigator found out the truth about the rest of Conrad's under-the-table deals. The history of how he really made the company what it is, it would destroy Stafford Oil. Destroy our family's name." Her gaze bored into his, as if she was willing him to listen. "Wanting to protect you, to protect our family… it's the most natural thing in the world."

"Natural?" Mark got to his feet. Even if she hadn't set the bombs herself, she was responsible for killing dozens of people. For power, for ego. And she had tried to kill Letty. Not just to protect his father or the company, but her own role in covering it all up. That's what this was really about. The anger burning inside him went cold, like molten metal forged into something hard and sharp. Something permanent. Whatever Kath had been to him before, that relationship was over. "There's nothing natural about any of this." He turned his back on her, muttering to the officer as he walked away. "She's ready for you." He didn't bother looking back. Kath was just one more rotten root in his twisted family tree.

CHAPTER 32

Sallow Bay, Alaska
October 28, 2018
Wet flakes smudged against Letty's window. Snowfall turned the
ground outside the clinic a pure white and the sky an odd gray
green in the still-dark early hours of morning. Everything empty
and silent now that the generator wasn't needed anymore, and the
nurses had finally left. Letty pulled an extra blanket from the foot
of the bed and tucked it tight around herself. All the signs of what
had happened in her room were gone. The blood wiped from the
floor. Letty's bandages and IV all good as new. Even a fresh pitcher
of water waited on the side table. Like nothing had happened.

What a lie.

She felt the stain of it clinging to her skin. So much had gone
wrong, in such a short time, she couldn't stop anticipating when
the next blow would fall. She took in a deep, shaky breath, ignoring
the burn in her lungs as she blew it back out again. She was alive,
she was going to be okay, and that was what mattered.

A soft knock came from the door, and Letty closed her eyes,
pretending to sleep. She wasn't ready for more company. She
watched the door inch open from under her lashes. Mark stood
silhouetted in the hallway light. He hesitated there, his shoulders
stooped in a way she hadn't seen before. Even in profile, his
posture looked like defeat. Because of the rig, or Kathryn? He
looked how she felt, like a battered mess.

And still, he'd come to see her after all. Her heart ached and, for some reason, after everything that had happened, this was what made tears prick behind her eyes. She pressed her lids the rest of the way closed, willing the tears to recede as she listened to Mark ease into the room and the door close with a soft bump.

She wanted to sit up and talk to him. She had so much to say, so many things to ask, but she couldn't make herself move. Since Jessa died, it always felt this way with Mark. All the feelings tangled up inside her got in the way of her words. Which was why she had been right to put distance between them. Even if it had meant making hard choices, like leaving the JDF.

His footsteps came closer, and she could feel his nearness. Sense that he was looking down at her. With anyone else, after what Kathryn had done, it would be creepy. But having Mark close was a comfort, even if she wasn't willing to let herself have it beyond this single, brief moment. For now, she let herself just lay there and be.

His fingers brushed her cheek, a lock of hair whispering against her skin as he brushed it out of her face and tucked it behind her ear.

Letty couldn't help it, she opened her eyes and smiled. "Hi."

If he'd looked tired in profile, he looked exhausted now. Shadows under his eyes, his hair standing on end from where he'd been running his hands through it. The way he always did when he was stressed. He smiled back, but sadness lingered on his face. "Hi to you, too."

"Are you okay?"

He laughed, and the skin around his eyes crinkled. "I think I should be asking you that."

"I'm better." She struggled up to a sitting position and lifted the sling. "Especially now that they fixed this."

Mark pulled a chair to the side of the bed, and his gaze swept over her, as if searching for other injuries. "What happened?"

She blew out a long breath and stared back out the window, where the snow had finally stopped falling. Where should she even start? Adam, Crawford, the rig, the terrifying moments after she'd fallen in the water... Kathryn. A lump grew in her throat, and she swallowed hard, trying to clear it.

"You don't have to talk about it now, if it feels like too much." Mark kept his voice gentle, but she could hear the tension behind it. Even dimmed by sadness and exhaustion, his eyes were a clear, bright blue. He had to be brimming with questions, but he didn't push. Which was such a Mark thing to do.

"It's okay." She steeled her nerve and launched into it, starting all the way back at the beginning. She talked until her throat got raw, drank two cups of water, then kept going until she got to Kathryn laying broken and bloody not two feet from where he sat now.

"I don't know why she did it, Mark. I really don't. Everything seemed fine, and then when I got to the part about the flight log, she just... lost it." She shifted uncomfortably in the bed, the memories too real, too present. A sheen of sweat broke across her forehead as her fight-or-flight response kicked back in, her exhausted nervous system no longer able to tell a real threat from a remembered one. She closed her eyes, waiting for her heart rate to come down. Waiting until she had control over herself again. "I can tell the board what I told her or testify or whatever." She found his eyes again, drawing strength from what she found there. Understanding, compassion, and something else — a fierceness she didn't quite understand. Maybe anger on her behalf. She cleared her throat. "Whatever you need, I'm here."

"You've done enough. Been through enough." He put his hand on her good arm and squeezed. "My godfather, Jimmy, called just now, when I was on my way to see you. He's on the board. With the explosion and the men still missing, plus the storm making it so hard to get the help we need in place, it's a lot. But I told him everything. About Kath, about Crawford. Jimmy will make sure the rest of the board knows the truth."

She leaned into his touch, needing the contact too much to care if he noticed. She'd just add it to the pile of things she could worry about later. "Mark, if I can help, I want to."

"I know." He said, his voice rough. He cleared his throat and let go of her arm, his expression tightening. "I spoke to Kathryn in the hallway."

Letty's gaze flicked to the closed door. She tensed, and her muscles sang out a protest. Still, she forced herself backward on the bed, gripping the side rail with her good hand. "She's still here?" She had assumed Kathryn had been arrested. Letty's heart bounced against the walls of her chest like an animal trapped in a too-small cage.

"It's okay, she's gone now." Mark mother hen-ed her back onto the pillows, tucking the blanket around her. "Kath's in custody. She was only still here at the clinic because they had to set her nose… and she's confessed what really happened, at least to me." He leaned back. "I'm not even sure where to start, but I'll try." Now he was the one that looked away. The pain she'd seen in his eyes when he'd first come in rose back to the surface as he explained what Kathryn had done, with Stafford Oil, with Crawford — who was, apparently, Mark's half-brother — and why she'd ultimately come after Letty.

Letty worried the strap of her sling while he talked, her mind racing. So many things made sense now. How Crawford had always known where to find her. Kathryn would have had access to the email updates Letty had been sending back to the foundation, including the one where she'd flagged the fact that the research facility's door had been unlocked the day she arrived. Crawford would have known he could get in to leave his little present of the bullet, if he just kept trying. Letty wrapped her good arm around the sling and hugged it to her chest.

"I'm so sorry." Mark leaned forward, put his elbows on his knees, and dropped his head to stare at the floor. He looked absolutely broken. "She attacked you because of me."

A flush of anger heated Letty's face. "It's not your fault. None of it is." She hated that Kathryn had done this to him. To all of them. Kathryn had hurt so many people, and in the end, it had all come down to power. Mark had it, and Kathryn wanted it. Letty rested a hand on the top of Mark's head, his hair thick under her fingers. He and Kathryn had been so close, more mother and son than aunt and nephew. To be betrayed like that... she couldn't imagine what he must be feeling. They sat in the quiet, until his shoulders finally relaxed.

She moved her hand back to her lap. "It'll all be okay."

His gaze shifted from the floor to her face, one eyebrow raised.

"Eventually." She gave him a weak smile. "It'll be different, but it'll be okay. And, I know it's not everything, but now that the board knows the truth, you can at least put the investigation behind you. You can take back your company."

He shook his head. "I resigned, for good this time."

But that didn't make sense, not now. "You what?" She straightened. "Why?"

"Kath was wrong about a lot of things, but not about that. Heading both the company and the JDF is too much for one person. The truth is, I never wanted to be Stafford Oil's CEO. I just thought it was what I was supposed to do, what my father expected of me. More than that, though, it was a chance to do something important, to steer the company in a better direction than he ever had." He sat back up. "I think some part of me knew there were things going on under his watch that shouldn't be. I was afraid of what would happen if I stepped down. Worried the company would fall into the wrong hands." The muscles of his jaw ticked as he clenched his teeth. "I just never realized which hands those were."

"And now?"

"Kath won't be in any boardrooms any time soon. Jimmy's agreed to step in as interim CEO, to work with the rest of the board to handle the disaster here and to make sure whatever happens now is on the up and up. I don't need to be there anymore. I need to be at the JDF." He held her gaze. "We both do."

Letty's fingers found the edge of her sling again, picking at the nylon weave. "I don't think that's a good idea." As glad as she was to have this moment with Mark, to feel like they were finally talking again, the way they used to... they had already tried the experiment of working together. And it had failed, miserably.

"Listen, I know I messed up when I first got here. I was worried and—" He cut himself off, shifting uncomfortably in his seat.

What had he been about to say? Jealous?

No, that didn't make any sense. She was projecting.

Mark raised a hand to his chest, his fingers pressing what looked like some kind of pendent he wore under his shirt. "I had no right to say what I said. I was wrong to pull you from the project. And I want you to come back. You belong at the JDF."

"I'm not sure I do." She used her good arm to pull her knees to her chest, ignoring all her body's aches. She had tried her damnedest and, for what? "We've still got God knows how many polar bears on the loose, those poor campers still missing in Denali, and a toxic red tide heading for Canada."

He shook his head. "Not even you can track every animal. I should never have implied that any of what happened since Katmai was your fault." He grimaced. "And while you might not have pulled the final set of water samples yourself, we would never have known Alexandrium diabli existed without your work. At least not until after it had made landfall. We would have missed a critical window to get out in front of it. Your work gave us the time we needed to figure out what to do, how best to stop it from destroying other ecosystems, from making God knows how many more people sick... Musa got the test results back from the biological samples you took on the fast ice. All of them showed toxic levels of

Alexandrium diabli." He paused as if waiting to make sure he had her full attention. "We've got a chance to manage this thing because of you."

Heat rose again from Letty's neck up her cheeks, but this time it had nothing to do with anger. His words meant more to her than she could admit to herself or him, but "even if it worked out this time…" She choked on the rest of what she knew she needed to say. "I don't think I can keep working for the JDF." She hoped like hell he didn't ask why, because what reason could she give? Certainly not the truth.

"Why?" His gaze bore into hers.

Kill me now.

"I'm not sure we can work together." She made herself hold his gaze, even if it meant he could see the truth behind her eyes. She didn't want to walk away. She hated the idea of not seeing him anymore, but she didn't have a choice. "We don't communicate well, and that's a problem the JDF can't afford. Especially not now, not with the tide and the bid to Congress still pending." He started to cut her off, but she held up a hand and went on. "If I'd told you about the letter I found in Crawford's things when I found it… If I had talked to you back then, how much of this could have been avoided?"

"None of this is your fault. Even if we'd known Crawford was my half-brother when he first went missing, we would have had no way to know what he had planned or how to stop it. You can't take that on yourself." He crossed his arms over his chest. "But you're right that we haven't been communicating. Not the way we should. And I'm sorry for whatever part of that is my fault. I think when you came on board at the foundation, I expected things between us to be the way they were… before Jessa died. Which… maybe wasn't fair." He ran a hand through his hair again, which left it standing up in all directions.

She fought the urge to smooth it down. "I could have handled it better, too. I should have. Not just what happened after I joined the

JDF… but what happened after Jessa died." This time, she let the tears fall free. They tracked hot trails down her cheeks. "Neither of you would have been on that boat if I hadn't cancelled our plans at the last minute. And I should have been there for you after it happened. I should have apologized a long time ago."

"None of what happened was your fault. I can't believe you ever thought it was." He shook his head. "And, it wouldn't have mattered if you'd come to the hospital to see me after Jessa died. I was too out of it to know who was there and who wasn't. Besides, Letty, you were grieving. We both were. I don't hold anything about it against you."

More tears trailed down her cheeks. He might not, but Kathryn certainly had. And Letty did, too.

"Is this why you were avoiding me when you first started work?" He pulled two tissues from a box beside the water pitcher and handed them to her.

"I wasn't—"

He cocked his head at her, and she stopped the lie before it could get the rest of the way out of her mouth. "Yeah." She blotted her face with the tissues.

Something like relief crossed his face. "Well, that was dumb."

She snorted out a laugh. "Thanks."

"And we're talking now, aren't we?"

She nodded, still wiping tears from her face. "I guess so."

"And there's nothing to keep us from talking going forward?"

Her feelings hadn't changed, not really. But the weight of them did feel lighter somehow. Like, even if she hadn't told him everything, she'd shared enough so that she could look at him, talk to him, and not feel consumed by the shadow of Jessa's absence. "I suppose that's true, too." She crumpled the damp tissues up in her hand.

"The JDF needs you, Letty." He said the words softly, but they landed in her heart with a thump. The JDF wasn't just a foundation, it was Mark's whole world — especially now that he'd resigned from Stafford Oil. Which meant what he was really saying was that he needed her.

He might have forgiven her for not being there for him before, but she wouldn't let herself make the same mistake again. Especially not when she knew, deep in her core, the JDF was where she belonged.

"Okay," she finally said, dropping the tissues onto her blanket and extending a hand for him to shake. "I'm in."

"Welcome back." He took her hand in his, and his face split into a grin.

She couldn't help but match it.

EPILOGUE

November 3, 2018

San Diego, California

In some weird twist of fate or logic, it had taken going away to finally make San Diego feel like Letty's home. Or maybe it was tonight's company that had done that. Letty smiled to herself as she grabbed a half-empty bottle of Prosecco from her refrigerator and carried it into the living room. She refilled Gemma's glass and settled back on the couch, careful not to crush the mountain of snacks piled between them.

Gemma's contribution toward her "welcome home dinner" looked like the entire contents of a 7-Eleven. She pulled two gummy worms from a bag of candy and dropped them into the sparkling wine. Letty grimaced, but Gemma didn't seem to notice. She took a deep drink of her sugary concoction and gave a deep, happy sigh. "You seem different since you got back."

"I do?" Letty sipped her own, thankfully worm-less bubbles, not sure if different was a good thing. "Different how?"

"I don't know." Gemma propped her feet on Letty's coffee table. She wore long mismatched socks that came up over her knees, one cobalt blue, the other green and orange stripes. On anyone else, it would have read Pippy Longstocking. But on Gemma, it was pure punk chic. "Better."

"Really?" Letty had only been back in the office a couple of days. Most of that, she had spent wrapping up her part of the Katmai case. She'd confirmed a bear captured trying to break into a hunting cabin near the Ahklun Mountains was the second, missing bear from Katmai, then turned her attention to preparing communities across Alaska for the continuing Southward migration of polar bears and other potentially dangerous animals. They had no way to know how many animals had been displaced by Alexandrium diabli's destruction of their ecosystem, but it was a safe bet they would continue to find their way into populated areas.

It had been good, satisfying work. But it hadn't exactly left her time for self-care. Or even to shower regularly. Letty gestured toward Gemma with her sling. "I'm not sure what that says about how I was before."

Gemma winked. "You had your moments." She dug through the snack pile until she unearthed the remote, unmuted a rerun of The Bachelor, and wiggled deeper into the sofa.

Truth was, Letty did feel different. Happier, more focused. She still showed no sign of any of the aftereffects she had feared would come from being submerged in the toxic water. Thank God. Her other injuries were healing and, slowly, life seemed to be moving on.

She had thought it would be hard to let go of the Alexandrium diabli project, but today's hand-off had actually felt good. Especially given the team the foundation had put together to tackle it. Hilde had excelled so far in managing on-the-ground care to the people of Sallow Bay, while also handling fall-out from the moratorium on fishing in affected waters. Musa and Ines had been tasked with managing the foundation's plan for a national response, while a team of other top-notch scientists managed the threats the tide posed abroad.

She had hardly seen Mark since they'd been back. He had been caught up with the aftermath of the rig explosion, then on a plane again, headed back to D.C.. But, it hadn't felt awkward. They'd even talked on the phone, once or twice.

A quick check-in on travel plans and upcoming projects. Nothing major, but it was enough to make her confident coming back to the JDF had been the right choice. And not just because Gemma would have killed her if she hadn't. They were buried in work, which was why a stack of case files now crowded Letty's coffee table. She shifted them aside and propped her feet up beside her friend's.

"Can't remember how long it's been since I had a girls' night." Gemma took another big drink from her glass. "Wasn't sure we'd ever get here, to be honest."

"You mean with the divorce?"

Gemma nodded. "The lawyers finally hammered out a deal. I'll keep primary custody, and Noah will go back and forth between our houses. Splitting holidays and school breaks. More or less the standard sort of schedule."

"That's amazing." Letty clinked her glass against Gemma's. "How'd you manage that?"

"Donny finally realized he didn't hold all the cards." Gemma balanced her glass between her thighs, poured Skittles in her hand, and sorted out the red ones. "The promotion helped."

"What promotion?"

"You are looking at the JDF's new VP of Technology and Logistics." She popped the candy into her mouth and chewed, chasing it down with the last of her bubbles.

"Congratulations?" Letty said, without meaning it to come out as a question. Even for business-speak, that one was hard to parse. She pulled open a bag of popcorn, which was awkward, given that she had to hold it in the hand still pinned to her side so she could rip it open with the other. "What does that mean exactly?"

"Hell if I know." Gemma smiled at Letty from behind her glass. "But the judge seemed to like it. Mark sent a character reference, too. Told the court the JDF couldn't have completed the research necessary to fight the red tide without my 'invaluable effort and support.'"

Letty laughed. "Yay, Mark." He wasn't wrong but, still. "Way to sell it." Letty swiped a piece of popcorn along the inside of the bag to soak up as much of the butter and salt as she could.

A nightly news graphic swirled across the TV. Gemma turned up the volume and tossed the remote onto the top of the snack pile. "Here we go."

The graphic faded, replaced by a video of Mark jogging down the steps of the capital building. Musa and Ines followed closely behind. All three wore suits and somber expressions as they pushed through a hoard of press to where a dark SUV waited at the curb. An anchor spoke over the footage. "Representatives of the Jessa Duquesne Foundation, now widely known as the JDF, appeared again earlier today before a Congressional committee reconvened to address the imminent threat posed by the toxic red tide known as Alexandrium diabli, which is currently floating in the Arctic Ocean off the Canadian Archipelago. While the tide has not made landfall on any inhabited coastline since Sallow Bay, that is soon expected to change." Senator Hilliard appeared at the top of the steps and veered off in the opposite direction, a hand up to block his face from the cameras. The anchor went on, as the frenzy of press diverted their attention to Hilliard like a swarm of pissed-off bees. "In light of these recent events, the committee is expected to approve the JDF's bid to act as a centralized hub for both the nation's gathering of information and response to this ongoing crisis. We have been unable to confirm…"

Letty turned the volume back down. Whatever the news could tell her, Mark would know more than they did, and he'd promised to call with an update before the team got on the plane to come home.

"What's that smile for?" Gemma plucked one of the soggy gummy worms from her glass and popped it into her mouth.

"What smile?" She forced her face into neutral. "I'm not smiling." She busied her traitorous mouth with finishing her own glass of Prosecco. Under no circumstances was the thought of talking to Mark making her grin. She was just relieved that, so far, no signs pointed to Congress or the press trying to lay responsibility for the rig's explosion at the JDF's feet. There would be questions and press and probably even more police statements… but for now, the foundation was doing exactly what Jessa would have wanted. They were hard at work making the world better, doing everything they could to save lives.

"Okay." Gemma fished out the second worm. "If you say so." She pushed one of the files on the table toward Letty with her blue-socked foot. "Brought you a present."

"Did you?" Letty raised an eyebrow but couldn't ignore the bubble of excitement expanding in her chest. A new file meant a new challenge. A chance to get out into the field. To get her hands dirty doing the thing she loved.

"I think you'll like this one. It's right up your street."

Letty pulled the folder into her lap and flipped it open. "I can't wait."

THE END

ACKNOWLEDGMENTS

The research for this book was at once overwhelming and fascinating. I fell in love with the idea of setting a book in the Arctic before I realized how little I actually knew about it, much less how a scientist would conduct her research there. I couldn't have written Unnatural Intent without the help of a bunch of people who are much smarter than me.

A giant thank you to Kyle Dilliplaine, Researcher and PhD student in Biological Oceanography at University of Alaska Fairbanks; Maren Fulton, PE; Stephanie Fulton, Research Associate at Pacific Northwest National Laboratory; Andy Mahoney, Professor of Geophysics, Geophysics Institute, University of Alaska Fairbanks; David G. Ortiz-Suslow, Research Professor at Naval Postgraduate School, studying ocean surface waves and their role in air-sea exchange mechanisms; and Sally Walker, Professor of Geology and Invertebrate Paleobiology with a focus on Marine Sciences at the University of Georgia.

These people collectively spent hours of their time with me. They answered long emails. They got on Zoom to show me how their equipment works. And, ultimately, they helped me figure out how to build a new, more terrifying natural menace. Everything I got right is thanks to them, and anything I got wrong is a problem entirely of my own making.

I also need to thank Heart Dominguez (again). Heart is my go-to veterinary medicine source and always willing to help. Even when I email him at inopportune hours or chase him around our kids' school events asking gruesome questions. Not that I don't do this to most people who have the misfortune of meeting me in person. Consider yourself warned.

No set of acknowledgments would be complete without thanking my writing family. Heather Lazare, editor extraordinaire, what would I do without you? Eboni Harris, Janice Rocke, Sarah Pruitt, Kelly Yarborough, and Spencer Lipori, my Sundays are never the same without our critique group. Will Pruitt and Penny Righthand, thank you for making my Thursdays, and this book, so much better. Susanne Lakin, thank you for teaching me how to be a better writer. To my beta readers, Laura McCune-Poplin, Lauren Gesselin, Penny Righthand (again), Katy Liner, Andrew Stillman, and Melissa Bowers, thank you for helping me whip this book into shape.

Thank you to the team at Black Rose Writing for bringing me into the fold. I am so grateful you took a chance on me with my first book, and second, and now third. Here's to us doing many more successful projects together.

Finally, a thank you to my family, friends, and readers for giving me so much love and support. I know we're not meant to have favorites among our children. But as far as book babies go, Letty's story is mine. I hope you love reading about her adventures as much as I love writing them.

ABOUT THE AUTHOR

Brooke L. French is a recovering lawyer, author, and boy mom. Her debut thriller, *Inhuman Acts*, hit number one on Amazon's kindle charts in both medical thrillers and suspense in 2023, and her second novel, *The Carolina Variant,* continues climbing the charts. Brooke got her undergraduate degree in English from Emory University, followed by a law degree, which after many long and sometimes fulfilling years of practice, she mainly uses now as a coaster for the cup of coffee she puts down only to type. Brooke lives with her husband and sons between Atlanta and Carmel-by-the-Sea, California.

DO NOT MISS THE BEGINNING OF THE
LETTY DUQUESNE THRILLER SERIES

"*Inhuman Acts* is a timely, taut, edge-of-your-seat, page-turning thriller."
– Joseph Swope, author of *Dark Age Monarch*

BROOKE L. FRENCH

INHUMAN ACTS

NOTE FROM BROOKE L. FRENCH

Word-of-mouth is crucial for any author to succeed. If you enjoyed *Unnatural Intent*, please leave a review online—anywhere you are able. Even if it's just a sentence or two. It would make all the difference and would be very much appreciated.

Thanks!
Brooke L. French

We hope you enjoyed reading this title from:

www.blackrosewriting.com

Subscribe to our mailing list – *The Rosevine* – and receive **FREE** books, daily deals, and stay current with news about upcoming
releases and our hottest authors.
Scan the QR code below to sign up.

Already a subscriber? Please accept a sincere thank you for being a fan of Black Rose Writing authors.

View other Black Rose Writing titles at
www.blackrosewriting.com/books and use promo code
PRINT to receive a **20% discount** when purchasing.

Made in the USA
Las Vegas, NV
28 October 2024

10649170R00177